THE MIDNIGHT PACK

JERICHO JAMES: BOOK 1

JASMINE KULIASHA

orbitbooks.net
orbitworks.net

This book is a work of fiction. Names, characters, places, and incidents are the product of the author's imagination or are used fictitiously. Any resemblance to actual events, locales, or persons, living or dead, is coincidental.

Copyright © 2025 by Jasmine Kuliasha

Cover design by Alexia E. Pereira
Cover illustration by Luisa Preissler
Cover copyright © 2025 by Hachette Book Group, Inc.
Author photograph by Lisa Joy Photography

Hachette Book Group supports the right to free expression and the value of copyright. The purpose of copyright is to encourage writers and artists to produce the creative works that enrich our culture.

The scanning, uploading, and distribution of this book without permission is a theft of the author's intellectual property. If you would like permission to use material from the book (other than for review purposes), please contact permissions@hbgusa.com. Thank you for your support of the author's rights.

Orbit
Hachette Book Group
1290 Avenue of the Americas
New York, NY 10104
orbitbooks.net
orbitworks.net

First Edition: May 2025

Orbit is an imprint of Hachette Book Group.
The Orbit name and logo are registered trademarks of Little, Brown Book Group Limited.

The publisher is not responsible for websites (or their content) that are not owned by the publisher.

The Hachette Speakers Bureau provides a wide range of authors for speaking events. To find out more, go to hachettespeakersbureau.com or email HachetteSpeakers@hbgusa.com.

Library of Congress Cataloging-in-Publication Data
Names: Kuliasha, Jasmine author
Title: The midnight pack / Jasmine Kuliasha.
Description: First edition. | New York, NY : Orbit, 2025. | Series: Jericho James ; book 1
Identifiers: LCCN 2024058719 | ISBN 9780316587334 trade paperback | ISBN 9780316587327 ebook
Subjects: LCGFT: Detective and mystery fiction | Fantasy fiction | Novels
Classification: LCC PS3611.U418 J47 2025 | DDC 813/.6—dc23/eng/20250303
LC record available at https://lccn.loc.gov/2024058719

ISBNs: 9780316587327 (ebook), 9780316587334 (print on demand)

*For anyone who tells their friends to
look at the moon.
And for Deidre.*

PART I

JERICHO

CHAPTER 1

Jericho is known as the oldest city in the world, and according to the Bible, it was cursed by God.

My mom wasn't thinking of the Bible when she named me. She just wanted me to have a boy's name to put on my résumé and thought Jericho sounded cool. She'd say, *"Jericho James,* an extraordinary name for an extraordinary girl!" I don't know about *extraordinary*, though. A better way to describe my special brand of charmed life would probably be *unusual*.

Have you ever known someone whom things just sort of happen to? Like a friend who goes to the mall and ends up thwarting a jewelry store heist? Or maybe she sets out for a short hike but meets a park ranger on the trail and winds up tranquilizing and tagging black bears with him? Or she gets her private investigator license as a last resort to avoid working retail but, instead of tailing cheating husbands or suspected parole violators, becomes somewhat famous for solving the crazy animal cases nobody else wants to take?

Yeah, that's me.

Chupacabra sightings? Call Jericho James. (They were shaved goats. All of them.)

Swamp-monster in the Everglades? I'm your girl. (For the record, it was a giant anaconda.)

Cthulhu sightings off the coast of California? My phone was ringing nonstop with that one. (It was an injured giant Pacific octopus who's now convalescing nicely at the Monterey Bay Aquarium.)

Cthulhu again, this time in southern Florida? An even crazier, but still normal, set of animal circumstances. Hint: It involved pythons. Lots and lots of pythons. And it was my first time on the news. I got to describe the ins and outs (pun intended) of a mating ball on live TV.

Then something truly bizarre happened: People started looking past my bubbly blonde-ness and seeing my inherent talent for cracking cryptid cases. I'd gained a reputation, and now whenever there was some unusual animal activity, most police stations across the country had me at the top of their call list. Which was how I found myself heading to Stillbridge, Maine, at the frenzied request of a frustrated police captain.

The last time I was in the Pine Tree State was to investigate a Cassie sighting. But Maine's own Loch Ness–style monster turned out to be a record-breaking fifteen-foot-long Atlantic sturgeon weighing in at over eight hundred pounds. The sheer size of the fish was incredibly strange. But in this job, I've found that truth is always stranger than fiction.

This new assignment, however, brought me away from the water and into a small town nestled on the edge of the woods—which is ostensibly every small town in Maine, since the state is almost 90 percent forest. Stillbridge sounded woodsier than most, though, as the self-proclaimed "Gateway to Mount Katahdin and the 100-Mile Wilderness." The largest mountain in Maine loomed just north of the accurately named wilderness, and Stillbridge was tucked right between them.

A seemingly endless wall of trees blurred past my red VW Beetle as I drove to my destination. Fall had arrived in full force, and the forest was a vivid tapestry of scarlets, oranges, and golds, peppered with deep evergreen. I allowed myself to get lost in the colors for a brief minute—a practically magical sight to my Florida girl eyes—before turning my thoughts back to the police file and news article I'd read earlier.

A woman's savaged remains were found in these woods, bitten and clawed apart. Katherine Waller, age twenty-two, on vacation to hike the Appalachian Trail in the 100-Mile Wilderness after graduating from college earlier this year. She was only a handful of years younger than me. I chewed my lower lip thoughtfully. It wasn't the first death I'd investigated, but that didn't make it any easier. The wampus cat murders of East Tennessee had made the news, too. A six-legged cougar-type beast was a shoo-in for a headline, especially since the attacks mirrored the Knoxville incident in 1918, right down to the slew of stray animals killed... their livers ripped out, but the rest of the carcasses intact. A college freshman was also a victim in the new attacks—a gaping hole on the right side of his body is a vivid image that still haunts me. I arrived to find the mayor organizing a wampus cat hunt, which I was able to talk him out of after a rabid cougar with a bloodstained muzzle was caught and put down. Poor thing must have been insanely iron-deficient, and instinct took over. The killings stopped after that.

This time, the local authorities had determined that the trauma was indicative of a single animal, and the bite radius was in line with either a small bear or a large wolf, though neither was a perfect match. So this poor woman had been hiking alone and was attacked by some sort of creature. No foul play suspected. As far as the police were concerned, the death itself was case closed. Except for the matter of this mystery animal that was bold enough to attack a human, big enough to inflict fatal damage, and still at large.

Since local animal control couldn't find an animal to control, they called me. Both the policeman leading the case and Katherine's distraught parents wanted the creature found, identified, and ultimately *subdued*, which I took to mean *dead meat*. Large mammals weren't exactly my specialty, but I had plenty of faith in my abilities—and in the semi-automatic gun I kept on me for emergencies. I hadn't had to use it yet, and I hoped I never would, but better to be prepared in these situations.

What if it was a new, apparently violent and toothy species, though? It sounded far-fetched, but looking out the car window at the passing forest, I could almost believe that there was some hitherto-unknown creature living there. People were still discovering new species around the world, and no way *all* of Maine's woods had been explored.

If I'd learned anything through these cases, though, it was that the simplest explanation was usually the correct one. With Occam's razor in mind, I pulled into Stillbridge.

THE MIDNIGHT PACK

As far as towns go, it was unremarkable in its normalcy, but definitely very cute. Main Street, with all its brick buildings and hand-painted signage: cute. The coffee shop on the corner, whose window said ESPRESSO YOURSELF in big, cheery, hand-painted letters: cute. The bed-and-breakfast where I was staying, with its crisp, white wood siding and wraparound porch: cute. Christopher at the front desk, who winked at me when he took my bags: *double cute*. I glanced at his hand: no ring. I hoped I'd have time to maybe invite him for a drink later, life being short and him being adorable, but...first things first. As soon as my suitcases were settled, I rushed out into the crisp Maine day for some info gathering.

The ground was still wet from recent rainfall, but the fall sun had come out and was shining brightly, making the puddles on the sidewalks glisten. I shivered. Even with the sun, the air was spiked with a brisk coolness that hinted at the winter to come, and this warm-weather girl hadn't brought anything heavier than a flannel shirt. At least the day was serene—in juxtaposition with my life of chasing wild stories. It might be nice to live somewhere like this someday.

Yeah right, Jericho, like you could ever live someplace this *quiet.*

I paused in front of the police station, which luckily was not too far from where I was staying. The small, whitewashed building was weather-worn but well kept, and the big black lettering of the station's sign was clearly (and tidily) handwritten. I had an appointment to talk to the sheriff later that afternoon. Sheriff Jackson—whose father and grandfather were also Sheriff Jacksons, and whose daughter was shaping up to be the first female Sheriff Jackson—was the one who'd contacted me about the case. We'd spoken on the phone several times, but I had a fresh slew of case-related questions for him after reading and re-reading the police file. My arms prickled with goose bumps as I recalled the grisly photos that were included—Katherine's body twisted at an unnatural angle, her left arm torn off at the shoulder and flung several feet away. Three deep claw marks marred her face, completely mangling her jaw on one side. I blinked, shaking the image from my mind.

The station's white wooden sides made the building stand out from its vintage, brick-walled cousins that sandwiched it. The entire Main Street had an old-timey look to it, which I enjoyed. I leaned against a weathered telephone pole that had been peppered with posters, absentmindedly fingering some of the tacked-up papers. There was a sale at the local pizza place. A lost dog. An advertisement for babysitting services. But sticking out from behind the general notes, I noticed another, mostly hidden paper. I lifted the babysitting page and revealed Katherine's faded image, front and center on a MISSING poster. Her once auburn hair had become a caramel-blonde on the rain-washed flyer. She was smiling and wearing a graduation cap. She looked a little bit like me.

And now she's dead.

I shuddered in the sunlight as a chill passed through my shoulders. Then I yanked the poster down.

"It was a monster, ya know."

The voice came from behind me, pulling me out of my reverie. "What?" I turned and shaded my eyes against the afternoon sun with my hand.

A young boy with a mop of black hair and round glasses a

little bit too big for his face pointed at the paper in my hand. "What killed her. It was a monster. Maybe a dogman. Maybe the Tote-Road Shagamaw." He pointed to his shirt, which had an image of a muscle-bound bear-moose bursting out of the words STILLBRIDGE ACADEMY SHAGAMAWS.

I couldn't tell if he was joking. "Uhh," I said intelligently. I did not want to talk about this with a kid.

The boy suddenly looked unsure of himself and jammed his hands in the pockets of his jeans. He turned to face the sidewalk, nudging at some pebbles with a ratty red tennis shoe.

Now I felt bad. "What do you mean?" I asked.

The boy contemplated the pebble a moment longer, as if he was deciding how to respond. He nodded to himself, then looked up, pushed his too-big glasses higher on his nose, and sighed. "My mom doesn't believe me. She thinks I'm crazy. But I hear them at night."

I pulled my phone out of my pocket and opened a recording app, showing the screen to the boy as I pressed RECORD. He nodded his consent. "Tell me more," I said into the phone.

He stepped closer but avoided my eyes as he focused on the sidewalk behind me. "My house is the last one on the street, at the edge of the woods. I can see all the trees right from my window. That's where I hear the sounds. It sometimes starts with a snapping, like, like when you step on a stick and it breaks. Then snarling, scratching…" He raised his hands, fingers curled into little claws, slashing them through the air while trying to roar in a low voice. He turned his attention back toward me, the sounds trailing off as he looked into my eyes. "You don't believe me, either."

Hurt was written all over his face. Poor kid. I knew what it felt like to not be believed. I bent down so my eyes were level with his. "I definitely believe you heard something. What's your name, buddy?"

"Mikey." Mikey eyed me dubiously.

"How old are you, Mikey?"

He scowled. "I just turned ten, and I'm old enough to know what I'm talking about. I've lived here my whole life, and I'm not stupid. I know what sounds all the animals around here make. These are different."

"Actually, I was going to ask if you should be in school right now." I smiled at him gently.

"Oh. We get out early on Wednesdays. All of us used to walk home together, but since that lady was killed, most of the other kids get picked up by their parents. I don't have a dad, though, and my mom works all day, so I still walk."

"Does it bother you to walk alone?"

Mikey shrugged. "I'm safe out here. The monsters are in the woods." A cloud passed overhead, as if punctuating his sentence. He continued, adjusting his glasses again. "You're that detective lady, right?"

I nodded and raised an eyebrow. "What made you think that?"

I didn't dress in any way that screamed *detective*. The closest thing I have to a uniform is yoga pants and a tank top, but only because that's what I wear most often, like every other warm-blooded female into the athleisure lifestyle. My nail polish isn't what you would consider "professional," either. My color choices are exclusively based on witty names. Keep your pastel pinks and ruby reds—give me Ice Cream and Shout, Indi-Go-Round, and Not Red-y for Bed. Today's was One in a Melon—a particularly warm and intense pink.

The boy responded with a small smirk. "All the grown-ups have been talking about it, how a special detective was coming here. I saw you coming out of the hotel, so I just figured that's who you were."

"Hey, that's some decent detective work yourself."

He grinned, and his attention quickly shifted back to his red tennis shoes. "Anyway, I thought you should know about the monster. I tried to tell my mom that I know what I'm talking about, but she still thinks I'm crazy."

"Can I tell you a secret?"

"Yeah?" His eyes met my face again.

I leaned closer and whispered like we were a couple of conspirators on the street. "People call me crazy, too. But you know what? I'm glad. I'd be offended if someone ever called me normal."

Mikey smiled up at me. "In that case, catch you later, crazy!"

I laughed. "Right back atcha, buddy. Have a good walk!"

He turned to leave but suddenly whipped his face back around. His smile was gone, his expression hardened and serious. "Don't go into the woods."

———————•———————

"Katherine was missing for about a week before her remains were found," Sheriff Jackson said, offering me a paper cup full of steaming black coffee. I gratefully accepted, wrapping my hands around the cup for warmth. It was surprisingly colder inside the station than it was outside, maybe to keep delinquents spending the night in the lone jail cell on edge.

"The body was a shock to us all, real nasty injuries as you know. I wouldn't wish that kind of death on anyone. Anyway, we tried to keep the official investigation going, but the chief was eager to chalk this one up to an unlucky encounter and call it done. Luckily, the animal being on the loose means we could bring you in." The sheriff smiled at me with a mouthful of slightly yellow teeth.

"Yeah...lucky," I said, taking a small sip of the coffee and trying to hide my grimace at the lack of sugar. "So I've talked to the other officers on the phone, and I'm meeting the hunters that found Katherine's body next. I also plan to chat with the guy at the B and B where Katherine stayed, but I'm not quite sure where to turn to after that, besides just marching on into the woods. Is there anyone else it might be worthwhile to check with?"

The sheriff reached up and scratched the back of his neck, frowning as he thought. "Well...he might not be the best person for conversation, but there is an old fella who actually lives out in the woods. A hermit, of sorts. Keeps to himself most of the time. If he didn't come into town for feedstock every once in a while, I'd say he was a figment. I can give you a general direction to where he stays, though I haven't been out that way in years. He doesn't take kindly to visitors. His name's Kermit."

I choked a little on the coffee.

"Kermit...the hermit?"

"Well, yeah, I suppose you could call him that."

I couldn't help laughing at the ridiculous name, though Sheriff Jackson just eyed me strangely, like a rhyming moniker shouldn't surprise anyone. *Oh well.* I thanked him for his offer on directions to Kermit the hermit's place in the woods, and his generous container of case files and recorded interviews, and made my way back to the bed-and-breakfast.

Finally cuddled up in the cozy four-poster bed with a hoard of pillows, I played the interviews given to me by the sheriff, as well as the few I'd recorded on my phone. It had started to rain on my way back, and the gentle sound of droplets pattering on the window combined with the comfort of my pillow-nest threatened to put me to sleep, but I blinked my eyes stubbornly. I ran my fingers through my shoulder-length hair, fanning it around my head like a golden crown on the pillowcase. The full moon, already shining brightly despite the early-evening hour and the rain, illuminated the small room with a pleasant, almost pearlescent glow. I listened to an animal expert, Joseph, speaking about the bite wounds.

"...No, nothing like this. It's similar to a couple o' things. Similar to a lone wolf, maybe similar to a bear. But if you forced me to pick between 'em, I couldn't. It was something big, though, that's for certain."

It just didn't make sense. Large animals don't generally disappear without a single trace, and everyone I'd spoken to had universally agreed that it was undoubtedly an animal attack, though no tracks were ever found. That contributed to the

differing opinions when it came to what type of animal, with three schools of thought:
1. Bear with a unique bite structure
2. Wolf (a really big one)
3. Unidentified species (Mikey's "monster")

There were plenty of black bears in Maine, and I supposed it wasn't out of the question for one to be different from the norm. I'd also done some research on wolves. While there weren't any known wolf packs in the area, occasionally wolves did meander down from the Canadian woods to the north. Case in point, the local legend about the "dogmen" Mikey mentioned. The creatures who'd attacked a family home in Palmyra years ago were clearly either Canadian wolves or coyotes. General size was an issue now, though. Both the coroner and this animal expert pronounced that whatever had attacked Katherine was *definitely* larger than a wolf.

Something tugged at my memory, causing me to sit up and open my laptop. *Weren't there actual giant wolves once?* I sat cross-legged on the bed with the computer on my lap, tucked my hair behind my ears, then typed "giant wolf" (the technical term) into the search bar. An entry on dire wolves was one of the first hits. *Yes, yes, that's right!* I had watched a show that featured these guys once when I first started my journey into being a cryptid critical. Dire wolves were prehistoric cousins of today's wolves, and about twice as big and strong. They were thought to be extinct, but then again, so was the coelacanth until some unwitting fisherman hauled one up on his boat.

I tapped the laptop absentmindedly, studying drawings of

the latest addition to my list. Dire wolves were *huge*, probably larger than a linebacker in most cases. In fact, if you ran into one of those at night, in the dark shadows, it might be entirely possible to mistake it for...

I laughed out loud and ran my fingers through my hair. I'd long ago learned that anything was possible. But these attacks, these sightings? They always turned out to be normal animals.

Always.

CHAPTER 2

I woke up the next morning to a beautiful fall day. The rain had stopped, the sun was shining, and the air was crisp. I opened the window of my room and inhaled deeply. Everything smelled like petrichor and pine. I kept the window open to let the morning air filter in while I compiled my to-do list and reviewed my notes from the previous day.

I'd fallen asleep with my laptop open. I pulled it onto my lap at the edge of the bed and tapped on the keys. The article about dire wolves lit the screen as the computer groaned awake. I shook my head and closed the laptop with a sigh, then looked over to my handwritten notes.

Kermit's name sat beside an unchecked box, along with "visit crime scene." I'd been putting off the trip to where the body was found because (a) I'd seen all the pictures, and (b) I knew that any clues outdoors would have been long gone by the time I arrived, so waiting a few extra days for nicer weather wouldn't hurt. But with no other real leads, and the fact that I couldn't wait forever for the hermit to come into town, I knew it's what I had to do. A fall breeze from the open window kissed my hair and a little chickadee landed on my windowsill, chirping happily, as if to drive the point home.

By the time I'd finished compiling my notes, packed a day bag, had my all-important cup of hot, sugary coffee (I espresso-ed myself), ate a granola bar, and let Christopher at the front desk know where I was going (safety first), it was already noon. I walked toward the woods, pausing by a school at the edge of town. It must have been recess, because the playground beside the trees was packed. The tinkling sound of childhood laughter made the air sparkle as kids ran and played, their exuberance palpable. *I wish I had that much energy.* I was already fantasizing about another cup of coffee.

As I continued past the playground, two girls jumping rope sang loudly, drowning out the other kids' joyful play.

Wolf, wolf, where is the wolf?
He is coming to take your sheep!
Wolf, wolf, where is the wolf?
He'll come and get you in your sleep!
Wolf, wolf, there is the wolf—
He has come and eaten your sheep!
Wolf, wolf, there is the wolf—
He's here to get you in your sleep!
Wolf, wolf . . .

The song became muffled as I stepped into the shade of the trees, but the girls' voices rang in my head. *Kinda morbid, but a catchy tune.*

I had just lost sight of the playground when I heard the leaves crunch behind me.

Something grabbed my wrist, and I quickly jerked my hand free as I whirled around, reaching with my other hand for the knife I kept at my side.

"Whoa!" squeaked little Mikey as he put both his hands up and took a step backward.

"Shit!" I breathed deeply and felt my heart pounding in my chest. Mikey said nothing, but just stared at me with wide eyes. *Jericho James, you can't say "shit" in front of a kid, even if he did just scare it out of you.* "Shit!" I reiterated wholeheartedly.

Mikey shook his head as if he knew what I was thinking, dislodging his glasses in the process. "Don't worry, I've heard that word before. You just startled me."

"*I* startled *you*?" I asked incredulously. I didn't give him a chance to respond. "Mikey, what are you doing here?" He didn't answer but pushed his glasses back up and tugged on my hand, silently urging me a few feet back to the edge of the trees. I walked with him until the playground was in sight. The girls were still singing.

Wolf, wolf, where is the wolf?

"Don't go into the woods."

I sighed and opened my mouth to respond, but Mikey continued, "I heard the monster again." The rest of his words poured out in a hurried rush, "Since you took a recording of me before, I thought maybe I could take a recording, too. Like, maybe that could help? So yesterday I borrowed my friend's playback mic."

Mikey pulled a bulky, metallic pink microphone out of his

backpack. He held it up proudly. "I didn't even need to wait long! The monster came back last night."

The monster. I looked at my watch, then back at Mikey's expectant face. "Nice detective work, kiddo. Let's hear it."

Wolf, wolf, there is the wolf—

Mikey rolled the microphone around, exposing a panel of buttons on the back. He hit PLAY. For a moment, there was nothing but the sounds of rain and static; then suddenly an eerie, high-pitched screech erupted from the device, splitting the air around us. The otherworldly scream diminished into a low groan, followed by cracking and popping sounds, then sniffing and a low growl. The hair on my arms stood up.

He's here to get you in your sleep!

The singing stopped as the girls looked toward the source of the screeching sounds. They pointed at the boy beside me and started laughing.

"Mikey, you're so weird!" one of them called out. Mikey looked back at me, pushing his too-big glasses up the bridge of his nose. Tears threatened behind his eyes.

I knelt, locking eyes with him. "Don't listen to them. Crazy is a compliment; remember that. So you've been hearing this from your room regularly?"

He nodded solemnly. "Every month since summer vacation, so almost forever."

"You are one brave dude. Thanks for getting this." I patted him on the shoulder and turned back toward the trees.

"Wait! Y-you can't go in there," he stammered. Then he continued forcefully. "I recorded this to prove the monster was real. I thought you'd believe me."

"Of course I believe you, buddy. That's exactly why I *have* to go. It's my job to track down stuff like this." I shot him a smile and waved, then went back into the woods.

He was still standing there, unmoving, when I turned to look one last time. I sighed and kept going, picking my way down the thin but visible path through the trees. Whatever it was that Mikey had recorded last night *was* extremely creepy, and frankly I was shocked that he wasn't more disturbed. *I guess he's used to hearing it now?*

The otherworldly calls certainly didn't sound like any animal I was familiar with, but every other one of my cases that started out with folks crying "monster" ended with a perfectly regular animal who'd been victimized by overactive imaginations. More than once, I've felt like I was living out a Scooby-Doo cartoon. Even so, I gave a gentle pat to the silver-and-abalone-handled knife I kept strapped to my left leg, and the small gun in the holster on my right. I'd never fired it on the job, but I knew how to use it. I was a regular fixture at the local gun range and a more-than-decent shot.

I thought about my last time at the range as I made my way through the woods. I'd hit my target every time, to the point where the men there stopped their own practices to watch me. I was in the zone that day. Even with the audience, I felt like I was on my own, my steady breath guiding the rhythm of my shots. I was in that same zone now, breathing in time with my steps.

I paused to check the map the sheriff had given me the day before, taking in the stunning beauty around me. The orange-and-gold canopy gave the sunlight that filtered down an extra-warm glow, and the small insects that darted before me glittered in the golden light. I smelled fresh pine, felt the loamy earth under my feet, and heard the warbling of birds flitting through the colorful trees. I suddenly felt very Zen and one with nature. Had Katherine felt that way just before her death?

Wolf, wolf, where is the wolf?

I hummed along with the birdsong as I turned from the map to my wrist. I knew that my phone wouldn't have any signal, but I'd turned on a step-tracking app before I left, and my watch told me I'd gone just over four miles. Only half a mile more to reach the clearing where Katherine's body had been found. Kermit's house was four and a half miles farther in and to the left. *I've got this*, I thought, though it'd been a while since I'd done so much hiking. I ran track and cross-country in both high school and college, so I figured the distance would be manageable, but I was still breathing a bit more rapidly in the cold air.

Hopefully the visit to this hermit's house would be quick. Sheriff Jackson's gravelly voice was gentle but stern, giving a warning that the hermit would be "none too happy" to have unexpected visitors, even though he encouraged me to use the lead. I ran through my list of questions for him in my head: Had he seen or heard anything the night of the attack? Had there been any strange animal activity in the past few weeks? And I definitely wanted to ask him if he'd *ever* heard sounds in the woods like the ones Mikey had recorded.

Damn—I should have borrowed that kid's recording thing. I shook my head ruefully. Maybe I could convince Mr. The Hermit to come back to town with me, because that recording was... something. The only noises now were the birds singing, and I was glad for their pleasant company. But all thoughts of animal sounds left my head as I reached the clearing. This was it—the site of the attack. I took a deep breath and dove in.

Turning on my PI brain, I examined the packed dirt in the middle of the trees. The clearing was about fifteen feet across and looked completely benign. Not that I'd expected to find anything, but I still had to see it for myself to be sure. I had pored over pictures of this place in news articles about Katherine's death, as well as the fully detailed set of photos in the police report, but seeing something in person is always different. Being here made it *real*. This wasn't a story anymore. A young woman died *right here*. And it was my job to bring her family closure, or as much as I could give them.

I looked around, noting the bushes and tightly packed trees that circled most of the clearing. Had Katherine paused here for a break and been caught unawares by something leaping from the shadows? There were certainly enough of those to hide something. I walked farther into the clearing, wondering what the younger woman had seen in her last moments of life.

A twisted root caught my foot, causing me to stumble a few steps. *Shit, shit!* The poor girl's mangled body had been sprawled out exactly where I was standing. A chill raced up my spine. *It's bad luck to stand where the dead have lain.* I don't remember where I'd heard that, but I quickly stepped aside. From where I now stood, I could see the sky through the trees, clear and cloudless and *darkening*. The sun was already beginning its descent in the horizon. I mentally kicked myself, groaning as I looked at my watch. I'd completely lost track of time. My fitness tracker was still running in the center screen, and the clock was minimized to a corner. I still wasn't accustomed to the earlier sunsets that go hand in hand with winter's approach. But at least I'd gotten to see the clearing.

Well, time's up, Jericho. The still full moon would provide some light, but I didn't want to be caught in the woods at night. I was already cold, and what if I tripped on another exposed root disguised by shadows? I needed a broken ankle like I needed another lecture from my mom on finding "someone to settle down with."

Not to mention that whatever had gotten Katherine remained at large. I glanced in the direction of Kermit's house, dismayed. My chat with the hermit would have to wait for another day. With my mind made up, I turned back the way I came, my footsteps loud in the silence.

Silence?

The birds had stopped singing.

An icy chill snaked through my blood, and I froze, my ears straining, listening. The forest was eerily still. The soft pressure of unseen eyes sent a tingle between my shoulder blades. Adrenaline flooded my veins, and I started moving on autopilot. I slowly lowered my hand to my gun and raised it in one smooth motion, pointing it in front of me and toward the path back to town.

My heart beat once. Twice. But all I could hear was my own breath. On the third heartbeat, there was a loud snap from behind me, and I whirled around in time to see the bushes shaking by the trail near the opposite side of the clearing. I trained my gun in that direction and, with eyes locked on the shuddering bushes, began backing toward the path I'd just come from.

I steadied my breath, my mind running through possibilities.
Maybe it's a trick of the light and the lengthening shadows.
Maybe it's just a bunny and you're an idiot, Jericho.
A low growl rumbled from the bushes I was headed toward.
Not a bunny.

I stopped moving and whipped my head around, searching in vain for the source of the growl. It was echoed by another on the opposite side of the clearing. *Were there two? Or was it the same one?* Could some beast be blocking my path back to the town, and another closing in? A twig cracked from the trail toward town, followed closely by another rumbling growl. The hairs on my arms and the back of my neck rose suddenly as my arms prickled with goose bumps.

I was being hunted.

The realization washed over my jumbled thoughts like cold water, clearing my mind. I had to assume that both the path forward and the path behind were blocked. If I could see whatever was threatening me, I was fully confident I could get at least two shots in before the creature, or creatures, came closer. *But what if there's more than two?* I couldn't see anything aside from the bushes and the deepening shadows of the trees. I would be firing blind.

I guess that leaves door number three. I jammed my gun back into its holster and quickly pivoted to the left. I ran through a gap in the trees, off the trail and into the forest, in what I hoped was the direction of the hermit's house.

THE MIDNIGHT PACK

A cacophony of sounds exploded behind me, but I didn't look back. Branches clawed at me, scratching my face and grabbing at my hair like so many gnarled fingers as I scrambled through the tangled undergrowth. An uneasy silence fell, and for a moment the only sounds were my adrenaline-charged steps and my ragged breath. The stillness lasted long enough for me to wonder if I'd just imagined the commotion from the clearing.

Then that moment ended and there was a definitive crash in the underbrush behind me. I gasped and looked back over my shoulder but saw no signs of my pursuers. I faced forward again then choked on a scream—the forest had abruptly opened to a small but steep ravine at my feet. Forward momentum carried me over the precipice, where my body lurched into space before tumbling down the slope.

The fall wasn't far, but it was hard, and I heard as much as felt a sharp crack in my ankle when I met the rocky bottom. I managed to lift my head, but the rest of my body wouldn't follow. At the top of the ravine, dimly outlined in the fading light, was the hulking silhouette of a person.

Jericho James, you fresh idiot.

Everything went black.

CHAPTER 3

I woke up slowly, relishing the lazy space between wakefulness and dreaming. The warmth of the sun caressed my face, and my soul soaked it up like a sponge. I needed some sunshine. I hadn't had a nightmare like that in a *long* time. I shuddered as I remembered the terror of being chased.

It was just a dream, Jericho. I rolled over and opened my eyes with a satisfied sigh...

This is not my room.

The thought was the mental equivalent of getting dunked in a bucket of ice water. I jolted up and took in my surroundings. I was sitting on the plushy mattress of a queen-size bed, surrounded by a veritable sea of blankets and quilts. I fingered the edge of the quilt on top. The daisy-patterned mustard-and-burnt-orange fabric was worn but well kept. I wore the same black tank top and gray tights from *when? Today? The day before?* Either way, my ensemble was worse for wear with holes, dust, and grime, and I had inadvertently covered the crisp white sheets in a layer of dirt.

The sunlight paid no notice to my strife and continued to pour in through huge bay windows to my left, highlighting the dust motes that floated languidly in the air before me. I felt rather dust-motish myself, not knowing when or where I was, suspended in sunlight and time. The room smelled fresh and woodsy, all pine and cedar. There was a full, somewhat spicy undertone as well. I breathed in deeply, but the movement made me wince in pain. I must have bruised my ribs in the fall. I stretched the rest of my body carefully, taking stock of any other injuries, and *ouch—okay, so moving makes that ankle angry.* But aside from my battered rib cage and what I decided must be a sprained ankle on my left side, everything else seemed to be in one piece. I was hungry and a bit disoriented, but I was alive.

The heavy bedroom door creaked open, breaking me away from my body examination. I froze, panicked—it made sense that someone had brought me here, but I hadn't given it any thought in my first moments of consciousness. *Oh God, what if it's some vagabond in the woods who wants to chain me to a radiator? Or someone from town who doesn't want me snooping around...*

I braced myself for the worst to walk through that door... but as it opened, the most beautiful human I'd ever seen stepped through. This man was positively angelic. If my life were a movie, this is the part where backlighting would frame his face in a gentle glow, his perfectly scruffy chestnut hair would start ruffling in a misbegotten wind, and a classic love ballad would play in the background as he moved in slow motion closer to me. He'd probably rip his T-shirt open for good measure.

Maybe I died after all.

As it happened, his shirt remained sadly intact and he took a slow step into the room, as if he were approaching an injured animal.

"Hey," he said gently, "I'm glad to see you're awake." He smiled.

I fell out of the bed and onto the floor.

"Ow!" I cringed as I started to right myself and lifted a hand to grab the side of the bed for support. He was already by my side, having crossed the room in a few quick steps, so instead of the bedpost I'd been reaching for I found his hand in mine. His broad palms were warm and rough, his fingers callused. He had the same spicy scent that I'd noticed before—*this must be his room.* That was a comforting thought somehow. He hoisted me up with ease, then with both hands on the small of my waist, he positioned me into a seat on the bedside.

When he seemed sure I wasn't going to spontaneously dump myself to the ground again, he let go, his fingers trailing briefly down my hips before he pulled his hands away. My skin tingled at the ghost of his touch, and the shirt-ripping daydream reappeared unbidden in my head. *Hey, you can live there rent-free.* He inhaled then stepped back, suddenly looking down shyly as he cleared his throat.

He glanced up at me and smiled, then without breaking eye contact reached behind himself to grab a simple wooden chair from the corner of the room. He'd known exactly where it was without looking. *Definitely his room.* He pulled the chair with one hand and flipped it around so the back of the chair was closest to the bed, then straddled the seat to continue facing me.

His clear blue eyes locked on mine, and I found myself pulled into his gaze. It felt like looking into a mountain lake, calm and cool on the surface. But I could tell there were hidden depths below. I had the sudden mental image of peering too deep and drowning in those twin blue pools, but strangely didn't mind. *Snap out of it, Jericho!*

He was looking at me expectantly, and I realized he had just asked me something.

"Wait, what?" I must have hit my head harder than I thought—I'm not usually one to lose myself in daydreams, handsome men aside.

"I said you must have lots of questions—"

"Well, yes. Who are you? How did I get here? How long was I out? And aside from this clearly being your room"—I grinned at the surprise that crossed his face—"where is 'here'?"

As he opened his mouth to reply, I patted my sides and looked down with a start: My two deadly accessories were missing. I looked back at him with narrowed eyes, reminding myself to not let the hotness overtake reality. "And where are my knife and gun?"

The man put his hands up in mock defense and smiled. "They're safe—see, your knife is over there." He pointed to the small table on the opposite side of the bed, where the silver handle glinted in the sunlight. It was a custom piece, the sterling silver inlaid with abalone and molded with clever grooves to fit my fingers. The five-inch blade lay neatly tucked inside. "I like your style, by the way. That's a good knife."

I would not be distracted by flattery. I gave him a wilted

look and raised an eyebrow. "Uh, okay, and your gun is right here." He patted the back pocket of his worn jeans.

With a scowl, I reached out, and he handed it to me. I inspected it as he continued. "We took out the bullets. I hope you understand." My mouth opened with an objection and some choice words ready, but he went on. "No loaded weapons inside. House rules." He shrugged and gave me an apologetic smile. "Besides, we don't know who you are or why you were heading toward our home, armed to the teeth. We keep all our own weapons locked up, but I figured you'd feel more comfortable with your gun on you, empty as it is." I nodded in acquiescence and tucked the weapons back to my sides.

He carried on. "As for the rest, my name is Benjamin Grey and I live here with my family. You might be familiar with my dad—um, Kermit."

I felt my eyes widen in recognition. *Clearly Kermit is* not *a hermit.*

Benjamin nodded, acknowledging my surprise. "We like to keep to ourselves, and we stay busy out here. Dad goes into town every so often for supplies and such. But anyway. As to how you got here, I was out hunting, and I heard someone running through the trees. I went to see what the commotion was and found you passed out in the ravine. I carried you back here"—he gestured around the room—"and the rest, I guess, is history."

Benjamin shrugged, but I wasn't ready to brush aside the details of his story that he'd left unsaid. His answers left me with an entirely new set of questions, like: Why didn't they want the town to know the truth about Kermit? Did

Benjamin see the man from the ravine? Was *he* the man from the ravine? What did Benjamin look like without a shirt on, and was he single?

I sat poised to continue my internal line of questioning, and I was about to ask at least one of the queries for real, but Benjamin gave me a crooked smile and jumped in first. "Not so fast there, cowboy. Er, cowgirl. You know who I am, and where you are. I think it's your turn to tell me who you are, and why you were armed up and on your way to my home."

My eyes narrowed slightly, but he continued in a gentle tone. "Don't try to tell me that you weren't, either. There's nothing out here but this house. So either you were very, *very* lost, or you were on your way here with a purpose."

I'd been tense throughout our exchange, but I let my body relax. Those were reasonable questions, and Benjamin had been nothing but chivalrous so far.

I sighed. "That's a fair point. My name is Jericho James, and I'm a private investigator. I was hired to look into the death of a young woman named Katherine Waller." I'd been watching Benjamin's reaction carefully, but at the mention of the murder he only looked puzzled.

"Yeah, we heard about that. My dad is something of an animal expert, and he says it was clearly a random bear attack."

I shrugged. "Maybe so. But that's what I'm here to find out." Benjamin stiffened slightly at this, so I gave him what I hoped was a reassuring smile. "I was hoping I could pick your dad's brain on the local wildlife."

Benjamin leaned back and chuckled. "Yeah, he knows what he's talking about, so I'm sure he'll tell you the same." He paused and ran his hand through his hair, ruffling it further. "So, um, how did I come to find you at the bottom of a ravine?"

My mind replayed the moments leading up to that frantic run through the forest, but my stomach rumbled before I could organize my thoughts.

Benjamin's eyes widened. "I'm sorry, you must be starving. We're not really used to company. Do you feel up to walking? We can head to the kitchen, or I can bring you something to eat here." He smiled again. "I make a mean peanut butter and jelly sandwich."

"That would be great. I *think* I can walk." I sounded much more confident than I felt, and Benjamin stood up and scooted the chair haphazardly back to its corner to give me some space. He offered a hand, but I pushed myself out of the bed without any aid. An injured ankle wouldn't keep me down (all evidence to the contrary). I stood up shakily and tested said ankle. It immediately buckled under my weight. *Dammit!* Benjamin reached out with a steadying hand, but I'd already grabbed the bedpost.

"I'm okay." I straightened up and tested my ankle a little more gently and found I could slowly and painfully manage a limp. Benjamin looked entirely dubious and seemed poised to catch me should I show signs of falling again. "Really, I can do it." I smiled up at him. "My mom likes to say that I'm as stubborn as the day is long."

"Well, in that case"—he gestured to a door past the foot of the bed—"there's the bathroom, but I've been injured enough times and in enough ways to know that you're supposed to rest an ankle like that, so I'll bring your food up here."

I was gearing up for a protest, but he was already at the other door. "Doctor's orders!" he called cheerfully, then left, closing the door behind him. His spicy scent lingered with me as his footsteps receded.

Benjamin left me with a lot to process. Like, did anybody in town know he existed? And how had he found me in the woods? Could he have been the shadow I saw as I fell? He certainly got there quickly if that was the case. Also, what was the exact shade of his lake-blue eyes, and why couldn't I get the smell of him out of my mind? Like some lustful teenager from a B movie, I was already looking forward to his return. I rolled my eyes at my own instant crush. It had been a while since I'd had a boyfriend, but this sudden rush of attraction made me feel like I was *desperate. Says the Jericho who was ready to skip work to ask front-desk-Christopher out for drinks.*

I sighed. First things first—I focused on walking across the floor to the bathroom, silently acknowledging that Benjamin might be right about needing to rest my ankle. *Benjamin.* I reminded myself that I didn't know anything about him and should not judge a book by its extremely attractive cover. *For all you know, he could be a murderer.* I shook my head again, immediately dispelling the thought as it entered my brain. I prided myself on my ability to read people, and my gut reaction told me he was one of the good ones. He did seem guarded, as well as concerned about my motives for visiting the house, but that was completely reasonable for the son of a hermit.

I smiled triumphantly when I finally made it to the bathroom, then quickly took a drink from the faucet. The icy water instantly soothed my parched throat. I hadn't realized how thirsty I was. I looked up to the mirror and breathed a sigh of relief, which turned to a groan as my battered reflection returned my gaze. I gently touched a bruise on my cheekbone. I'd never thought of myself as a 10/10 beauty, but most of the time I managed a solid "cute." This was not one of those times. My shoulder-length deep-blonde hair had come out of its classic ponytail and instead floated around my head in a mess of tangles like a wild halo. My eyes, my most striking feature, which typically ranged from amber to gold to caramel depending on the lighting and my wardrobe, peered out dully from a raccoon-like mask of dark circles. My usually tan skin had paled and was now bruise-mottled, looking especially lurid in the bathroom light. I washed my face and hastily combed through my hair with my fingers in an attempt to freshen up.

I almost felt like a regular human again when I limped my way back into the bedroom. There was a lonesome desk against one of the walls, so I hobbled over to the wooden chair and began to push it over.

"Oh, let me get that." I hadn't heard him enter the room, but Benjamin was beside me in moments. He pushed the chair with one hand and with the other set the sandwich plate atop the desk with a flourish. "*Et voilà!*"

"*Merci, monsieur,*" I said with a smile.

"*De rien, mademoiselle. J'espère que ça te plaît,*" he said smoothly. He noticed my confusion and blushed. "Uh, that is, I hope you like it."

"You speak French?" I asked, intelligently. *Duh, Jericho, he just did.* And did he just become even more attractive for it? *Oui.*

"Um, I thought you might, too," he said.

I shook my head. "No, you've now heard everything I've retained from my trip to France last year." *Almost everything.* I also knew that *cheval* meant horse, since I was chasing down sightings of the Cheval Mallet. But it seemed like too long a story to tell, so instead I smiled. "My strengths lie elsewhere."

I sat on the wooden chair, using the desk as my lunch table. Benjamin plopped down on the bed beside me. Even though we'd only spent a total of about thirty minutes together, his laid-back attitude already had me completely at ease. Benjamin exuded an almost palpable strength and serenity. If there was a storm brewing, there was no doubt in my mind that this man would be a rock unmoved by the torrent around him. It was a welcome calm. I always considered myself cool and collected, but my work had the habit of straining that peace. *Cthulhu sightings! Chupacabra sightings! And what did Mikey say? A dogman or Tote-Road Shagamaw!* Always a false alarm, always dramatic. But not right now. Surrounded by Benjamin's spicy cinnamon scent and sitting in the warmth of the sunlight, a tranquility washed over me that I hadn't experienced in a long, long time.

I really hope he's not some sort of drug lord.

By the time I finished my sandwich, we were laughing and chatting away like old friends. And maybe I was flirting a little harder than usual. I did keep brushing my hair away from my face, mostly to eat the not-bad sandwich, but also in the hope that he would notice my shoulders and neck. I didn't get to meet too many super-hot men in my line of lonely work, and I didn't want to pass up the opportunity for...something.

Benjamin was also a loner by happenstance. ("Happenstance" in this case being mysteriously secluded in the Maine woods with his dad.) As I ate, he told me that his father had already left early that morning to trek into town on a mission to both let the police and the hotel know where I was, and to kindly collect my things. There was no way to or from their home except for the hike through the forest, which I was in no condition to do with my ankle, so it seemed that I would be imposing as a guest for an indefinite while.

With his help, I cobbled together the timeline of events from the chase the previous day up until my peanut butter and jelly sandwich. The only piece I couldn't reconcile was this: How was Benjamin close enough to be at the ravine when I fell while still seeing neither hide nor hair of the thing that had been chasing me? If he really was that close—close enough to hear me running—shouldn't he have also heard some of the same growls that I did?

To my dismay, a little voice deep down kept asking, *What if it was him? What if he's the one who chased me?* I looked at Benjamin. He'd been gazing out the bay window, lost in his own thoughts. His face was calm, but when he caught me looking at him he smiled shyly, his blue eyes twinkling like sunlight on a mountain lake. I'd build a house on the edge of those waters just to see that sparkle daily. I silenced the voice. *No, there's no way.*

I yawned, and Benjamin left me to take a nap in his bed. The injuries from my fall were taking their toll. My body was begging for more rest, and I was in no mood to fight it. My eyes shut as soon as my head hit the pillow, and I instantly fell into a dream. I was back in the clearing, but I wasn't alone.

THE MIDNIGHT PACK

The two girls I'd seen at the playground yesterday, a lifetime ago, were skipping rope. I approached them, but they were oblivious to me as they sang.

Wolf, wolf, where is the wolf?
He is coming to take your sheep!
Wolf, wolf, where is the wolf?
He'll come and get you in your sleep!
Wolf, wolf, there is the wolf—
He has come and eaten your sheep!
Wolf, wolf, there is the wolf—
He's here to get you in your sleep!

They suddenly dropped the jump rope and stood completely frozen, staring at each other. I got the feeling that I'd fallen into a scene from *The Shining*, and I didn't like it. At this point, I was right beside the girls, but they still didn't acknowledge me. *Rude.* I reached out to get their attention, almost touching one of them on the shoulder. When my hand was mere millimeters away, both girls whipped their heads toward me in sync. Two pairs of eyes abruptly and intently stared into mine.

If they ask me to play with them, I'm so out of here.

One girl raised a finger to her lips as if cautioning me to silence. Then she slowly moved the finger away from her face and pointed down. My eyes followed the motion, and my blood ran cold with an electrifying chill when I saw what she was pointing at: Katherine's dead body lay at our feet.

"*It's bad luck to stand where the dead have lain,*" they said in unison.

CHAPTER 4

There were men's voices outside the door.

"You can't keep her to yourself forever, Benny boy."

"Come on, she's resting."

"Negative, Ghost Rider. She's awake, can't you tell?"

Were there more of Kermit's kin in this house? I listened closer to the other voices pestering Benjamin. They all shared the same soft lyricism, but one voice wasn't as mature as Benjamin's, and the other was tinged with sarcasm. By the way they were goading him, I figured they couldn't be anything but brothers. Just how many secret children was this "hermit" hiding? *This had better not be some kind of cult compound, preying on unsuspecting women.* The little voice was back. I frowned. Benjamin looked too nice to be in a cult. *But it's always the nice-looking ones who are the predators.*

I gently stretched my arms and wiggled my fingers, attempting to silence the voice and shake out the remnants of my creepy dream, which hadn't made my sleep exactly restful. As a result I wasn't entirely awake yet, and still so very tired, but trying to recapture my nap would only be prolonging the inevitable.

I called through the door, letting the men outside know I was indeed awake.

"I'm up, Benjamin! Just give me a few minutes!"

After somewhat more than a few minutes, I had freshened up (somewhat) again and hobbled back to the door to let in my hosts. No sooner had I turned the doorknob than three men piled in. They were all good looking and *definitely* brothers, but where Benjamin was tall and fair, the other two were slightly shorter and had darker complexions.

"Jericho, glad to see you're up! This is Theo and Seth," Benjamin said with an apologetic smile. "They're, um, well, they're really pleased to meet you."

I could tell he was trying to recall town manners but didn't quite know how to go about it. I gave him a reassuring nod. "Nice to meet you both."

I sat down on the edge of the bed, and Benjamin quickly pushed the chair over so I could use it as a footrest. As I smiled at him gratefully, I noticed his brothers exchanging a look between them. Benjamin glared in their direction, and one of them coughed, then came to sit on the bed beside me. Benjamin joined me on my other side, but the third brother kept his station near the door, leaning against the heavy wooden frame with his arms crossed over his chest. The man in the doorway had short black hair and stared at me with stormy, piercing eyes. I suddenly felt surrounded and exposed. As if he sensed it, Benjamin leaned closer to me, protectively. He reached out an arm as if to put it around my back, but hesitated and settled on resting it behind me on the bed.

"Come on, Seth, why don't you join us?" Benjamin offered his brother a smile.

In the doorway, Seth returned a grin, but the smile didn't touch his eyes. *Now, this guy has the look of a predator.* "Looks like the bed is full." His voice was snide and laced with annoyance.

"Don't mind our baby brother. He's just not used to guests." Theo turned to me and smiled warmly. His eyes crinkled when he did, and his black hair flopped downward. He laughed at himself and smoothed it back. *I can't believe I thought he and Seth looked alike at first. These two are night and day.*

In fact, Theo somehow looked familiar, but I couldn't put my finger on why. Maybe because when he smiled, he looked a lot more like Benjamin. I filed that thought to the back of my exhausted mind to reexamine later and returned my attention to the conversation at hand, which largely consisted of Theo peppering me with questions about the town, its people, and what had brought me to their home. As I recounted the story of my run through the woods and Benjamin's rescue, I steered the conversation to the mystery monster and their thoughts on Katherine's killing. The more I thought about it, the more I was certain that whatever had chased me and whatever had gotten Katherine were one and the same. Maybe Theo or Seth had some new tidbit of information.

"Well, if you had to guess, what would you think it was?"

Theo frowned, his mood suddenly sour. "Our father said a bear killed the woman. Maybe the same animal was after you."

The other brother was silent, so I pressed Benjamin on what creature (or creatures) had chased me.

He shifted his weight to his other arm. "I mean, the bear that got to Katherine could still be in the area. But my best guess is this was some dumb animal that got spooked." At this, Benjamin glanced at his brothers, and the air in the room shifted. Theo beside me looked pensive from a glance, but his eyes darted around the room like he couldn't focus on any one thing. Seth, still in the doorway, was studiously ignoring the rest of us as he picked at his dirt-caked fingernails.

It felt to me like somebody was hiding something, and these guys didn't seem to be very good at lying. Maybe they kept exotic animals illegally, like tigers or something, and one got out. It wouldn't be the first time. In 2021, someone's pet tiger roamed the streets of Houston for an entire week before it was caught—one of the few jobs I turned down, since I didn't own a tranquilizer gun. *An escaped tiger would explain a lot, actually.*

I broke the uncomfortable silence. "So, do you guys have any pets?"

The three brothers looked at one another and laughed, like I'd just cracked a joke, finally lightening the mood of the room.

"No," responded Benjamin, still smiling.

"Not even a cat or something?"

Seth laughed even harder from the doorway, and Theo shook his head. "Gross."

"What's wrong with cats? I like cats," I said, offended.

Theo stood up from the bed and looked over at Benjamin.

"This one's defective, Ben, you can keep her." He said it kindly, though, and gave me a smile and a wink as he walked out of the room. He took Seth by the elbow as he did, pulling the other man along.

We heard their footsteps receding down the hallway, leaving Benjamin and me alone again. I sighed and leaned against him automatically, resting my head on his shoulder before I realized what I was doing. Just as I registered that I was getting awfully comfortable with a complete stranger—*and my head fit so well there*—he leaned into *me*, lowering his head against mine. I pushed away and straightened up awkwardly.

"Uh, I'm sorry," I stammered.

"Don't be." He flashed me a lopsided smile. "You just look like you could use some moral support."

Well, if he's offering... I returned my head to his shoulder, near the crook of his neck, and inhaled deeply. The smell of him swamped my senses. *Benjamin*. He tentatively put an arm around me, and I closed my eyes, inadvertently making a small, contented sound as I relaxed against him. He was so warm. As a perpetually cold person, this was a massive bonus. I could practically sense Benjamin's mouth crack into a smile as he softly brushed the top of my hair with his nose.

"You smell so good," he murmured to himself.

My eyes popped open. I sincerely doubted that. More than likely, I smelled like sweat and dirt. But if he enjoyed that, I'd take it. *Is that a creepy thing for him to say, though, Jericho?* Maybe. *But did you like it?* Yes.

I leaned away. "Thanks, I needed that."

Benjamin looked like he wanted to say something else but

smiled shyly instead. His eyes turned to my hand, which he picked up in his own. He flipped my hand so my palm was facing up and traced the lines there with his thumb. His hands were so much bigger than mine and, again, warm. *Very warm.*

He spoke, still looking at my palm. "My mom used to say, 'Sometimes all we need is a hug to put the broken pieces back together.'"

"Your mom sounds like a smart lady."

"Yeah, she was." He stopped stroking my hand and set it gently back on my lap. "She, uh, she died a while ago."

Benjamin kept looking down, but his eyes weren't focused on me anymore. He seemed lost in thought. Then he shook his head, and when looked back at me, he was smiling.

"She'd have liked you, though."

"You think so?"

"Oh yeah. Someone like you? Brave enough to trek through the forest alone, looking for an animal that recently *killed* another lone woman in that same forest—and I suspect you were planning on taking it on all by yourself if you found it, right?" I blushed in answer, and he went on. "Yeah, I figured as much. Tough enough to refuse help walking, even though your ankle is clearly in pain..."

I laughed, interrupting him. "Others might say that's being nothing but foolish and stubborn."

He shrugged. "You need to give yourself more credit than that. There's a thin line between foolish and brave, and a thin line between tough and stubborn. You're a strong soul, Jericho. And looking into your eyes is like looking into the sun."

That's a new one. Like I was burning his retinas out? I turned my head down, but he put a callused thumb under my chin and gently angled my face back up toward him. His lake-blue eyes searched my amber ones.

"I meant that as a compliment. Looking at you, it's... well, frankly, it's mesmerizing. Your eyes are full of fire and life. I'm not sure how anyone could resist that."

I smiled slyly. "Are you saying you find me irresistible?"

He grinned back. "I don't see how anyone could stand a chance."

He moved his face closer to mine, hesitantly. He shifted his hand from my chin to my cheek, sweeping some wayward hair behind my ear. I leaned in closer, and his warm breath swept my neck, eliciting goose bumps. I hadn't been this close to an actual guy in... *far too long if you have to preface it with "an actual guy," Jericho.*

The sound of a door slamming reverberated through the house, startling us apart.

I jumped. "What was that?"

Benjamin looked pained. "That would be my dad, who always has impeccable timing."

He got up from the bed and put his hands in his pockets, as if he had to keep them locked up lest they develop a mind of their own and go back to caressing my face. *Yes, please.* I sighed.

Benjamin took a few steps over to the doorway and leaned against the doorframe expectantly. The sound of steady footsteps grew louder, and Kermit (the not-hermit) soon towered beside Benjamin. If I thought Benjamin and his brothers were big, then Kermit was an absolute mountain. It was painfully clear where Benjamin inherited his broad shoulders and lumberjack-like physique. I take that back; lumberjacks *wish* they had bodies like Kermit. Even his blue-and-white flannel shirt did nothing to hide the muscle-bound shoulders beneath. He glanced at his son, giving me a clear profile view of his strong jawline, though the wide-brimmed hat he wore shaded his eyes and nose. He made an intimidating figure, even as someone I guessed was around my own dad's age, but I consciously pushed the feeling down and sat up straighter.

Kermit stepped fully into the light of the room, and I immediately felt silly for being intimidated. He removed his hat, revealing wavy white hair and bright-blue eyes. He cracked a huge grin when he saw me, and the smile lines around his eyes crinkled. I love it when people have deep smile lines. It's like a permanent map of their life's happiness. I couldn't help but smile back.

"Tarry here, I pray thee; for the Lord hath sent me to Jericho." He slung a large pack off his shoulder and lay it on the bed beside me. It was all my things from the hotel in town.

"Oh, thank you."

"You are most welcome, Jericho James. Kermit Grey, at your service. Benny told me how he found you after a fall, and I didn't expect you'd be walking back to your hotel room anytime soon."

Benjamin blushed at being called Benny, but he didn't interrupt his father.

Kermit went on, picking up a grocery bag that he'd set down among my belongings. "I'll go start on dinner now, as I suspect Benjamin didn't give you more than a sandwich." Benjamin's blush spread.

"I do expect Benny gave you some fresh towels for the shower."

I didn't think it was possible for Benjamin's blush to deepen, but it did as he ducked out of the room.

Kermit paid no mind to his absence and carried on. "And I hope the boys have been letting you get your rest and haven't been pestering you too much." He exhaled in satisfaction as he set the last bag down. "They're good boys, just not used to having company over."

Kermit turned away and started walking slowly toward the door, then stopped. "By the by, Jericho, someone was looking for you," Kermit said, turning toward me. Noticing the surprised look on my face, Kermit didn't wait for me to ask who. "A boy was waiting for you where the woods meet the town. I wanted to ask you about him."

Recognition dawned on me, and I nodded. "Oh, that was probably Mikey. Little guy, with dark hair and big glasses?"

Kermit looked me in the eye. "The very same. Do you know him well?" I shook my head, and he continued. "Then is he a new friend of yours?"

"Er, kind of. He's been hearing some strange animal noises. I was actually hoping you could help identify them," I said, chagrined all over again that I didn't have the recording with me. "Why do you ask?"

"He made me think of..." He paused, still in the doorway. "Never mind, it was nothing." Kermit shook his head. "I would be happy to help identify what he heard. Perhaps you can describe it to me over dinner." He didn't wait for a response before he turned away again and walked out of the room.

Benjamin reappeared, perfectly framed in the door and holding a fresh stack of fluffy towels. He made to bring them into the room, but stopped when Kermit leaned back through the doorway, looking back to lock eyes with his son. "Benjamin, why don't you leave this nice lady to clean up for dinner? I could use your help in the kitchen."

"Okay, Dad." Benjamin quickly set the towels down on the bed next to my bags and gave me a small shrug. *Dammit, Kermit!*

The two walked down the hallway, their voices carrying as they spoke.

"You're a grown man and it's time for you to learn how to cook. Your mother would be rolling in her grave if she thought all you gave that poor girl was a peanut butter and jelly sandwich."

"But—"

"No *buts*, Benny, it's..." They were far enough away that I couldn't hear any more, but I smiled to myself at their conversation.

I hobbled my way to the door and shut it, pressing my back against the wood and biting my lower lip as I thought back to my own conversation with Benjamin. *"Your eyes are full of fire and life."* Who talks like that in real life? Still, his words sent a rush of warmth sweeping through my body, and I recalled, too, his spicy scent and warm breath on my neck. My skin tingled pleasantly at the memory. I reached my hand to my neck and cheek, trailing over the places he had touched. I pulled my hand away, rolling bits of grime between my fingers. *Gross. You need a shower, stat.*

Kermit hadn't mentioned anything about timing for dinner, but I assumed it would be soon if they were already cooking. I limped to the bathroom and twisted the hot-water handle as far as it would go. I wanted to scald myself to wash away the dirt, fear, and strange dreams that had accumulated over the last twenty-four hours.

I stood underneath the shower, the water as hot as I could manage without burning myself. Its cleansing feel against my head and back was heavenly. The water pressure was immaculate as well. I imagined it drumming away all my dirt and pain. Steam billowed around me like an ethereal cloak before sweeping into the rest of the bathroom, creating a beautiful but eerie effect. I had packed my own shampoo and conditioner for the trip to Maine, and Kermit had the presence of mind to grab them from my hotel bathroom. I lathered up my hair, loving the feeling of all the accumulated ick washing away with the suds. I watched the water swirl down the drain until it ran clear. My eyes caught on a small bar of brown-flecked soap sitting in a small stone enclave cut into the shower wall. I picked it up out of curiosity. It smelled like cinnamon and pine, just like Benjamin, and looked handmade. I took a few strong whiffs and let myself get lost in the heady scent. The cinnamon-pine smell carried lazily through the steam, and the heat around me mirrored the slow burn in my core as I thought back to Benjamin's fingers gently touching my face. Even the little voice that usually cautioned me was silent.

It was the best shower of my life.

Once I was out of my reverie and finally clean, I shut off the water and ventured out. The tile of the bathroom floor was *cold*, even with the leftover steam filling the room like a warm mist. Shivering, I reached for the white, fluffy pile that Benjamin had deposited earlier. What I thought was an armful of towels was in fact one extremely plush bathrobe, and I wrapped it around myself gratefully.

The shower had neither a curtain nor glass around it. Instead, it was a floor-to-ceiling semicircle of stone with an open space to enter. The floor was slightly tilted toward a drain in the center, and the semicircular walls seemed to catch all the water. *Clever design. I wonder who built it.* Not only the shower, but the entire home. I wasn't sure exactly how big it was yet, but either way I had a hard time imagining a construction crew out in the forest, especially with how secluded the family contrived to be. I had an equally hard time imagining Kermit doing everything by himself, though. I still didn't know his profession, if he had one. He struck me as a live-from-the-land kind of guy, but he clearly had money to shop in town and keep up the place, not to mention feed *three* adult sons, so there had to be some sort of money coming in.

I foraged through my bags for something suitable to wear to a family dinner. I knew I'd only packed my standard tank tops, tights, and a handful of flannels, but I was hopeful that something slightly more presentable—maybe even a dress— had somehow squirreled itself away in my bag. No such luck. I settled on a black tank top, black tights, and a mustard-colored flannel that I knew would bring out the amber in my eyes.

I brushed my hair until it shone, opting to leave it down. I tucked two bobby pins over my ear, holding back loose whisps of blonde. Nobody had come to retrieve me yet, so I sat down on the edge of the bed with my makeup bag beside me. I fished out some eyeliner and mascara, then flipped open my compact mirror and carefully outlined my eyes and swept my lashes. *Did I bring my concealer?* I wasn't doing it to impress Benjamin. *Yes, I am.* I just wanted to look my best. *For Benjamin.*

I'd just snapped my compact shut with a satisfying click when there was a knock on the door.

"Come in," I called.

The door swung open with a creak, and Kermit stepped into the room, alone. My heart fell a little when I saw who it was (or, more important, who it wasn't).

Kermit cleared his throat and came toward the bed, carrying something long and unwieldy. "Dinner is ready. And Ben reminded me about your ankle. These should help you." He held his arms out and I realized he was holding a pair of wooden crutches.

"Oh, thank you very much."

I stood up and maneuvered the crutches under my arms. The wood was grooved and pocked with divots, but sturdy. Surprisingly, they seemed to be just my size. All the men of the house were at least a foot taller than I was (and I am not particularly short), so it was a wonder they would keep a set of smaller crutches readily on hand.

Kermit answered my unspoken question as if reading my thoughts. "They belonged to my late wife," he said wistfully. "I made these for her myself when she broke her ankle, once upon a time. She'd be glad to see they're still making themselves useful."

I looked at the crutches with new admiration and smiled in response. "Well, I definitely appreciate using them."

Kermit's eyes trailed up from the crutches to my face. "And just so. You'll want to keep your weight off that ankle, if it's hurt as badly as Benny says it is."

I nodded in agreement. "I'll manage with these, thank you again."

"Well, all right," he continued. "This way to the dining room. Now that you have a way to get around, I'm sure Ben will give you a tour of the house tomorrow."

"That would be lovely," I said, and I meant it.

Kermit walked at a leisurely pace, allowing me to keep up with ease. We trailed down the hallway from my room, my eyes gliding over a series of family portraits hanging like birds on a wire. The pictures stopped abruptly as the wall gave way to a balcony overlooking a vast room below. I peered down over the heavy wooden railing and saw an open floor plan with couches and a fireplace on one side, and a long wooden table surrounded by sturdy chairs on the other. From my bird's-eye view, I could see the table was set, and the three brothers were milling around it with plates of food. I couldn't tell what it was, but the smells wafting to the upper floor were divine.

We reached a heavy oak staircase that headed down to the activity below, but Kermit paused and faced me, serious.

"They're good boys, you know. They're just not used to people."

I gave him a reassuring smile. "Are any of us really used to people?"

Kermit smiled back at that, though there was a seriousness radiating from his steely blue eyes. "I think you're one of the good ones, too. I also trust that you'll respect our privacy when you get back to town."

I took that to mean, *Don't tell anyone that I have three adult sons.* I nodded.

"Good."

We were poised at the top of the stairs, but Kermit hesitated and put his hand on my shoulder. His grip abruptly hardened, and he gently pushed me forward, still holding me tightly. Adrenaline electrified my blood in a sudden rush. He hadn't let me go, but it was clear that with a nudge he could send me down the staircase.

Kermit continued nonchalantly. "I'm glad I can count on your discretion." He pulled me back and made sure I had my balance, then gave me an apologetic look and offered his arm as he started down the staircase.

I shook my head even though my hands were trembling, and I was very much on edge from his not-so-veiled threat. *I can manage on my own, thank-you-very-much.*

Kermit stepped slowly, and I got the sense that he was waiting to catch me should I stumble. Well, I wasn't about to let *that* happen. I kept my hurt ankle between me and the railing, propping both crutches under the other arm. Leaning between the railing and crutches, I carefully picked my way down the staircase.

At the landing I could see what was hidden from above: A

kitchen was also part of the airy, open room. The entire floor was slate tile, though I stood on a red carpet that ran the length of the hall to the door. There was a matching oversize, well-worn rug in the living room to the immediate right. There was also a fireplace in the living room, happily roaring with flames. From my new vantage point, I looked up to see the hallway balcony we had just come from, and the vaulted ceiling high above. Straight ahead was the kitchen, underneath its own lower ceiling, and next to that was the dining room. The dining room table was gigantic; it wouldn't have looked out of place in an honest-to-God castle. Thick legs held up a long slab of solid, rough-hewn wood. It was topped with simple white porcelain dishes and lighted candles that reflected warmly against the wood grain. We headed there next, and Benjamin held out a wooden chair for me expectantly. I smiled as he helped me into my seat. I found myself at the corner of the table between Benjamin and Kermit, the latter at the head. Across from us were Theo and Seth. Seth's shifting eyes made me feel uneasy, so I was glad he sat in front of Benjamin.

Conversation turned from the food (perfectly cooked venison steaks, with a side of impeccably roasted mashed parsnips and carrots), to the wine (an earthy Pinot Noir), to my line of work (which they were very interested in), and finally to the men's life in the woods (which *I* was very interested in). Kermit was a particularly gracious host and conversationalist, keeping questions going whenever there was a bout of silence, and making the appropriate oohs and aahs when I regaled the group with stories of my past. He focused on me whenever I was speaking, and his eyes told me he was genuinely interested. *Maybe he's trying to make up for the incident on the stairs?* I didn't want to like him after he threatened me, but he was making it hard not to.

When the topic of woodland living came up, I got a chance to ask a question that Benjamin had been dodging all afternoon.

"So, what exactly do you guys do here?"

"Drugs," Kermit answered casually, as if we were talking about the weather, or a grocery list, or anything else equally mundane.

I promptly choked on my wine.

Benjamin's eyes widened in alarm, and I felt his hand give me a solid whack on my back as I coughed and sputtered.

"I'm fine." I held up a hand as a silent request for him to stop. I brought the linen napkin up to my face, gently wiping my mouth as I cleared my throat.

"Sorry." I looked at Kermit. "I thought you said drugs." I glanced around the table and laughed at the improbability of his answer.

Nobody else joined in my laughter, though Seth smirked.

"I did say drugs." Kermit cut another piece of venison and put it in his mouth.

Speechless at this revelation, I turned to Benjamin. He shot his father a pointed look. "Dad, you can't just say 'drugs' and leave her hanging."

Kermit shrugged and grinned lopsidedly. "I suppose. Jericho, we're working on a drug to kill bloodborne illnesses."

That was not at all the explanation I expected. "Oh," I said intelligently.

Theo interjected. "Are you familiar with bloodborne pathogens?"

I thought for a moment. "Viruses? You mean like HIV?"

"Exactly!" Kermit exclaimed, and slapped the dinner table, making everyone around it jump as utensils clattered against the wood.

"Wait, I thought there already was a cure for HIV." I looked around the table, and Theo shook his head.

"There's not a true cure for any bloodborne virus once contracted. So-called functional cures exist; these are usually drug cocktails that make a disease manageable. But what we're after is a *sterilizing* cure," Theo answered.

Kermit nodded. "The Holy Grail. Complete virus elimination."

My eyes widened. "So you're researching a complete cure for HIV? That's great!"

"Not specifically HIV." Kermit looked into my eyes. "But we believe our research could unlock the secret to curing all bloodborne viruses."

Benjamin cut in. "We think that there's a common thread in the nucleic acid, something linking them. Once we figure out what that is, we can target it and eliminate it."

"A sterilizing cure," I said breathlessly. "For *everything*?"

Across the table from me, Theo nodded.

My brow furrowed. "That's a big deal. A *huge* deal. Why all the secrecy around it?" I looked around the table at each man, trying to gauge their reactions. "And why aren't you with a science team in some tech-focused city?"

The men around the table exchanged looks, but it was

Kermit who answered. "We're well funded, of course, but our main backer would prefer that we stay out of the spotlight, all things considered."

I nodded, taking a sip of my wine, as if I completely understood the demands of a secret benefactor. I could tell they weren't going to give me more than that. Though I wondered who their mysterious donor was, and what "things" were being considered. I glanced around the room. Granted, I hadn't seen the entire house yet, but so far it didn't seem like the kind of place scientists would be conducting groundbreaking pathogen research and drug development. Not to mention the apparent scientists themselves. Benjamin and his family looked like they'd be more comfortable chopping logs than mixing chemicals. But then again, I supposed I didn't look much like a typical private investigator, either.

So many questions pounded against my brain, ready to storm out of my mouth, but I was cut short before I even started when Seth abruptly stood up. He pushed his chair back loudly.

"Why are we telling a stranger all of this?" At the word "stranger," he gestured to me, his voice hot with anger.

Kermit spoke gently to his youngest son. "Now, Seth, we can count on Jericho's discretion. She is a guest in our home until she's recovered enough to walk to town—and no, before you even think about suggesting it, she cannot go ten miles through the woods on crutches." Seth looked away testily, but Kermit continued. "And she is a detective. She would have figured out something was going on and come to her own conclusions. It's better that she knows the *truth*."

He put special emphasis on the word "truth." Benjamin and Theo nodded at their father, but Seth sat back down with a grunt, staring angrily at his plate.

I turned my head to Benjamin, but before he could say anything, Kermit cut in. "Don't mind Seth. Our lifestyle is just harder for him. Theo and Benny both got to go to college and have lives outside of this family before our research kept us in, but being the youngest, Seth never had the same chance."

I looked at the youngest brother, trying to give him a reassuring smile. Not that he was looking back at me at all. "I totally get it. I've been an outside force in so many of my cases. But hey, I'm not here to invade your life. Just going to heal up and find a bear, and then I'll be out of your hair for good."

Kermit nodded in agreement. *Good, put the old man at ease.* "Now, if you'll excuse me," I said, pushing the chair away from the table and grabbing the crutches. "I need to visit the ladies' room. Which is..."

Kermit gestured backward, to a hallway behind the staircase. "Back there, first door down the hall."

I flashed him the widest of smiles. "When I get back, I hope you'll tell me about how you prepared this venison, because it is divine with a capital *D*."

I hobbled off down the hall, much more dramatically than I needed to, making sure they could hear the crutches' tip-tapping from the dining room. That whole conversation was off, not to mention the family themselves. I wasn't about to let an opportunity for a little extra snooping pass me by. Leaning the crutches against the door of the bathroom for extra effect, I flipped on the light and gingerly walked farther down the hallway, wincing as a shooting pain ran up my foot with every other step.

The first room I found must have been Seth's—if the gaming system and haphazard pile of video games beside a small TV was any indication. Leaving the open doorway, I stepped quietly inside. It was sparsely decorated, as in zero personal effects besides the Nintendo, but otherwise similar to Benjamin's room the floor above. They each had a solid wooden desk and chair, though where Benjamin's bed had a mustard-colored quilt, Seth's had a less-worn quilt in shades of midnight blue. No adjoining bathroom either, I noted. Nothing crazy about it, though it was a little sad how lacking in personal touches it was.

Trying to be as quiet as possible, I crept toward the desk and slid open the drawer. The soft scrape of wood on wood sounded too loud in the silent room, and I glanced toward the doorway with a wince. Still empty. Inside the drawer was a pen, some Pokémon trading cards, and peeking from beneath the card stack something so starkly different that it immediately triggered alarm bells in my head: a thick strip of deep-blue fabric with mustard-yellow lettering. A chill snaked up my hand as I reached for the strip.

You are a guest in this house, you can't be snatching things!

But this thing bears further investigation. I can't not snatch.

Jericho James!

Silencing the voice in my head, I quickly pocketed the

fabric strip and backed out of the room. The next door was a few feet down the hall—surely that would be Theo's room, though I wasn't expecting anything much different from what I just saw. And I'd already found something, which had taken long enough that someone was bound to come checking on me sooner rather than later. I thought about abandoning my search and going back to that fantastic dinner (I may have been lying about needing the bathroom, but I never joke about meat)—though I'd already come this far. *Might as well, Jericho.* Reaching the door, I gently turned the knob and pushed. It was locked.

After a quick glance down the hallway behind me (still empty), I pulled the two bobby pins out of my hair. I bent the first into an L shape and straightened the second. Placing them both into the lock, I used the L-shaped pin as a lever at the bottom while I shimmied the straight pin until the lock clicked. *Oh my God, I love being me.* I pocketed my lock-picking arsenal, opening the door. The gasp was out of my mouth before I could stop it.

The inside was a wreck.

The bedding was torn to pieces. A single family portrait hung askew, the canvas shredded down the center between the brothers. Bits of what looked like quilt in shades of black and gray were strewn across the floor like so much dark confetti. *What the hell happened here?*

I took a hesitant step inside. It was less of a room and more of a...lair, for lack of a better word. Piles of dirty (but intact) clothing littered the corners. *How can he live like this?* I knelt, careful to keep my weight on my good ankle, and picked up a shred of the ex-quilt. Because that's what it was: shredded. Scratch that first question; *how could he even* do *this?*

I swallowed hard, feeling my heart pound in my chest as I fingered the raw edges of triple-layer quilted fabric. I tugged on either side of the scrap. Nothing. I wasn't sure how much time I had left before some enterprising brother launched a search party to the bathroom, but I tried again, muscles straining. And finally, the smallest rip. So tearing it was possible. I glanced around the room again, at the bits of quilt liberally sprinkled across the ground. *But still...*

Footsteps rang down the hallway, coming toward the room. I froze, dropping the shred of quilt.

Shit.

I whirled around to find Benjamin waiting for me in the doorframe.

"A little lost, Jericho?"

Benjamin's face was stern, though his voice was gentle. His eyes narrowed as he looked me up and down, as if he could discern what I'd been doing in his brother's room. His blue eyes flashed. *Fuck*, I hate it when people get hotter when they're mad, it's just not fair.

My heart was pounding. "Uh, yeah. I mean, no—I just uh, wanted to see a little more of the house." *Saved it.*

"Well, maybe you could have waited for me to give you a tour before you started snooping."

I felt my face flushing, not because I was embarrassed about looking around, but because I really didn't want my superhot rescuer to think I was some amateur who made sloppy mistakes.

"*Not* snooping," I said in the best defensive tone I could muster. "Simply peeking. Big difference. Just getting a feel for the layout, and I couldn't help but open the door *further* when I saw this hot mess express." I gestured to the destroyed room, hoping Benjamin would catch my inflection and assume the door was already open. I shrugged, trying to channel nonchalance. "I'm guessing your brother lost something and was having a dickens of a time finding it."

Benjamin's eyes widened as he took in the room, scanning each corner. I watched his face—though he was carefully guarding his emotions, I could see the slightest flicker of fear flash across it. *Weird*. Anger I could understand, or even worry, but what about this messy scene could possibly scare him?

"We should go back to dinner," Benjamin finally said.

I nodded in agreement, and before I knew what he was doing he had scooped me up into his arms as easily as picking up a book. My body type could be described as "clearly likes working out but also clearly likes tacos and doughnuts," so I was duly impressed when he crossed the hall to the bathroom where I'd left my crutches in what seemed like a few quick and quiet steps. And I can't say I didn't enjoy the ride.

When we arrived back in the dining room, Kermit and Seth were sitting silently, still eating slowly, though Theo was gone.

CHAPTER 5

I sat at the desk in my room, rolling my head to either side to stretch out the muscles in my neck. I was no stranger to muscle pain, but I was usually in a place where a masseuse, yoga studio, or someone with a medical license to rub me down until the hurt disappeared wasn't too far away. Benjamin's hands flashed across my mind: in mine when he'd helped me up after I fell, and splayed across my back when he carted me down the hallway to my crutches. *I bet he gives a great neck massage.*

I eased my own hands over my sore muscles, imagining his instead. Goose bumps pebbled my neck at the thought, and I quickly dropped my hands to my sides. Enough distractions. I fished in my pocket for the mangled bobby pins and the scrap of fabric from my foray into the brothers' rooms.

Bobby pins are almost impossible to straighten back to normal without pliers, but I did my best and tucked them back into my hair, for a possible next time. Which left Seth's fabric scrap. The strip was about an inch long and looked like a section of lanyard or part of a keychain. One side was blank dark blue, but the other side was embroidered with the letters *TC*. There was plenty of space after the *C*, but the mustard-yellow *T* sat on the edge of the ripped fabric. I racked my brain for any word that ended with *TC* and came up empty. It had to be initials.

T for Theo, maybe? But their last name was Grey, and it seemed odd that the youngest man of the house would hide something of his brother's. There was definitely a hierarchy among the Grey siblings that I'd noticed, with Benjamin clearly at the top. *Makes sense—I'd want him to top me, too.* I groaned at my own excessive horniness. *A secret girlfriend of Seth's, then?* That seemed more likely—a young adult trapped in the woods by his father comes across a cute girl out for a hike and hits it off. Could make sense. And... could it be my poor victim? But Katherine's initials were *KW*. As if on cue, the moment her name crossed my mind the trees outside shook in the wind, the leaves scraping against one another with a wild *shhhhhhhh*.

Wind moaned through a gap in the window as I looked around the room. The circle of lamplight around the desk was a cozy oasis, a stanchion against the surrounding dark. I shivered. You know what they say, you don't appreciate how much ambient light there is in a city until you're stuck in a dark house in the middle of the woods. Or something like that.

I made a mental note to ask Benjamin about the initials or somehow bring up Seth's relationship status as I fell onto the bed without changing clothes or washing my face, completely exhausted.

Jasmine Kuliasha

The dream came as soon as I shut my eyes. I was back in the clearing, *again*, but this time it was quiet: neither animals nor creepy singing girls. Just me. I glanced downward, at the mangled body a few feet away. *Make that me and Katherine.* The moonlight shone brightly in the open area, a contrast with the darkness beneath the trees around us. It meant I could easily see her, though, so I took the short steps to cross the clearing to where she lay and studied her face. I didn't feel cold, but I shivered. *She's dead. You have nothing to be afraid of.*

Her face looked completely at peace. At least, the side of it that was whole did. The other half was viciously shredded, with flaps of skin hanging loosely where they were torn. If it wasn't for the fact that half of her body was ripped apart, she could have been taking a really choice nap in the middle of the forest floor. I knelt to get a better look at the bite wounds. Moonlight glinted off her teeth, exposed by mangled lips.

Her eyes sprang open, inches from my face. "Run," she whispered.

I was frozen in shock.

"*Run!*" she yelled, urgently.

I woke up to the sound of Katherine screaming, then realized it was me. The scream died when I shut my mouth, and I sat up in bed, breathing raggedly. I heard a sigh in the dark, like someone breathing, and the hairs on the back of my neck stood up. I whipped my head around, half expecting to find Katherine's ghost in the room with me. The moon's brilliant light filtered through the bay window. It highlighted the rumpled quilts that enveloped me in uneven heaps, like a lone ship adrift on a choppy sea. I was alone. I drew my knees up to my chest and hugged myself, taking deep breaths to calm my nerves. *Ghosts aren't real.* The door abruptly sprang open, and I jumped in surprise as my heart pounded anew. Benjamin rushed inside, wearing a thin white T-shirt and blue plaid shorts.

"I heard screaming, are you—"

I cut him off before he could finish, "I'm okay. Just a nightmare." I smiled weakly in the moonlight.

Benjamin hesitated just inside the room, his eyebrows furrowed. I felt a flush of warmth rush through my body—even after everything that had happened this evening, I still wanted him, and goodness, I hoped he still wanted me. He took another step closer and raised a hand as if he was going to offer it to me, but smoothed his scruffy hair back instead. The wavy chestnut locks looked almost black in the moonlight, falling back to frame his face when he moved his hand. My eyes caught on his lips, and I realized I was staring.

"Uh," he stammered.

I sat up cross-legged in the bed and patted the empty space beside me, my words pouring out before I fully knew what I was saying. "Want to have a seat? I could use the company."

I was instantly thankful that I hadn't bothered to change out of my black tank top and tights—they were much more alluring than my pajamas, which consisted of one old extra-large concert T-shirt, complete with holes and threadbare patches.

He shut the door, stepped closer, and tentatively lowered himself onto the bed. He looked down at his palms, then into my eyes.

"Do you often have nightmares?" His voice was gentle.

I shook my head. "Usually never. I've had more in the last twenty-four hours than in the last twenty-seven years."

He chuckled dryly. "Yeah, I guess a lot has happened to you recently." He exhaled and lowered his head. "I have nightmares pretty regularly. So I get it."

He pulled his feet up from the floor and sat cross-legged on top of the quilt. This effort brought him closer to me, so we were sitting shoulder-to-shoulder. He shifted slightly and our arms touched, sending an unexpected thrill through my body. Goose bumps lightly peppered my arms.

"Oh, are you cold? I can get another quilt..." He trailed off as I looked at him.

My eyes traced his face, gliding from the dark stubble on his chin that promised a beard in the next few days, over to his sensitive lips, and up the angular slope of his cheekbones, until my gaze finally rested on his lake-blue eyes. Those eyes stared at me intently.

"What is it?" My eyebrows rose slightly.

It was hard to tell in the moonlight, but it looked like he blushed at my question. "Sorry, your eyes are...distracting."

"Oh." It was my turn to blush.

Benjamin abruptly looked down, absentmindedly rubbing the back of his neck. "So, is there anything I can get you?"

A very good question. I looked around the room that had seemed so cheerful and warm in the sunlight. Illuminated by the moon, the once warm colors had turned gray and cold, and shadows from the trees outside painted grotesque shapes on the walls. A breeze swept by the window, echoing the ghostly sigh I thought I'd heard. I was far from home, I'd been chased for my life, threatened on a staircase, caught in the act of investigating, and plagued by nightmares.

I really needed some company.

"Well," I started shyly. "To be honest, I don't really want to be alone right now."

Benjamin shifted and put a strong, warm arm around my shoulder. He held me tentatively at first, but I adjusted my seat and leaned into him. His grip tightened comfortingly. I rested my head on his chest and closed my eyes, enjoying the stillness of the moment and the heat of human contact. And God, he was *warm*. He drew me closer. I felt the steady rise and fall of his chest with each breath. In and out, like waves on a shore. I sighed, feeling my muscles slowly untense as I began to relax. His smell enveloped me, the pine and cinnamon invading all my senses. He bent his head down, leaning his cheek against my hair. I felt his mouth curve upward in a smile. The heat of his body flowed into mine until a sudden warm rush unfurled through me, like a tightly curled fern that was stretching up to grow. It pushed away my fears and doubt as it spread, until all that was left was contentment.

I adjusted myself slightly. We hadn't started out in the most comfortable position, but I was reluctant to break contact with Benjamin.

To my dismay, he pulled away. "Here, hold on."

He stood up and shook the sheets out then straightened them, drawing the sheet and quilt up around me like he was tucking me in. He smoothed the quilt on the other side of the bed and lay down on top of it. *How chaste.*

"Uh, is this good?" He was laying on his side facing me, his eyebrows raised in gentlemanly concern.

"Actually, you can get under the covers. If you want," I said, in what I hoped was a nonchalant tone. I tried not to look *too* excited, but it was hard to hide my delight as he slid under the sheets beside me.

He put a hand on my waist, gently turning me so my back was toward him. He lay on his side as well, with his arms wrapped around me. With my back pressed against his chest and my head just under his chin, I was completely ensconced. The stressors of the day (of which there were many) immediately began to melt away.

"How's this?" he whispered.

Uh, perfection. Even better than a hookup. Maybe.

I simply nodded against him, curling closer into his arms. I forgot how nice it was to be held. "Don't let go," I whispered back.

I felt his mouth crack into a smile in the dark, as his lips brushed the top of my head in what might have been a gentle kiss.

Any lingering desire my body might have been feeling was erased by sudden fatigue. With my nightmare forgotten, I closed my eyes, and sleep washed over me like a wave.

My eyes didn't open again until the fall sunlight poured through the large windows, drenching the room and everything in it with a soft golden glow. Benjamin was still pressed against me, his chest rising and falling in the measured rhythm of sleep. *What are you doing in bed with a strange man, Jericho James?*

THE MIDNIGHT PACK

Whatever I want, I thought back to myself.

There's something innately special about waking up next to another human body and having access to something different from your own. Benjamin was a solid, comforting presence that soothed me to my core. I snuggled in deeper, pressing up against him. His arms tightened around me automatically. A peaceful sigh escaped his lips, but his rhythmic breathing told me he was still asleep. In a lot of ways, truly sleeping with another person—touching and sharing the same space— was just as intimate as *other things*. It was as if in sharing our breath, we shared pieces of ourselves, and maybe we'd wake up knowing each other a little better than before.

Unmoving, I tracked my eyes around the room, taking everything in. I was completely at ease and wanted to soak it up: the sunlight, the cozy quilt piled around us, the bluebird-sky capping the dark forest outside the window, and Benjamin's body beside me. His spicy scent engulfing my senses. His heat mingling with mine. A perfect moment in time.

Benjamin's muscles tensed against me as he stretched, waking. I felt his mouth spread into a smile against my head, which brought out a grin of my own. I rolled over to face him and looked up at his blue eyes glinting in the early-morning light.

"You're really here," he said softly, chuckling to himself. "I was afraid that when I woke up, it would end up being a dream." He moved his hand from my waist to my face, tucking an errant blonde lock behind my ear. His hand hovered millimeters away from my cheek, as if he wanted to touch me but wasn't sure he should.

I answered his unspoken question by pressing my cheek

against his palm, and he gently stroked my hairline with his fingers. I closed my eyes to focus on his touch, relishing the tingles his fingertips left on my skin as they slowly swept over my face.

We were interrupted by voices elsewhere in the house calling loudly for Benjamin. The sudden noise broke the stillness and my calm as I sprang up, startled. At least, that's what I tried to do. Instead, I succeeded in falling valiantly off the bed. *Again.*

"I'm okay," I groaned as I struggled for my footing.

Benjamin was by my side in an instant. "Is falling out of beds a habit of yours?" There was laughter in his voice, but his hands were gentle as he helped me back up.

"Yes. It's highly effective for waking up instantly."

He laughed at my sarcasm and left to find his family while I quickly got ready for the morning.

To my immense pleasure Benjamin was waiting for me outside of the bedroom door. We went down the broad staircase for breakfast, finding the rest of the family already seated at the table. If they were disturbed by Benjamin's whereabouts this morning, they didn't show it. Seth smirked at us as we sat. Theo's face didn't give anything away, but I thought his eyes were sad. *Maybe Benjamin told him what I'd seen last night. Maybe he's embarrassed?*

Kermit led the conversation again just as he had the night before, with no mention of Benjamin's morning. Instead, he spoke exuberantly about an experiment they had been running in the lab.

"Preliminary results are exactly what we expected to see

from the antiretrovirals. We should be ready for next steps within the week!" He beamed at his sons.

Theo and Seth both nodded appreciatively, and under the table Benjamin squeezed my hand.

Kermit continued, "Theo and Seth, if you boys are done with breakfast, then let's get cleaned up and meet in the lab."

"Ben, won't you be joining us?" Theo asked his brother.

I silently willed Benjamin to say, *No way, I'm spending today with Jericho! All this important work be damned, ha, ha!* but Kermit interrupted my thoughts and answered for his son.

"I believe Benny promised this young lady a tour of our home and the grounds."

I grinned inwardly.

Seth scowled. "But Dad—"

"I've said my part, Seth. Among the three of us, we have enough hands in the lab for now. Benjamin can take a few days off."

The two men stared at each other for a moment, but Seth broke away and stood up, clearing his plates from the table. Theo followed suit, and Kermit stood up as his sons walked into the kitchen.

He looked at me and shrugged. "Don't mind them. They're good boys."

"Just not used to people?" I volunteered.

Kermit's mouth curved into a small half smile. "That too. Though I suspect right now they're jealous of their brother."

Benjamin blushed at that and looked down toward our hands, which were still clasped under the table.

Kermit joined the other two men in the kitchen before the

trio turned down a hallway in the back of the room that I hadn't noticed the night before.

Seth muttered something incomprehensible as they walked away.

"She'll be gone soon enough. Let him enjoy her company while he can," Kermit replied gruffly, though not unkindly.

She'll be gone soon enough. I pondered this as Benjamin and I finished our breakfast. He helped prop my injured leg onto an empty chair before leaving to clean up the kitchen.

He returned to the table, drying his hands on a dishcloth.

"Are you ready for the grand tour?"

I stood up, grabbing my crutches. "Obviously! Lead on, Captain."

CHAPTER 6

We started in the familiar hallway from the night before, standing at the base of the stairs. Staring up, I saw a mirror image of the hallway I was currently in. One side of the upper hall led to my—Benjamin's—room, the other to parts unknown. From where I stood on the sprawling ground floor the dining room sat on my left, and the kitchen at my back. The bathroom and two brothers' rooms I'd "accidentally" discovered the night before were farther down the hallway as it ran under the staircase. To my right was the living room, and then more unknown.

"My dad and I have rooms upstairs. There's also a little attic up there for storage and such. I won't bore you with that just yet." Benjamin beamed as he turned me around, more smoothly than I thought possible given my crutches and the cushy red patterned rug beneath us. As I spun, I noticed that the white stucco walls were bare—no family photos or art of any kind hung anywhere that I could see. In fact, the rug was the only note of color beyond the dark slate of the tile floor and warm wood stairs.

The rug abruptly ended in a patch of sunlight, illuminating the slate floor in stark contrast with the rest of the hallway. I looked up to see a thick wooden door with a wrought-iron handle and a cheery cut-out glass window.

"This is the front door. I figured we should start at my favorite part."

I laughed and raised an eyebrow. "This door is your favorite part of your home?"

His eyes widened momentarily. "Oh." He laughed. "No, it's what's on the other side."

He opened the door, and we stepped into the sunshine together. We stood on a huge wooden porch that ran the entire length of the facade.

"Oh my," I gasped as I took it all in.

The railing around the porch was lovingly carved with woodland scenes. Pine trees circled each post, reaching toward the roof. It was so life-like that the forest appeared to have taken up root in the railing. Carved squirrels, bunnies, raccoons, and wolves all danced amid the wooden trees. In the middle of the porch hung a gorgeous wooden love-seat swing—porch swings are my love language—and on either side of the swing stood matching rocking chairs. There were five chairs total. I guessed one had belonged to Benjamin's mother.

Peering over the edge of the porch, I looked back toward the house. The home was built on a hillside, but the roof was high and level even as the ground sloped downward. Swaths of land had been flattened into terraces along the slope, still verdant even in the cooling grip of fall. From the side view, the house was much, much larger than it looked from the front. The dark wooden siding of the home went back far enough that I couldn't tell where it ended, though I *could* tell that I hadn't seen nearly all of it yet. I walked back across the porch to the front door. From the front, the home looked like nothing more than a simple log cabin with an ample and expertly carved porch. Altogether it was a very cozy, Southern-style scene that I was surprised to find hidden in the woods in Maine.

I said as much to Benjamin, and he laughed.

"Once upon a time, my parents honeymooned in Savannah. My mom fell in love with big Southern porches, rocking chairs, and sweet tea. When they moved to Stillbridge—" He paused. "Well, to the 100-Mile Wilderness—which, let's face it, is pretty much the opposite of the South—Dad promised Mom she would have a Southern porch, and so he built this." He swept his hand out, motioning around us.

"He *built* this porch?" I looked at Benjamin in disbelief, and he nodded.

"By himself?" I asked, and again Benjamin nodded in answer.

"Not just this, the house, too," he added with a proud smile.

"Also by himself?" I was incredulous.

"Well, the first part anyway. As we walk through, you'll be able to tell where parts were added later. My brothers and I helped with those additions."

"That's really impressive."

Benjamin shrugged nonchalantly, but he looked pleased.

I shook my head as the implications of what Benjamin was

saying sank in. "Hold on, you picked up and moved your lives to the middle of the woods in Maine, just because your mysterious drug benefactor asked you to?"

Benjamin gave me a tight-lipped smile. "Well. We were pursuing a cure already, we just needed funding. When the council heard about what we were doing, they pounced. As for moving, well, the council is...persuasive."

The way he said "council" made me think it was Council with a capital C. "What kind of Council would ask you to do that?" I asked.

"The kind with a lot more money than they know what to do with, and a lot more clout than they should have," he said grudgingly.

Very interesting. I wanted to press him further, but the look on his face said he was done with the matter. *Very interesting indeed.* I made a mental note to bring it up again later as I made my way down the length of the porch, admiring the posts. I ran my hand over a wolf carving that looked so realistic, I half expected it to leap out of the wood and run for the trees. Beside me, Benjamin's lips curved into a sad half smile.

"Dad hand-carved each of those for Mom, too. She always said her favorite part about the woods was the wild creatures living in it." He stared at the wolf with me, smile falling.

Benjamin stepped around me and sat down on the wooden swing, which rocked under his weight. He leaned back and crossed his arms over his chest.

"This was her favorite place in the house. She'd come out here to read, and to think. I'd sit with her sometimes. Seth too."

Benjamin's eyes were locked on the trees in front of him,

lost in thought. I leaned the crutches against the porch railing and limped over to the swing.

"Mind if I join you?"

Benjamin grinned. "C'mon over."

He stopped rocking so I could sit down, and once I was settled, he began again.

"How long ago did she die?" I looked at him as I asked, trying to read his face.

"Five years now. It's strange to think that we've been in this house just as long with her as without her. I miss her. I mean, we all do, of course. We're grown adults, but she was still the glue that really held us together."

I rested a tentative hand on his leg, and he uncrossed his arms. He put his palm over my hand and linked his fingers with mine.

"So anyway, this is my favorite place. It reminds me of my mom, but it's also relaxing to sit, and to just *be*, if that makes sense."

I nodded. "It does."

We rocked in silence for a moment. The golden and ocher tones of trees in their fall splendor surrounded us, and I smiled listening to the sounds of the forest. The wind through the trees almost sounded like waves on the shore.

It was truly relaxing. I leaned against his shoulder without thinking—it just felt so natural, you know—and in response he kissed the top of my head.

His body tensed abruptly. "Uh, sorry, I just—"

I looked up at him. His eyes were trained on mine and creased with concern. I couldn't help but smile.

"It's okay." *It's more than okay.* "Actually, you can do it some more, if you want," I offered slyly. *What happens in the woods, stays in the woods, am I right?* But I wasn't entirely sure if he felt similarly, and the uncertainty loomed large enough to make me hesitant. *What if he was just being polite yesterday?*

To my relief, Benjamin's expression relaxed, and he smiled so warmly my face started to flush. My breath quickened, and I leaned in closer. And he looked right past me. I turned my head to follow where his eyes were tracking: the blue light of a video camera blinked in the rafters of the patio.

Benjamin stood up and offered me a hand, pulling me out of the swing.

"Maybe no one is watching?" I offered. *Kiss me, dammit!*

He chuckled dryly. "Someone always is. They probably know how I feel about you. But they don't need to watch." He motioned for me to accompany him as he started walking down the length of the porch.

They know how he feels about me? "Oh? How *do* you feel about me?" I asked, grinning like an idiot as I picked up my crutches and followed.

He stopped, and I caught up to him. His eyes were focused on the trees around us, clearly in thought. Then he swallowed hard and looked at me, taking both of my hands in his own.

"I, uh..." he stammered. "This might sound crazy, but I feel like I want...to be with you." My eyes widened, and he quickly continued. "Not like that. Or maybe like that. I mean, in any capacity. Just sitting here, or last night, or..." His voice was rough with sudden emotion. He shook his head and ran a hand through his hair, tousling it further. "Anyway, it's overwhelming. When I found you at the bottom of that ravine, I don't know, something opened inside me. Or maybe something broke. Maybe *I'm* broken." He looked at me anxiously, face flushed and eyes hopeful. "Sorry, that sounded way better in my head. Out loud it's just...so, so dumb. Forget I said anything."

I felt my cheeks heat in a blush and chuckled softly. "No, not dumb. " I smiled up at his face. "It's sweet. And I don't think you're any more broken than I am."

He returned my smile and we walked to the end of the porch in silence, then down wooden steps that hugged the side of the house. We stopped at the first terrace, emerging in the middle of a sprawling wildflower garden. I gasped. A sea of flowers swayed in the wind before me, like rainbow-tinted waves. Light glinted off the translucent wings of dragonflies as they hovered around, and colorful butterflies sprinkled the top of the landscape as they fluttered and swooned.

Seeing my obvious pleasure, Benjamin grinned broadly. "I thought you might like this."

"Like this...I love it," I said breathlessly, eyes widened to take everything in. "If fairies were real, this is where they'd live."

Benjamin cocked his head to the side, but then he smiled and guided me off the stairs and down the garden path. I was a bit baffled by their choice of garden decor, however. A shining black spire stood at the entrance to the garden. It spiraled upward about six feet from the ground as we picked our way along winding flagstones to the flowers. It looked like a menacing black unicorn horn, the tip so sharp you'd probably cut yourself just by being near it. It sat in shocking contrast with the colorful garden around it; the spire glittered in the light but seemed to suck in extra darkness when a cloud briefly blocked the sun's rays. *How Garden-Goth-core.*

All thoughts of the statue were quickly forgotten, though, as we walked farther into the garden. The view from the stairs was distant enough that the flowers had combined to create a dazzling ocean of color, but I saw as we approached that it was clearly overgrown and unkempt. Moss and grass peeped through the gaps in the flagstones, and wildflowers desperately leaned across the pathway as if trying to whisper secrets to their neighbors on the other side.

I ran my hands over the tops of the flowers as we meandered, my fingers grazing the soft petals and stirring up a brilliant shimmer of butterflies. I recognized purple coneflower, goldenrod, and the bright-yellow bushes of witch hazel (Benjamin told me his mother used to call it winterbloom), though there were many more I wasn't familiar with.

I took my time on the path, partly because of my ankle and partly to revel in the beauty around me. I loved flowers but mostly admired them from afar. I wasn't home often enough to take care of any plants. As a result, I had what my mom lovingly called a black thumb. I even tried my luck with plants that supposedly thrived on neglect, but I gave them either a little too much neglect to survive or too much attention on returning from a trip. *Plants are such drama queens.* But that made me like them even more.

The path was laid in a spiral shape that ran the length of the terrace, ending at a small gazebo in the center. We stepped inside and to my delight found another wooden swing, a twin to the one on the porch. I laughed excitedly as I sat down.

Benjamin chuckled at my unexpected laughter. "I take it you like swings?"

I smiled in response. "Well, why sit when you can swing?"

He joined me and we rocked together in comfortable silence, simply enjoying each other's company and the splendor around us. I was grateful that thus far Benjamin's tour included lots of pit stops for resting. The crutches were a great help, but my ankle was annoyed about walking even a short distance, and the rest of my bruised body protested anything other than stillness.

It was a perfect fall day, sunny but cool. Butterflies floated lazily in and out of the gazebo, interspersed with the more frenetic dragonflies. I closed my eyes, savoring the splashes of sunlight that filtered through the gazebo's slatted roof, warming me in stripes and patches with its subtle touch. When I opened my eyes again, I found Benjamin looking at me.

"Uh, hi," I said, suddenly shy under the intensity of his gaze.

"Hi," he whispered gently.

He reached out a hand and stroked my hair, delicately tucking some loose strands behind my ear. A velvety black swallowtail butterfly alighted on his hand and paused, languidly opening and closing its dark wings as if showing off their beauty. Benjamin carefully pulled his hand away from my head and held it aloft between us, butterfly still posed.

"She's beautiful," I whispered.

Benjamin smiled at my wide eyes. "She likes you."

As if understanding, the butterfly landed on my shoulder with a delicate flap before taking off to rejoin the revelry of her brothers and sisters in the garden.

My gaze followed her to the scene before us, all sparkling wings and tangles of blooms.

I was truly in awe. "This place is magical."

Beside me Benjamin nodded in agreement, though he didn't speak.

Wings fluttered overhead as the insects danced through the breezy gazebo. My eyes followed them upward as they swirled around the vines that climbed the gazebo's posts.

"It's mostly wild now," Benjamin said softly.

"Yes, but there's this uninhibited beauty to it," I said appreciatively.

"Yeah," Benjamin started. "You should have seen it when my mom was alive. She planted everything here. She loved flowers—all living things, really. This place was her pride and joy."

He trailed off, but I stayed silent, leaving space for him to continue.

"She..." He paused, clearing his throat. "We found her over there." He gestured to the part of the garden we had entered, to the dark spire that marked where the staircase ended and the terrace began. "She jumped."

Jumped? I followed his gaze up the high sides of the house to a flat space on the roof above, standing tall and imposing beside the garden.

She jumped.

From the roof.

Shit.

"Oh, Benjamin. I'm so sorry."

He shrugged, though sadness haunted the depths of his lake-blue eyes. "I guess she'd been depressed but knew how to hide it. Seth's the one who found her. He hasn't been quite the same since. Anyway, that dark, twisty spike-thing marks the spot in her memory." He gestured to the spire near the stairs.

"Oh," I said again. "It looks sinister." I immediately regretted my choice of words. *Probably not what you should say about his mom's memorial.*

"Yeah, it does." Benjamin chuckled humorlessly. "My dad was in a dark mood when he carved it, and it shows. It's made of black marble. But after the, well, after *it* happened, Dad really lost himself in our lab work. The cure we're searching for, it's something we all want to accomplish for Mom. We feel like we owe it to her to succeed."

I wondered if perhaps Benjamin's mother had the rare blood disease they were trying to cure. That could explain her depression as well as the family's drive for their work. But Benjamin didn't volunteer any more information, and I didn't feel like it was the time to pry.

"We buried her over there." He pointed to the other side of the garden, nearest the woods. I could barely make out a slab of gray through the overgrown flower-scape: her headstone. I hadn't noticed it hidden in the jungle of blooms even though we must have passed right by it before.

Benjamin continued. "Dad couldn't bear to come out here anymore, and neither could Seth, understandably. Theo's not one for plants, so he washed his hands of it. I do what I can, but a garden like this really needs more attention than I can give it." He shrugged.

"It's gorgeous," I said softly. "And any work you do here is a beautiful way to honor her memory."

He tilted his head toward me and gave me a half smile. "Thanks. I hoped you would like it."

We rocked on the swing in silence for a moment, then Benjamin sat forward, stopping us.

"Hm. I think my dad is calling me."

I'd heard nothing. Was this the woodland equivalent of faking a text to get out of a conversation?

After a few moments of straining my ears, I also heard Kermit's voice carrying across the yard, just as he appeared in the distance on the terrace below. I turned to Benjamin with my eyebrows raised. "Wow, you have really good hearing."

He looked surprised by my compliment, but then chuckled and shrugged again. "Thanks. I guess we should go see what he wants."

We stood up together, and Benjamin called back to tell his father we were coming, though I wasn't sure the older man would hear his son from the distance. Surprisingly, Kermit yelled back, saying he needed to show Benjamin something in the lab, and excitedly waved for us to follow before disappearing over the edge of the terrace and back inside the house.

We picked our way down the overgrown path, this time pausing when we reached the far end. Benjamin's mother's gravestone resided amid a wild cloud of pale-pink flowers that I wasn't familiar with. I knelt to get a closer look at the blooms, admiring the soft golden ring around a lime-green button in the center of each flower.

"Japanese anemone. My mom always loved these." Benjamin knelt beside me and gently pushed the wild plants to the side, uncovering the headstone.

Though it was weather-worn, the words stood out clearly.

BETH: BELOVED WIFE AND MOTHER. LOYAL TO THE LAST, FOR ALL TIME EVERMORE.

"Loyal to the last," I whispered.

"It's our family's thing." Benjamin's mouth quirked up in the ghost of a smile as he looked away from the carving, his eyes catching mine. "You know, like the saying—loyal to the last, to the..." He coughed as he trailed off, shaking his head. He ran a hand through his hair and cleared his throat. "Actually, I'm guessing you've never heard that before. It's just something kind to say about someone committed to a cause."

My heart was suddenly somehow in my throat, and I swallowed hard as Benjamin looked away. I wondered what cause his mother had pledged her life to besides her family, but I'm guessing it was something to do with the pathogen work. Benjamin's fingers brushed along carvings of intertwining flowers along the stone's outer edge. "My dad carved these, too. Wildflowers for a wildflower."

I raised an eyebrow at him.

"Dad always said that my mom was a wildflower in a sea of roses." He shrugged. "It was kind of their inside joke or something." Benjamin's blue eyes were facing the gravestone, but unfocused, as if he was looking through it or maybe peering into memories past.

"A wildflower. She does sound like my kind of lady," I offered with a gentle smile.

Benjamin turned toward me, eyes back in the present. He returned my smile and nodded. "Yeah."

He stood up and offered me a hand, which I accepted, and he waited beside me as I readjusted my crutches for the walk back to the house.

Since Kermit apparently needed Benjamin's input in the lab sooner rather than later, we didn't stop as we walked back to the wooden staircase that hugged the edge of the house. We passed a second leveled terrace, which up-close boasted an abundant vegetable garden, and ended at the third and final terrace (home to a truly expansive patio and what looked like an outdoor pizza oven), all of which Benjamin promised we'd see later.

Off the patio, we came to an enormous pair of rustic French doors. I wasn't surprised to see them open, since the weather was a flawless example of what a perfect fall day should be. As we stepped through the doors together, I *was* surprised when a sharp blast of cool air roared down from above, whipping my hair around my face and snapping the bottom of my flannel shirt. I threw my arms up in startled defense, but the air had already stopped.

"Oh, sorry about that—it keeps any bugs out when we have the doors open. I forgot what a surprise it is if you're not expecting it!" Benjamin grinned apologetically, and I narrowed an eye in mock irritation in return. I opened my mouth for a witty retort but lost my words when I saw what else was in the room.

THE MIDNIGHT PACK

We stood in a long but narrow hallway. On one side was the white stucco wall of the house, but the other side was lined with floor-to-ceiling glass. Through it I saw a room filled with gleaming metal and white machines: the laboratory. Unlike the hallways upstairs, this was brilliantly lit, making its contents shine.

"Whoa," I gasped. I wasn't sure exactly what I'd had in mind when I found out about the lab the night before, but it wasn't this. The scene in front of me looked like it belonged in a top-tier hospital or university, and most definitely not in the backwoods of Maine. Every one of my senses was suddenly on edge again.

"Uh, wait here for a minute." Benjamin put his hand on my shoulder then let it fall, walking to a cleverly cut door that blended seamlessly with the rest of the glass. He stepped into what looked like an anteroom to the lab. It was small but also boasted walls of glass; I had almost missed that it was a separate room. He let the door close behind him and reached for a white lab coat with a *B* embroidered on it. It was the lone coat left on a rack that occupied most of the tiny space. He hastily buttoned the coat to the top, then washed his hands at a small sink. When he was done, he grabbed a hairnet from a box perched on a small metal table, adjusting it over his scruffy mane. Under the table was a trash can, nearly full of discarded hairnets identical to the one that rested on Benjamin's head. Next, he plucked out two purple latex gloves from a similar box and slid them over his hands. Fully outfitted, he turned around and gave me a quick wave before going through the next glass door and into the main lab. His movements were fluid and practiced. I suspected he could prepare for lab work in his sleep. *I wonder how many times they walked into these walls in the beginning, though.* The glass was so clear that I barely registered its existence. Woe betide any birds that flew in here. *Thank goodness for the wind-blast zone.*

My breath left hints of condensation on the glass, I stood so close. I resisted the urge to press my hands and face against it and get a better look. The better angels of my nature kept me from getting fingerprints all over the immaculate surface.

There were four long metal tables in the lab, each home to a dizzying array of microscopes and other machinery that I recognized from movies but didn't have a name for. A lab-coat-clad Benjamin joined his similarly clothed family around one of these tables, peering through a microscope.

My gaze passed over the men to a row of glass-doored refrigerators that lined the far wall of the lab, each filled to the brim with vials and petri dishes. They were accompanied by two big, boxy, white machines in a corner that looked kind of like mini freezers. I squinted and noticed they were both labeled THERMAL CHAMBER—DON'T TOUCH ME SETH! I smiled as I continued my self-guided visual tour. Opposite the thermal chambers stood a stack of small wire cages—for rats, I guessed—but each was empty.

A loud whirring brought my attention to a machine on one of the tables closer to the center of the room. It was large, round, and white with a panel on the front that reminded me of my beloved Crock-Pot at home. It had a clear top and what looked like something spinning inside. I dug into my dusty memories of high school science class. A centrifuge, maybe?

THE MIDNIGHT PACK

The four men were chatting eagerly around it, and though I couldn't hear what they were saying, I could guess the topic of their conversation by the way they pointed at the whirring machine and nodded to one another. There was something inside that they were excited to look at.

As if on cue, the machine let out three long, loud beeps, and the spinning slowed to a stop. The men proceeded in practiced motions. Seth opened the lid and carefully removed a gleaming vial, which he passed to Theo. Theo took the vial to the next table, then returned with a small glass slide. This he handed to Kermit, who inserted it into the nearest microscope. Kermit leaned over the eyepiece of the scope and turned the knobs on either side, focusing it. The brothers stood to his side, waiting for their father. All three had their arms crossed, and Seth fidgeted, rocking on the balls of his feet.

Kermit abruptly took a step back and rubbed his eyes as if he was wiping away tears. He wrapped Benjamin in what looked like a backbreaking bear hug as Theo and Seth took turns peering through the eyepiece of the microscope.

Seth pulled a laptop over and typed something into the keyboard. An image appeared on the screen that I assumed must be the contents of the slide under the microscope. Benjamin peered into the scope while the other three leaned over the laptop, pointing to different blips of color on the screen.

When Benjamin pulled away, his face was lit with a bright smile. He clapped his father and brothers on the back and strode back to the anteroom, still grinning.

Have they found it? The—what was it?—sterilizing cure? I walked back to the door in anticipation, watching as Benjamin washed his hands thoroughly, hung his coat, and removed his other accoutrements. He caught my gaze and smiled broadly before sauntering through the glass door. Once out, he immediately swept me up in a dramatic twirl, as if we were at a ballroom dance and not a tiny hallway beside an expansive secret laboratory in the middle of Maine.

My crutches clattered to the ground as we spun together, but I was laughing too much to care. Benjamin pulled me into an embrace as we stopped, our laughter echoing down the long hallway.

The three men in the lab had turned to look in our direction at the noise, but Kermit quickly waved them back to work. Benjamin paid no mind, his blue eyes locked onto mine.

"So...?" I raised both eyebrows eagerly.

He answered with another brilliant smile. "I think we did it."

"A cure?"

He nodded. "Preliminary results show almost zero viral load." Excitement shone in his eyes, making them sparkle.

"Meaning, total virus elimination? Benjamin, that's amazing."

His smile fell the barest amount. If I hadn't been so close to his face, I would have missed it.

"*Almost* total elimination. We should run some additional tests, but we're nearing the finish line."

I wanted to ask the question that was blaring in my mind: *For what virus?*

Instead I nodded. "So, what now? Will you pop some Champagne and call up the medical journals?"

He chuckled. "Not quite. In vitro is done. The next step is in vivo—live testing. It's possible that this works even better when it's inside something living and breathing." He looked through the glass at his family in the lab and frowned. "Or that it doesn't work as well as we hope. Or at all."

Concern etched his brows, so I searched for a subject change. "What will you do the live tests with?" I thought of the empty cages that lined the wall inside the lab.

We both spoke at the same time.

"Rats?" I asked, but it sounded like Benjamin had muttered "us."

Unease prickled my arms as I stepped back, startled. "What?"

He shook his head, as if shaking himself out of a daydream, and turned his gaze away from his family and back to me. "Uh, rats, yeah, something like that. My dad is in charge of testing."

At that, he glanced quickly in his father's direction, but turned back to me again with a smile. "You know what, it's about lunchtime, and on second thought, Champagne sounds like a great idea."

Benjamin picked up my crutches from where they'd fallen on the tile floor and waited as I adjusted myself on them. He turned toward the dark end of the hallway, casually flipping a light switch as he walked. A series of small, round lights, both hidden in the floor and tucked cleverly into the ceiling, blinked on. In the newly lit path, I could see that the hallway ran the length of the lab before ending in a wrought-iron spiral staircase. I started walking, but I couldn't shake the feeling that something was *off* with Benjamin's answer.

Jasmine Kuliasha

Did he really say "us"?

As I followed him down the hallway, I reminded myself of how much I still didn't know much about him or his family.

Keep your eyes open and your head up, Jericho. Mystery is your element, and this is where you shine.

Energized by my mini self-pep-talk, I picked up my pace, but gave one last look over my shoulder at the lab.

All three men were standing stock-still, unblinking, and looking directly at me.

CHAPTER 7

A jolt ran through me at the force of their combined stare. Their eyes had been so still, so trained. Like...

Like predators targeting prey.

I stumbled forward on my crutches. Benjamin turned, eyebrows furrowed, but I waved him off. When I glanced back at the lab again, Benjamin's brothers and father were busily at work, as if they had never been doing anything else.

Benjamin was waiting for me at the stairwell, but I walked past him and started up the stairs with my thoughts. I made it one step before he grabbed my arm. I turned, scowling.

"Not that way..." He trailed off as he saw my expression. "Whoa, are you okay?"

"I'm *fine*," I lied.

Benjamin laughed mirthlessly. "I may live in the woods in a houseful of men and get virtually zero interaction with other humans, but even *I* know that when a woman says she's 'fine' like that, it actually means there's a problem."

"That's not necessarily true." *Yes, it is.*

"Yes, I think it is."

I huffed. *Why is he this insightful?* I was not in the mood to be understood. I'd been chased through the woods, beaten up in a fall, set adrift among strange people, threatened directly by one of them, and stalled on the job I was supposed to be doing. Now I was in the middle of some sort of drug development and testing that didn't seem to be quite *on the level*. And his family was creepily staring at me.

I felt like I was in front of a complex jigsaw puzzle with one missing piece. A piece that would give sense to the rest of the puzzle, if only I could see it.

I couldn't, though, so instead I looked into his eyes. From my vantage point on the first step, we were at a height with each other, so I could clearly read his expression. It was completely open, waiting. There was no judgment there, only Benjamin.

I knew how deep my stubborn streak ran, and I had full confidence that I could forcefully insist everything was okay until long after we'd both died of starvation. Which would ultimately accomplish nothing. I was frustrated by my own lack of understanding of the situation, but intellectually I knew this was nothing more than an opportunity to further unravel the mystery.

"Okay," I sighed. I thought about Theo's wrecked room, the mystery fabric in Seth's, and Kermit's not-so-veiled threat. "I have been getting some... weird vibes from your family," I said tentatively.

Benjamin looked at me with a grave expression, then his mouth twitched as he snorted, unable to contain his amusement. His eyes squinted with mirth as he erupted in a hearty, full laugh.

I widened my eyes in indignation as he gasped for breath between bouts of laughter, with tears glistening on his face. "It wasn't a joke—" I started hotly, feeling my frustration bubble up again like the lava of a barely dormant volcano.

Benjamin waved a hand for attention. His laughs grew more infrequent, and his breath became deeper and steadier, until he finally cleared his throat to speak. He wiped his eyes and gave me what I gathered was his attempt at a somber look, then his mouth curved upward in a smile he couldn't contain. "That's about the nicest thing anyone has ever said about them."

He snorted and broke out in another chuckle at the thought. This time I joined in as well, laughing at the ridiculousness of it all. After a moment, Benjamin shook his head and sighed. "I am truly sorry for any *weird vibes* or otherwise seemingly strange behavior from myself or my family. We're all kind of..." He trailed off, thinking.

"Not used to company?" I said, the steady family line coming so readily to my lips.

He tilted his head, considering. "Horses of a different color, so to speak, is I guess more like it. But yeah, that too."

Benjamin continued, smiling. "As much as I'd prefer that your ankle wasn't hurting you, I have to admit that I'm glad to have an excuse to keep you here for a few days." His cheeks blushed a light pink. "So hopefully my family isn't scaring you off."

"Hah," I retorted. "I don't scare *that* easily." Though truth be told, I'd rather face down a giant snake than find his family staring at me like that again. I frowned as the force of their gaze popped into my mind and rubbed my arms as they pricked with goose bumps at the memory.

Benjamin reached out with concern on his face and placed his warm hands over mine. "Are you cold? I was going to bring you down to the wine cellar to pick out some Champagne, but it's even chillier down—"

I didn't let him finish. "Did you say wine cellar?" *Ah, my kryptonite.*

"Yeah, but—"

I interrupted him again. "I'm fine, really." He raised his eyebrows at that, so I smiled at him. "I'd love to check out the wine cellar."

He took my hand and guided me back down the stairs, then behind the staircase to a round metal manhole-type cover inset in the floor. It looked exactly like a sewer cover.

"Are you hiding the Ninja Turtles down here?" I asked jokingly. Benjamin laughed and lifted a plastic casing on the wall, uncovering a small white button and a switch on the inside.

"Stand back," he said. He pressed the button while gently holding an arm out to block me in case I did not stand back to his satisfaction.

One loud, long *beeeeeep* burst from somewhere overhead. As I searched upward for its source, the sound of metal scraping on rock rumbled at my feet. I looked down to find the manhole sliding neatly into the floor and disappearing beneath us, revealing another spiral staircase, this one leading into the darkness below. *Mind the gap.*

"Whoa," I gasped, "that's really—"

"Unnecessary? Ostentatious? Overly elaborate?" Benjamin offered.

"No, I was going to say cool." I smiled up at him.

"My dad, as down-to-earth as he is, has a secret love of the dramatic," he said by way of explanation.

"I approve. Can we go down now?"

Benjamin reached back to flip the switch beside the button, and string lighting that wound around the staircase flared to life below. The string lights glowed with an inviting warmth, drawing me down. It dawned on me that if I was in an adult Hansel and Gretel situation, this is exactly how I would be lured by the witch.

"Follow me," Benjamin said as he started down the winding staircase. He didn't need to tell me twice. He moved slowly, so I could easily keep up even with my crutches. I stepped onto each stair as he left it, anxious to see what was promising to be a one-of-a-kind wine cellar.

I'd always wanted a wine cellar. There was something inherently romantic about them. They made me think of old-timey France, rolling hills of tangled vineyards, and running barefoot through a castle in slow motion, wearing a dress with yards of flowing skirts billowing behind me. Far superior to the bottom shelf of the pantry where I stored my wine at home.

I paused my castle-and-gown daydream when we reached

the bottom of the staircase, where Benjamin flipped on another light switch. Dim lights blinked to life above us, only partially illuminating rows of wooden shelves. Each was about five feet high and packed from top to bottom with bottles. I could see at least three rows, but the shadows beyond could have easily been hiding more. It was hard to gauge how far back the room went. The air was indeed much cooler in the wine cellar, but I suppressed the urge to shiver. I didn't want to admit that Benjamin was right—but more important, I didn't want him to think I was too cold to examine this wine collection. I'm never *too anything* to check out new wine.

I ran my fingers along the cool stone wall as we ambled down the first row. I went even slower than usual on my crutches to avoid hitting anything in the slender rows, so I had time to notice that the bottles were growing progressively dustier the farther we went. By the end of the row, the labels were so coated in dust as to be completely illegible. I stopped, trying to make out the words on the last one. Benjamin noticed and paused with me, lifting the grimy bottle. He brought it toward his mouth and blew hard. He uncovered the words, but in doing so effectively transferred a cloud of dust directly onto my face.

"Ack!" I coughed and hastily wiped at my eyes to clear them.

"I'm sorry! That move went a lot better in my mind," Benjamin said, abashed.

I felt something soft gently wiping my face—*a handkerchief?* And when I opened my eyes again, Benjamin was neatly folding an off-white square of fabric, which he tucked into a pocket of his jeans. A modern-day gentleman complete with matching handkerchief: *ah-dorable*.

When he noticed me looking, Benjamin grinned, then cocked his head to the side to indicate the next row of wine bottles. I followed him as he walked, dusty bottle forgotten, though I read the date he'd uncovered as I passed by. *An eighty-six-year-old wine? I wonder how much that must be worth.* I was even more careful not to stray from the center of the aisle to avoid bumping any of the racks. We got about halfway down the third row (and there were indeed more rows after that) when Benjamin stopped and knelt, eyes locked on the middle of the shelf before him. His long fingers swiftly brushed over several bottles before hovering over one and lifting it. He looked up at me and tilted the bottle, showing me the label.

"Oh, Dom Pérignon. Fancy," I said appreciatively. I'd never tried it before on my PI income. The last "Champagne" I'd had was better mixed with orange juice. I always enjoyed Champagne, though. Much like the idea of a wine cellar, it was another thing I highly romanticized in my mind. It made me think of sparkly dresses and having a droll laugh with friends. *I have no idea what one might consider a droll laugh, but I'm sure it's achievable with the right Champagne.* Also, I once read about an elderly celebrity who said the key to her long life was a diet that consisted mainly of Champagne and popcorn, and I'd like to believe that's true.

"Well," Benjamin paused, turning the bottle over in his hand. "Like you said, we should celebrate. This is the closest we've ever come to a breakthrough in our research." He stopped talking, then blushed and looked down before continuing, his voice softer. "And. It's, uh, it's special to have you here to share it." He stood up and faced me, his eyes still an intense blue even in the dim yellow lighting of the wine cellar. They were focused directly on me. I felt my cheeks flush.

Benjamin leaned in slightly, peering into my eyes as if he was trying to see behind them. He was close enough that I could feel his warm breath on my cheek, like a gentle caress in the coolness of the cellar. His breath smelled like mint. I felt my heart speed up.

"Golden-eyed girl," he whispered, almost to himself. "I'm so glad I found you."

I searched his eyes, finding a potent mix of hope, desire… and fear. It was the same fear as the night before, but I still couldn't figure out what he could possibly be afraid of. Rejection? The thought was almost laughable. His chestnut hair had a ruddy glow in the lighting of the cellar, and I imagined running my hands through it as we tumbled onto a bed together. Not to mention his eyes, his smile, his laugh… *No, I'm sure no woman will ever reject him as long as he lives.*

I was scared, though. Scared of falling too hard into desire. Scared to eventually leave him and go back to my life, which suddenly seemed like a faraway memory from a faraway dream. *Do I really have to go back? Wait, what are you doing, Jericho? You don't even know him!*

Also, weren't you looking for something?

Yeah, a kiss.

I felt like a ship adrift on feelings inside of myself. I'd never been swept up so completely just… lusting after someone, and it absolutely terrified me.

He leaned in closer as if he could read my thoughts—and maybe they were his thoughts, too—but he paused hesitantly. His eyes locked onto mine, questioning. *Is this okay?* they said without speaking. *Yes, a million times, yes.* I closed the gap between us, and my nose brushed his as I tilted my face upward.

My lips parted in anticipation, and a loud clatter abruptly rang out from the staircase. My mouth formed into a startled gasp instead of a kiss, and I fell into Benjamin in surprise. He caught me easily. *Thank God for those muscly arms.* Even though I wasn't in danger of falling further, he didn't let me go. *Thanks again.* I didn't want to think about crashing into the rows of vintage wine bottles. I was certain that the contents of the cellar were worth more than my condo and my parents' house combined.

"Hey, Theo," Benjamin called out wryly.

How the hell does he know it's Theo? I squinted toward the staircase, but I couldn't make out who was on it.

"Oh, hey there, little brother. Did I catch you two canoodling down here? You know Dad would hate to find any of his priceless wine bottles broken in... *action*." Theo paused sarcastically before that last word. I supposed it was a typical brotherly comment (not that I had any brothers to know what was typical or not), but I was annoyed by his oily tone.

I also hadn't realized Theo was the oldest—it was hard to compare ages due to the hulking size of each Grey son, but I would have thought Benjamin was the eldest, given his self-assuredness and the way the other brothers seemed to defer to him.

Theo ambled down the stairs, reaching the bottom with a cocky bounce. He was smiling amiably. He *looked* perfectly nice. Well, I could have misinterpreted his tone. And maybe I wasn't annoyed by his tone as much as I was annoyed by the interruption. I sighed.

"Just getting some Dom to celebrate," Benjamin said, holding the bottle aloft.

"Nice choice. I was...coming to do the same," Theo replied. His eyes were pinned to me, and I couldn't help but feel like that wasn't quite how he'd found himself following us.

Benjamin grinned. "Great minds!"

"Why don't you bring two bottles up? I'll let Dad know you've got the goods." He didn't wait for an answer but started back up the stairs.

Benjamin held me, but his eyes didn't leave the stairs until he was sure his brother had thoroughly departed. After a moment, he turned back to me, and his arms relaxed. I hadn't realized he was so tense.

"Ah. I love my family, I really do. And I truly believe in what we're working on, and it's exciting, and it's important." He paused. "But sometimes it would be nice to be alone." He gave me a lopsided grin.

"I understand." *Kind of.* As an only child of highly individual parents, I'd spent plenty of time alone. I'd only continued the trend into my adult life with a job that didn't lend itself to company. But I certainly appreciated solitude, and so far, that seemed like a rarity in this family.

"Well, I guess we'd better go up," Benjamin said, though he made no move to release me.

"Yeah, I guess we'd better," I agreed, hesitantly. I ran my fingers up the length of his arm, marveling at the strength I felt there.

Benjamin turned his attention to the shelf beside us, and he put the Champagne bottle back in one of its grooves. I raised an eyebrow at him, questioning.

"Maybe we don't have to go up right away," he offered hopefully.

"Indeed not," I agreed with a wide smile. I leaned in. I wanted desperately to kiss him. He made me feel safe, somehow. I thought about being wrapped in his arms the previous night. Rushed though it was, it hadn't felt awkward at all. It felt natural. I hadn't slept like that in *years*. I craved the sight of him, the feel of him, the smell of him... I breathed in deeply and closed my eyes. *Yes.* I felt his now-free hand move to my upper back, bare in my tank top, drawing me closer to his body. *YES.* The skin on my back tingled with his touch. And then he abruptly stopped and moved both his hands to my shoulders, where he began rubbing my arms up and down.

I opened my eyes, confused.

"Jericho! You're freezing!" he admonished, looking chagrined. I tried to argue but he flung the crutches under my arms and scooted me toward the stairs. "Let's go get you warm," he said in a tone that brooked no argument.

"There's more than one way to get warm, you know," I muttered.

Benjamin blushed and cleared his throat to respond, but we heard voices calling from above. *Ugh, men are so impatient.* But I guess I was, too, sometimes. *Like when I'm waiting to be kissed.*

"Okay, fine," I said, acquiescing.

Benjamin let me go, then retrieved the first bottle of Dom and tucked it under his arm. He plucked another bottle from the same shelf, then we set out through the rows and out of the cellar.

We met the rest of his family in the kitchen—which was absolutely beautiful, with top-tier appliances and gorgeous black-marble countertops—where they'd already laid out leftovers from last night's dinner along with some fresh sandwich-making supplies. The three men were laughing together when we walked into the room, though they stopped to cheer when they saw that Benjamin came bearing Champagne.

"There they are," Kermit said with a smile. "I was about to send a search party down!" Theo winked at Benjamin, and Seth smirked. I blushed. I didn't think I could ever grow accustomed to this level of sibling attention.

Benjamin took it all in stride, however, and grabbed two ceramic plates from the stack as he moved down the line of leftovers, piling on a selection of food for us as he chatted eagerly with his brothers about their lab findings. I was content to simply watch their interactions. Kermit was all smiles and loving backslaps. Benjamin had a compliment or a kind word for each brother and his dad. Theo was sarcastic, but in a playful way, and even Seth was smiling.

We walked back down the hallway between the kitchen and dining room that led past the lab, and soon we stepped out into the sunshine of the patio terrace. I squinted against the bright light and followed Benjamin across the flagstones to a glass-topped table nestled in the shade of a vast triangular canopy that spanned the length of the space.

Kermit pulled a chair out for me and nodded when I thanked him. Again, his seat was at the head of the table, but he didn't sit down right away. While the brothers settled in, Kermit held up a bottle of Champagne and a long carving knife. He tapped the side of the bottle several times, the knife chiming delicately against the glass.

"Boys." He paused, waiting for their attention. "And Jericho," he added with a small nod in my direction. "Today is a very special day. You have each literally put blood, sweat, and tears into our work. We made sacrifices for it. And today, well, it looks like those sacrifices are paying off." He looked at his sons, making eye contact with each of them in turn. "Your mother would be so very proud of each of you." He peeled the wrapper and the wire cage off the top of the bottle, then stepped away from the table, holding the Champagne horizontally in an outstretched arm. He rotated the bottle until the seam of the glass pointed upward. With his other hand he brandished the knife and swiftly sabered the bottle top with a loud but satisfying *shiiink* and *pop*.

Champagne burst forth from the severed top. Theo, who either knew beforehand what his father was going to do or had otherwise anticipated it, was already holding empty flutes, and he rushed to catch the outpouring of liquid from the sliced top. "Dad," he chastised, "you're not supposed to do that with good stuff."

Benjamin leaned close to me and whispered. "See, I told you. Dramatic."

I scoffed at Benjamin's comment. "That...was awesome," I said loudly, turning to Kermit.

Kermit smiled at me. "Ah, a girl with good taste."

Theo passed full glasses to me and Benjamin as he sat down, and once everyone was seated with drinks in hand, we clinked them together with a celebratory "Cheers!"

Benjamin sat beside me, and his shoulder brushed mine as he laughed with his brothers. The Champagne was delicious, light and bubbly, a perfect counterpart to the crisp fall day. You hear a lot about wine and food pairings, but what about wine and weather pairings? I want to know the best Chardonnay for a summer breeze, and the best Merlot for a thunderstorm. I closed my eyes and smiled, relishing it all. I was so lost in the moment that I almost didn't hear Kermit asking me a question.

"So, Jericho, how about my wine cellar? Was it to your liking?" Kermit asked between bites of his lunch.

"Well, it's not a giant room full of books, but I'll take what I can get." Books were one thing I could never get enough of, and sadly hadn't brought on this trip. I opened my eyes and smiled at him. I still couldn't decide how I felt about him after our...interlude...on the stairs, but it did feel like he was making an effort to smooth things over.

"Who says we don't have a giant room full of books?" Theo asked.

"Benjamin, have you not taken this girl to the library yet?" Kermit sounded appalled, but I couldn't tell if it was just a mock exaggeration of incredulity, or if he was truly shocked by this news.

"Well, er, we've been busy."

"Oh, is that what the kids call it these days?" Theo teased. Seth rolled his eyes.

I blushed, but Benjamin waved a hand nonchalantly. "All right, all right. I'll show her after lunch," he said.

"Benny, be sure you're letting that girl get enough rest, you hear? She can't recover if she's always on the move," Kermit said, giving his son a wilting look.

Theo leaned back lazily in his chair, gazing casually at me. "Rest *is* best. Isn't that what they say?"

I cleared my throat to change the subject before any more men could run a commentary on best practices for my health. "So, how about that cure? Will you be starting the testing soon?" I asked Kermit.

All eyes at the table shifted over to the large man. Kermit met his sons' gazes and shifted slightly in his seat. "Oh, probably after a week or so." He shrugged. "It will be sometime after you're gone."

"Oh, interesting. Do you need some time to order testing animals?" I asked.

The three brothers still had their eyes on Kermit, like they were as intrigued by his answer as I was.

Kermit tilted his head marginally to one side and pursed his lips. "Well, I am going to start by testing it on myself, as it were." He must have noticed my eyes widen, because he continued quickly. "It's not *common* practice, per se, but in this case I'm the best option we have." He looked at his sons pointedly as he said this. He paused before continuing. "You see, Jericho, I myself have the disease we are trying to cure. It's quite uncommon, and only apparent in humans, so animal testing—the kind that might be done on a lab rat—is impossible in this case. Human trials come after animal testing anyhow, so I'm just skipping ahead."

Not common practice indeed. He sounded unconcerned, but even I knew that you don't "just skip ahead" in lab work like this. I couldn't keep the giant question to myself any longer.

"What disease is this again?"

"Something so extremely rare that most people haven't even heard of it," Kermit answered smoothly. "I won't bore you with the details."

I noticed that Theo and Seth were still looking at their father in disbelief, as if they were shocked by either his revelation or—more likely—by the fact that he was telling *me*, an outsider, all of this. Benjamin, on the other hand, was staring directly at me with his brows creased. *Is he trying to gauge my reaction?*

I thought about this for a moment. Kermit was edging around actually telling me what this mystery disease was, *but why?* Could this be part of why they were hiding out in the woods?

Is he worried about infecting other people?

"Is it contagious?" I finally asked, simultaneously dreading the answer and fighting the urge to scoot my chair away from his.

"If any of my blood or saliva were to directly enter your bloodstream, then yes, very. But excepting that, then no, not at all," he said easily.

The men's full attention was on me now, and the weight of their gaze felt heavy around me. I mentally shook it off and considered Kermit's words. "So as long as you don't bite me, or spit into any of my cuts, then we should be golden?"

Kermit smiled at that. "Just so, Jericho."

"Maybe don't ask him to be a blood donor, either," Theo added.

Seth's eyes were locked on his father, with a piercing gaze that was quickly turning into a glare. Benjamin was still studying me. Theo crossed his arms and narrowed his eyes into slits, like a large jungle cat. He leaned back in his chair as he regarded the entire table silently. His mouth curved into a hard-lined smile, as if he was privately amused by the conversation.

I frowned. "I guess I'm confused—why even wait a week, then, before doing the test?" I asked Kermit. "Haven't you waited long enough?"

Theo raised an eyebrow, though the thin smile never left his face. "Why indeed, Father?"

Kermit gave his eldest son a somewhat exasperated look. "Frankly, it's something better done when we don't have company. I thought you'd know that, Theo. And I'll need all three of you boys to help me prepare." Kermit turned his attention to me. "Jericho, I do reckon that you'll have recovered enough for the walk to town in a week. I'm sure you're anxious to get back to your job and your life."

Seth stopped glaring at his father. "That," he said, "actually makes sense." He relaxed his stance and looked at me with slightly less distaste now that he was certain my visit had an expiration date.

One week. I decided I didn't want to be around when they were doing their unsanctioned human testing, but a week didn't seem like enough time. *Not at all enough time to learn more about the Greys.*

But the job—*my* job—suddenly popped back into my mind. Along with a macabre image of Katherine's ghost from my dream, nodding. I'd gotten completely sidetracked in Benjamin's company.

While I was grappling with my thoughts, Kermit continued speaking to his sons. "In the meantime, you boys have earned some rest after all this. Let's go camping for a few days and enjoy this glorious New England autumn."

"A great idea!" said Theo. Seth's sour expression melted into a smile. My own smile fell as I turned to Benjamin, anticipating his excitement for the trip. It would be selfish of me to ask him to stay while his family vacationed without him. Suddenly a week seemed like a long time when it would be spent all alone in the secluded house.

"Uh, actually, I'm going to sit this one out, guys."

For a second, I thought I'd imagined Benjamin saying exactly what I'd hoped he would, but then his brothers reacted.

Seth shot him an annoyed glance. "Really, Ben?"

Theo raised an incredulous eyebrow in his direction but didn't say anything. Instead, Kermit spoke up. "Excellent, my boy, I was hoping you'd say that."

Theo raised his other eyebrow in surprise, and Kermit turned to his eldest son. "There are a few simple but time-consuming things that would be beneficial to get done before the test. Benny can lay the groundwork while we're gone."

My face flushed in relief. Theo and Seth were still staring dubiously at their brother, but Kermit tilted his head toward me and winked. I got the distinct sense that Kermit knew exactly how glad I was to have Benjamin to myself for a few days, and that he even *approved.*

Kermit directed Theo and Seth to clear the table after we finished our meal. As soon as the two men had walked into the house and out of sight, he spoke again.

"Ben, I need to show you some things in the lab. Why don't you take Jericho to the library and then come find me? I'm sure she'll spot something there to keep her occupied."

Kermit said the last part with a grin in my direction.

Benjamin nodded at his father, then offered me a hand up from the table. With my interest fully piqued, I took his hand, and we walked back into the house.

CHAPTER 8

I like big books and I cannot lie.

Benjamin pushed on the solid oak doors that led to the library, and my eyes swept around the room in awe as the heavy doors creaked open. Floor-to-ceiling bookshelves lined the four main walls and a smaller reading nook. The only wall space not occupied by books was home to the door we just walked through, and two enormous windows on the opposite side of the room. The reading nook was lit by cleverly disguised bulbs set into the floor, along with an abundance of standing lamps. They surrounded a very plush-looking navy-blue velvet couch, and it looked cozy to the extreme. *I want to sit on you.*

"First the wine cellar and now this. If I didn't know any better, I'd think you were trying to woo me, sir."

Benjamin smiled. "Hey, it worked in *Beauty and the Beast*, and you're definitely a beauty."

"But you're no beast," I said playfully. I nudged him with my shoulder, and Benjamin's smile faltered for a heartbeat.

If it wasn't for my eyes, trained from years of tracking snakes in murky water (I wasn't the three-time winner of Florida's annual Python Challenge for nothing), I might not have noticed it at all. When he glanced my way his smile had returned, if slightly tighter, and he watched me as I approached the nearest shelf.

I walked along slowly, partly because of my crutches and aching ankle and partly because I wanted to read the titles as I navigated the sea of literature. I fingered the spines of several books as I ran my hand down the shelf. As far as I could tell, the collection was separated by genre and alphabetized by author. There were timeless classics by Brontë and Dickens, looking well-worn in their faded bindings, interspersed with newer fiction. I nodded approvingly. More than one of these was on my personal book-bucket-list, and I was already mentally planning how I'd spend my reading time.

After doing research for my case. That is, if they had any books that would be useful.

Benjamin put a hand on my shoulder and pointed out different sections, which, in addition to the standard fiction, fantasy, and sci-fi, also included medicine, horticulture, history, comic books ("For Seth," Benjamin said with a shrug), mythology and folklore, and—incredibly for me—zoology.

What were the odds of finding an entire section on zoology in a home library? And it was an expansive shelf, with rows and rows of books on animals of all sorts. Though oddly, they all seemed to be focused on mammals, and mainly large ones. *Lucky break for me, I guess?*

I was amazed by the number of purely animal physiology

titles. They ranged from what looked like kids' picture books to university textbooks, and everything in between. My eyes paused on *Animals of Maine* and *Mammals of the American Northeast*. I pulled out the latter and flipped through the pages. It had detailed drawings and photos of each animal's skeleton, including teeth and jaws. I turned a section over at random, and the book opened to a page about black bears. Kermit's voice rang in my ears: "Clearly a bear attack." *Well, we'll just see about that.* I could almost feel Katherine's ghost from my nightmare, again nodding approvingly. "Can I read this one?" I asked Benjamin.

He grinned. "Of course! You're welcome to read anything while you're here. Just make sure you put it back where it came from. Dad is a real stickler for a tidy library."

With that many titles to keep track of, I could totally understand why. If the books became unorganized, it would be nearly impossible to find what you were looking for. Benjamin walked over to an old wooden writing desk in the corner that I hadn't noticed before. He opened a drawer and pulled out a handful of multicolored paper bookmarks.

"Here you go," he said as he came back. "You can stick one of these anyplace you take a book. That'll make it easier to return them."

"I can tell you've done this a time or two," I said as I accepted the slips of paper, trading two for the books I'd removed.

"Yeah, my dad isn't really the kind of guy who lets you make the same mistake twice." He shrugged.

I could believe that. Kermit seemed jovial enough, but he'd also threatened to push me down a staircase. I shuddered at the thought of seeing Kermit *really* angry and looked away from Benjamin. *What was Kermit like as a father?* My thoughts quickly collapsed to the background, though, as my eyes focused on the desk behind Benjamin. Sitting on top of the desk was a cherry-red telephone. A very old phone, but still. My cell phone had gone missing during my run through the woods and subsequent fall, and with everything that had happened I'd kind of forgotten about it. But now I was keenly aware that I hadn't had contact with anyone outside of this cabin in nearly forty-eight hours.

"You have a phone?" I asked in disbelief.

He snorted. "Well, yeah. We live in the woods, not the Stone Age."

I turned to him with an eyebrow raised. "I mean, it *is* a rotary phone, Benjamin."

"Fair enough," he laughed. "Do you want to use it? You're welcome to—just, uh, maybe don't be too specific on the details about your stay here, if you talk to anybody?" He shifted his weight as he spoke.

"Don't worry about that," I said, with my eyes locked on the phone. "Your dad and I have an...understanding." I turned to Benjamin. "Whatever secrets you have are safe with me. I hope you know that."

He nodded and gave me a half smile. "I do."

Something else occurred to me. "Benjamin, wait, do you also have—"

"Wi-Fi? No." He'd interrupted me before I could finish. My shoulders slumped at the news, but in a way, it was also nice to be disconnected. He looked into my eyes, and his shoulders tensed for a moment, as if he wanted to say something else. I waited expectantly, but he just ran a hand through his hair. A lock fell forward, covering his eyes, and I resisted the urge to tuck it back, and maybe let my hand linger on the crest of his cheekbones, and—

Benjamin coughed. "Uh, anyway, I'm pretty sure my brothers are going to want my help rounding up camping supplies, and there are a few things my dad wants to show me in the lab, so—"

He trailed off, but I nodded. "Yeah, of course. I'll just be here. I'm going to call my mom and check out some books."

Benjamin walked to the door with the promise that he would be back shortly, and I told him to take his time (which I didn't really mean, because I wanted him back sooner rather than later). Though either way I had business to attend to.

I maneuvered over to the desk and sat down in front of the phone, propping my crutches against a neighboring bookshelf. The phone's only companion on the sparse desktop was a squat lamp with a green glass lampshade boasting a friendly warm glow. *Cozy.* I smiled at it and reached for the phone.

I silently congratulated myself for memorizing my mom's phone number as my fingers spun the numbers on the old rotary dial. I once read a study where researchers claimed they could accurately guess participants' ages based solely on how many phone numbers they had memorized. The pre-smartphone generations of course retained vastly more numbers than those post-smartphone. I believed it. I only knew three by heart, including my own. The third? A restaurant in my hometown that delivered tacos. *Hello, priorities.*

THE MIDNIGHT PACK

The last number spun back into place, and I held the phone up to my ear. It hadn't occurred to me to ask about a phone earlier. Not that I didn't want to update my parents on the fact that I hadn't died in the woods, but it didn't seem urgent. My mom and I have always had a mutual understanding that the other would have the good sense not to get killed, and my dad gets his news from my mom. In the past, we've gone weeks without talking when one of us was traveling, but I was glad for the chance to chat, regardless.

The phone continued to ring until I finally got my mother's voicemail. After her high-pitched "Leave me a message, darling!" and the beep, I gave her a small rundown of where I was and assurance that I was all right in the woods of Maine.

I put the receiver back on the phone base, and with animal books in hand (rather haphazardly with my crutches), I made a beeline for the couch. Before becoming a PI, I'd thought the job would be all-glamour-all-the-time. I'd envisioned a life full of stakeouts and exclusive access to highly classified areas. As it turned out, there's a massive research component. And much less access to those classified areas. But as it also turned out, I didn't mind at all.

I sat lengthwise on the couch so I could keep my feet up. I hated to admit that Kermit was right about me needing to rest, *but*... I sighed. *This has been a sigh-inducing few days.* That thought, of course, made me sigh again. My injured ankle throbbed annoyingly, so I grabbed one of the pillows from the side of the couch to prop up my foot before settling in to read. I quickly found the page with the black bear that I'd flipped to earlier. Joseph, the animal expert from the sheriff's recording, wasn't fully convinced that it was a bear, but it was still his favored culprit. Kermit, on the other hand, had proclaimed Katherine's death a *definite* bear attack. I figured that was as good a place as any to start.

Frankly, mammals weren't my specialty. Aside from a few cases involving goats, cougars, and horses, I'd fallen into reptilian cases by happenstance, until that became what I was best known for and what I knew best. So despite having an Indiana Jones–level aversion to snakes when I started, I'd grown to appreciate them. And other reptiles besides. Now I knew *all* about snakes, lizards, alligators... you name a reptile, I've probably seen it, and possibly captured it. I didn't know a lot about bears, though, or wolves. I had made sure Sheriff Jackson was aware of this fact when he requested my services, but he'd just said that I "came recommended." Though I'd never thought to ask, *Recommended by whom?* Maybe he'd heard about the wampus cat case, though I was working with both a biologist from the Knoxville Zoo and local animal control that time.

Either way, extra research was necessary. I didn't expect to crack the case with a single book, of course, but I needed independently acquired information to help confirm the men's suspicions. Getting to know Kermit only solidified my sense that he was an outdoorsy type who was also intelligent enough to create some kind of cure for an illness. So, a smart guy like that: It made sense that he'd know what he was talking about when it came to the local fauna, right? Frankly, I was betting on the bear as well.

Until I read about them.

THE MIDNIGHT PACK

The only bear species found in Maine is the smallest and shyest of all Ursidae (that's a champion bear vocab word), the black bear. *Small* is a relative term here, with the largest of these bears getting close to five feet tall (standing) and weighing around four hundred pounds. But they're not known for being aggressive, and the bear physiology just wasn't in line with the bite marks on Katherine's body. I thought about the photos in the police report. Whatever attacked her had much bigger and longer jaws. Unless this particular bear was some sort of mutant. *Stranger things have happened*, said part of my brain. But it just didn't feel right. According to this book, black bears are so docile that the best defense if you see one is to literally *scare it away*. Incidentally, this is also my defense against unwanted advances from men at the bar.

But that didn't sound much like an animal that would attack a human unprovoked. *Okay, so what if it* was *provoked?* A startled animal could certainly react in self-defense, though that didn't explain how the bite marks were simply *different*. Vastly different. *Why was I the only one who couldn't reconcile the bite pattern?* I supposed I wasn't the only one, though. If Sheriff Jackson really had zero doubts about the bear, he wouldn't have hired me. I reached for the next book, *Animals of Maine*, to corroborate what I'd just read.

My typical research pattern was simple: Find and verify. Regardless of how I came by information, I always, *always* worked to verify what I learned. *This would be a lot easier with the internet.* I flipped through the book and almost missed the section on bears—it was only one page, since there is only one type of bear found in the Pine Tree State. All the information was the same as the previous book's. I scanned the last paragraph, then paused. My heart beat faster when I saw the word *fatal.*

"*. . . at the time of writing, there have been no fatal bear attacks in Maine.*"

I exhaled and slammed the book shut. The thump reverberated around the empty library. I drummed on the hard cover with my fingers. *It wasn't a bear attack.* Only Katherine could know for certain, but my gut told me it was true.

My temples flared with a sudden pain as my head started to ache—I wasn't used to drinking in the middle of the day. A wooziness caught up to me. I closed my eyes and propped the book on my chest, then leaned back on the couch, massaging my forehead.

"Not a bear," I murmured.

"Yesss," came a slow whisper. *See, even the wind agrees with me.*

Though I tried to keep my eyes open, I promptly drifted into sleep and back to the instantaneous dreamland that these woods seemed to cultivate.

I was on the track at my high school, running. My feet thumped on the padded ground as I flew through the course. I'd always felt at home on a track. Running was a way to clear my mind and lift my spirit through the dramas of my teen years (then later in college, and finally life in general).

Something was wrong, though. I shifted my head back and

THE MIDNIGHT PACK

forth as I sprinted, trying to pinpoint the source of my unease. Then it dawned on me: I was alone. Goose bumps peppered my arms. I was *never* alone on the track. There were always at least two or three other students either running, watching, or making out under the bleachers. Not this time. Rows of silver bleachers circled the track, all empty.

I shook off my nerves as I ran. Never mind—there *was* someone there. A figure stood on the other side of the track, just around the loop from where I was. *Thank God for some company, this was getting creepy.* I sped up to reach the mystery person. Auburn hair and stormy eyes came into focus, and my heart shot into my throat.

Katherine.

Mercifully, it seemed to be the Katherine I'd seen on the MISSING poster, not the corpse version. She wore a deep-blue sweater with UTC MOCS splashed across the front in mustard-yellow lettering. Her jeans were tattered, but in an I-bought-them-like-this kind of way, and a short lanyard that matched her sweater hung from a pocket. Something tickled at my brain, but it was forgotten as I noticed she was holding something, though I couldn't see what. I ran toward her as fast as I could manage, stopping only when I reached her. She nodded at me and slowly held up the dark object in her hands: a book. She continued lifting it until it blocked her eyes. The worn cover was a faded navy blue that matched her sweater, but the gold-leaf title gleamed in the sunlight: *Wendigo*. I barely had time to wonder who on earth Wendigo could be when Katherine's body suddenly lurched forward. She heaved the book at my face.

I flinched and raised my arms, tensing to absorb a hit that never came. I shot up gasping, awake.

I must have been asleep for a while because the sun had already set and the room was dark, save for the floor lights rimming the walls. Eyes wide, I looked around furtively, orienting myself. I was still in the library, and I was alone. I half expected to see Katherine standing beside me with another book in hand.

"I'm alone," I said aloud. As if saying it would make it true.

It was just a dream, I reminded myself. *A nightmare.* My breath evened out, and I sighed and slumped my shoulders. *Just another nightmare.* I straightened up again and swung my feet over the edge of the couch to stand. My shoes met something hard on the floor, and I looked down curiously.

A familiar dark-blue book with gold-leaf lettering sat on the hardwood beside the couch.

It can't be... I took a few deep breaths then leaned closer to read the title.

Wendigo.

My arms and legs prickled with goose bumps as my brain tried in vain to reject what I was seeing. *Oh no. Nope, nope, nope, nope.*

"Ghosts aren't real," I said aloud to the book, in my bravest voice. It came out as a squeak.

"Probably not."

I screamed, and the unexpected voice from the other side of the library also let out a startled yelp.

"Whoa, sorry, Jericho, I didn't mean to scare you," Benjamin called out as he quickly covered the space between us in long, powerful strides. He flipped a switch on the wall, and the standing lamps blinked to life in unison. "Is everything all right?"

I took several deep breaths and put a hand on my chest over my poor fluttering heart, as if I could press it back into submission. "Er," I stammered.

Benjamin knelt and retrieved the offending book from the floor. "*Wendigo*, huh? That's some heavy reading."

"That's just it, though, I'm not reading it." My words poured out in a rush as I proceeded to tell Benjamin about my dream and finding the book at my feet. Goose bumps dotted my arms again as I spoke. The story did not get any less creepy with retelling. By the time I was finished, I again half expected to see Katherine standing beside me, and Benjamin's face had paled slightly as well. My words hung in the air as I waited for him to say something reassuring.

He didn't.

He looked at me, blue eyes reflecting the silver moonlight that now peeked through the window. If I concentrated, I could imagine the pale light revealing new depths in those twin blue lakes. Was there a darkness hiding there?

"Benjamin, who are you?" I whispered softly.

He lifted a hand to my face, brushing a stubborn stray hair behind my ear. "I'm someone who cares about you. The rest is only shadows in the dark," he said gently. Then he shrugged and shook his head. "But I admit I'm confused about this, uh... wayward book."

He looked away from me and frowned at the book in his hand. Then he turned his attention behind us, to the wall of books at the back of the couch. There was a conspicuously empty spot directly behind and above me.

"Ah—" He smiled. "Look, it came from right there. It must have slipped and fallen."

"'Slipped and fallen'... Benjamin, it's a book, not a person on a wet floor."

He turned back to me with an eyebrow raised. "Would you rather I say it was a ghost?"

"Erm, that'll be a hard no. My, what slippery bookshelves you have."

He slid the book into the empty space on the shelf. The gold-leaf lettering on the binding seemed to glare at me, so I turned away and leaned into Benjamin's arm.

"I think I'm done in the library for now," I said, my voice muffled against his shirt.

Ghosts aren't real.

"Let's go upstairs." Benjamin stood and offered me a hand, which I gratefully accepted. There's something inherently comforting about physical contact with another human when you're scared. Which I wasn't, because there was nothing to be scared of. *Because ghosts aren't real.*

We walked to the door, and I paused as Benjamin reached over to turn off the lights. He flipped the switch, blanketing the library in a quiet darkness. I nodded at him and we stepped out, closing the doors behind us. As they shut, something thumped loudly on the floor from the depths of the library. A chill washed over my body, and my eyes widened to an alarming degree. I didn't need to check to know that *Wendigo* had fallen again. Because of an inexplicably slippery bookshelf. *Ghosts aren't real.*

After a pit stop in the kitchen to grab a bountiful charcuterie board that Benjamin had made during my lengthy library nap, we made our way to the living room. We sank together onto the cozy leather couch, warmed by the cheerfully roaring fireplace. He set a platter heaping with cheeses, meats, and crackers on a coffee table in front of us and poured two glasses of red wine from a bottle that had been waiting there. My mom always said if I couldn't find an attractive man, then I should find one who was prepared. It seemed Benjamin was both.

My bravery returned with the wine, the heat, and the pleasant light of the fire, so I asked Benjamin about the book.

"So, who's Wendigo anyway?"

"Ah. Uh, it's not a *who*, it's a *what*," he started. I waited for him to go on. My eyes were on him, but his gaze was locked on the flickering orange flames. The firelight made his face look particularly warm and soft, and his hair seemed to glow bronze in the reflected light.

He cleared his throat and continued. "The wendigo is an old legend from the Native Americans here in the US and First Nations in Canada. It's a person who transforms into some type of cannibalistic creature after tasting human flesh."

Something about the way he said "tasting human flesh" made my arms and legs prick annoyingly. I rubbed my calves and scooted closer to Benjamin as he went on. "When Europeans came over, they witnessed this firsthand, supposedly.

That book you saw is a collection of their accounts." His eyes left the fire, and he looked at me. "They compared the wendigo to werewolves." He shook his head to himself. "Not similar at all, though, really, other than both conditions being infection-based."

I decided to ignore the fact that he was talking about these creatures like they were real. "Werewolves? Did they believe in werewolves?" I asked with an eyebrow raised.

Benjamin chuckled. "Well, yeah. Actually, lots of people do. Especially here. Have you heard of the Palmyra dogmen?" I nodded. I'd done my cryptid due diligence before I came to Stillbridge. A family in Palmyra, a town not too far from Stillbridge, had claimed they'd been chased and harassed by five shapeshifting men.

Benjamin continued. "Well, those were basically werewolves."

"Sure, but weren't those proven to just be coyotes, or Canadian wolves who'd gotten addicted to that family's trash?"

Benjamin shrugged. "It doesn't matter if that one was real or not. The point is, every culture has a werewolf story."

"Every culture has a creation story, too, but that doesn't mean that God is real," I retorted.

"Doesn't it? What do you believe, Jericho?"

What do I believe? I looked out the window into the twilight sky. The full moon from Wednesday night had only just begun to wane. When I was a kid, I could never tell if the moon was coming or going. It was a mystery to me until it either became a tiny crescent sliver or grew into a full moon. One day, my best friend Maria and I were wondering about the curious nature of our lunar neighbor when her Mexican mother overheard us.

She said, with a lilted accent that I always adored hearing, "*Mijas*, the moon always tells you what it is doing. You just need to listen! When the moon makes a C, *como Cristo*, it's dying. Like Christ died for our sins. When the moon makes a D, *como Dios*, it is filling up again. Like God fills us with life."

Every culture has a creation story. Every culture has a werewolf story.

I turned back to Benjamin. "I don't know. Just because a lot of people believe something doesn't make it true." He tilted his head at me in a gesture to continue. "I mean, once I was called to investigate a Cthulhu sighting in Florida. *Cthulhu*, Benjamin, the fictional monster made up by an antisemitic asshole. Reports kept coming into the police station about it. Multiple people saw this mystery creature and they all believed the same thing. There was a media frenzy around it—I was even on the news."

Benjamin raised his eyebrows in appreciation, and I continued. "And you know what it was? A massive mating ball."

"Mating ball, huh?" Benjamin said slyly. "Sounds kinky. What is that, exactly?"

"It happens when male snakes sense that a female is single and, um, ready to mingle. They literally swarm her. Up to a hundred male snakes will tangle up as they fight for the right to *get it on*. In this case, pythons came back to the same place, night after night, to do their business. I took pictures, I took a video...the snakes had zero privacy from me. But I had *proof*, dammit. And the same people who cried Cthulhu in the beginning still wouldn't be swayed."

I paused and looked toward the fire crackling brightly in

the hearth. "I think people believe things because they want to, not because there's actually something to believe in."

I could feel Benjamin's eyes on me even though I was still facing the flames. He cleared his throat and started speaking softly. "Most stories are rooted in truth, you know. I believe in the wendigo."

I turned back toward him, incredulous. "You do?" He nodded. "But, Benjamin, you're a *scientist*!" I said, feeling strangely affronted.

"That's just it, though. There's science behind it."

I opened my mouth to object, but he continued before I could. "Wait, hear me out, Jericho." I shut my mouth and looked at him imploringly. He gave me a small half smile before continuing. "Do you know where mad cow disease comes from?"

Not where I thought he was going with this. "Cows?"

"Right, but do you know how they get it?" I shook my head. "They can get it from being fed brain matter from other cows."

"Oh, gross." I looked at the salami on the table, suddenly queasy.

Benjamin ignored my commentary and continued. "How about Ebola, or MERS, or even COVID?"

I hadn't heard of MERS, so I shrugged in response.

"Well, the best virus tracing points to exotic animals as the genesis for all of them. The fact is, it's known and proven that humans can contract new viruses from eating certain meats. And at least cows can get brain-altering prions from, uh, being fed cannibalistically." When he saw a wave of confusion wash over my face, he added, "Prions are like viruses, but even harder to kill."

He paused and looked out the window, then turned back to me. "So we know that viruses and prions are transmissible via meat. We know that mad cow disease causes extreme aggression in cows. It stands to reason that a human in the same circumstances would have a similar reaction."

When he explained it that way, it did make sense. *Gross.* "Are you saying that a wendigo isn't a cryptid, but a real disease?" The red wine in my glass suddenly bore a little too much resemblance to blood, so I set it down on the coffee table next to the meat.

I stared at his face, ruddy and warm in the orange light of the fire. The flames glittered against his wavy hair and danced in his eyes, giving him an otherworldly look. He shrugged, but there was no uncertainty there. "All signs point to yes, disgusting as it is. As for the Europeans comparing them to werewolves..." He paused, considering.

I raised an eyebrow at him. "You're not telling me you believe in werewolves, too. I mean, do you?"

He gave me another half smile. "If the wendigo is real, who's to say the werewolves of Europe and elsewhere aren't?"

I wasn't buying it. "Did you not hear my story about Cthulhu? There's always a logical explanation."

"Do you only believe in what you can see, Jericho?"

"For the most part, yeah," I said.

He shifted on the couch so his entire body faced mine. "What made that book fall downstairs?"

The goose bumps were back. I rubbed my arms as I answered grumpily. "A slippery bookshelf. We discussed this."

"But you said it was the same book you dreamed about?"

"Coincidence," I grunted.

"So do you want to go back to the library now? Maybe hang out down there instead?" Mischief glinted in his blue eyes. I knew what he was doing, where he was going with this line of questioning, and I didn't want to play along.

I sighed. "No. No, I don't. I don't believe in ghosts, I don't believe in dogmen or werewolves... I don't believe, but I still get scared. I do believe our hearts are whimsical and our instincts are trained to be cautious of these *things that go bump in the night*. So I admit: It's nighttime and apparently I get creeped out by falling books. Enough so that frankly I'd rather not... I'd rather not be alone tonight."

That was the truth, for more reasons than one. Last night—which I'd spent in Benjamin's arms—was one of the most comforting nights of my life. As this evening approached, I'd been wondering how to broach the topic of repeating it. I looked at him with a shy and hopeful smile. He'd turned back to the fire as I was talking, and I admired his chiseled profile in the firelight as he ran a hand through his scruffy hair. I used to smirk when books described someone's heart as skipping a beat, but here I was with a flutter in my chest. When he looked back my way he was smiling, too, which made the corners of his blue eyes crinkle upward.

Then he laughed.

Not the response I was hoping for. My smile faltered.

"To be honest, I was trying to figure out how to ask you

that all day," he said. Relief swept through me. He laughed again, and this time I joined in.

I looked down, still smiling, and I felt his thumb under my chin. He gently angled my face upward, so I was looking into his eyes. I was acutely aware of his touch on my skin. His eyes searched mine, and the sudden warmth I felt wasn't just from the fire. Time seemed to slow, and all at once the minor details in the room sharpened around us. The fire crackling in the hearth lazily spit out embers onto the well-worn rug that sat stoically in front of it. The wind moaned softly at the window, but it wasn't dark or ominous. It reminded me of someone humming deeply but sweetly under their breath. The light of the moon and the fire combined to give the entire room an ethereal glow, beautifully illuminating Benjamin before me. My breath caught in my throat—*is he finally going to kiss me?* He edged closer, and I leaned in to meet him. I closed my eyes. My senses were engulfed by the campfire smell of the fireplace and Benjamin's spicy scent. The two mingled together in a comforting way that rooted me in place. I parted my lips, anticipating.

Then instead of meeting his mouth, my face pressed into the crook of his neck as he swept me into a powerful embrace. I sighed inwardly, but only briefly, as I let myself be held. It felt so good to be in the security of his arms that I almost didn't miss the would-be kiss. *Almost.*

I felt his heartbeat against my chest, a powerful rhythm that swept up my own. I snuggled in deeper, enjoying the feel of his body against mine. He breathed in and leaned against the top of my head, exhaling in a contented sigh. I tilted my head upward, locking eyes with him. He smiled.

"Do you like stars?" he asked abruptly.

What? "Um, yes?"

"I want to show you something," he said. He relaxed his arms as he unwrapped himself from me, then stood and offered me a hand up from the couch.

CHAPTER 9

After Benjamin asked me if my ankle was okay with more walking and if I'd like more wine (fine, and yes, but white), we climbed back up the stairs and past the bedrooms on the top floor. Benjamin carried a large wicker basket filled with cozy-looking blankets that he had borrowed from the living room. A carefully nestled bottle of white wine sat atop the blanket pile: the proverbial icing on the cake.

With Benjamin laden down with supplies and myself with my crutches, we slowly made our way down the long upstairs hallway. We headed the opposite direction from Benjamin's room, until we reached what looked like a dead end: an empty wooden bookshelf.

My disappointment at an empty bookshelf (who has an *empty* bookshelf?) quickly dissipated when I noticed it was not a bookshelf at all. It was a short set of very steep stairs, going straight up the wall and into darkness above. In fact, *staircase* was a generous term. The rough-hewn, almost vertical steps shared a lot more in common with a ladder.

"Ooh, spooky," I said. I peered into the gaping maw where the stair-ladder disappeared into the shadows of a room above us.

"Let there be light," Benjamin responded. He deftly flicked a light switch in the corner with his elbow.

A dim but warm light filled the room above my head, and I could just make out an assortment of shapes in the visible corners. "What's up there?" I asked.

"Just the attic. It's mostly for storage and currently home to a bunch of junk, and some of my mom's stuff that my dad couldn't part with."

"Oh," I said, confused.

He laughed at my tone. "We're not here for the attic, I want to show you what's *behind* it."

We climbed into the attic (some of us Benjamins more gracefully than us Jerichos), and I could see that he wasn't wrong. The sides and corners were piled high with boxes and lumpy shapes that might have been children's toys. The box nearest me had a small pile of dusty photos strewn over it. Three small children that could only be Benjamin and his brothers smiled up at me from the picture on top. I smiled back at them. Two dark-haired boys with glasses sandwiched a shaggy-caramel-blond-haired boy in a group hug. Something tugged at my memory when I looked at the boys in the photo, but I pushed it aside as my attention fell on the tall thin doorway on the other side of the room. It was a strange size for a door, especially in a house full of burly men. The window beside it was equally thin and long.

I squinted to peer out the window. Beside me, Benjamin

pulled what looked like a TV remote from a small wooden box that was attached to the wall. He added the remote to his blanket-filled basket. He walked to the doorway and flipped another light switch. This time string lights, like Christmas lights, winked into existence in the night beyond the glass panes.

"Ooh," I gasped. I'm a sucker for good nighttime string lighting. It's on the Jericho-approved list right next to porch swings, wine cellars, and big libraries.

He smiled at my reaction, then held the door open for me and gestured into the night.

I gasped. The lights across the rooftop illuminated something I can only describe as a homemade Ninja Warrior course. Wooden ramps led up to crevices that looked like they were meant to be jumped across, an assortment of ladders and ropes connected various platforms like a deranged spiderweb...and a large trampoline sat squarely under one of the more precipitous drops.

"For safety," Benjamin explained when he saw my gaze pause on the trampoline.

"Benjamin, what is this place?"

Benjamin chuckled. "Well, um, as you might imagine, gym memberships are hard to come by in the 100-Mile Wilderness. So we built our own training course."

I guess this is less of a shocker than the atomic-grade laboratory downstairs.

"Training for what?" I peeked at Benjamin out of the corner of my eye. Strong muscles ran in grooved lines down the length of his arms. *Does it matter what he's training for if this is the result?* I wanted to trace those lines with my fingertips, and also with my—

"Just for life, I guess." Benjamin shrugged, interrupting my thoughts.

I blushed, thankful for the shadows cast by the ninja course. Benjamin caught my eye and smiled warmly, continuing. "But that's not why we came here."

We made our way across the roof to the trampoline, where Benjamin laid out a stack of blankets before helping me up beside him. It was a warm night by New England fall standards, which meant it was still cold to me. I was grateful for the enormous bundle of blankets that Benjamin had commandeered. We lay down on the pile together, and Benjamin covered both of us with a soft and woolly comforter. The trampoline shifted beneath us anytime Benjamin moved. It reminded me of lying on a waterbed, albeit stiffer and bouncier, though it wasn't uncomfortable. We shared sips from the wine bottle, and I hummed contentedly. Said contentment was cut short when a distant animal call rang through the night air. It was a rough howl, followed by a cracking sound.

I jolted up, straining into the darkness behind the string lights.

It sounded just like a wolf... but with the cracking? It was more like Mikey's monster.

All of my alerts were suddenly on red. That was it, I was certain. The thing that made that noise. That's what I was searching for. My chest ached from the sudden pounding of my heart. I knew I should go after it. So what if it was dark?

I made to sit up, but Benjamin put his arm around my shoulders and directed me back down to the blanket, his weight an insistent barrier between me and my job.

"Ah, don't worry, that's just some harmless animal, likely tearing through the underbrush. Besides, nothing can get us up here," he said confidently.

"You sure it won't come this way?" I patted my sides, but I'd left my knife and empty gun back in my room. Another reason to not charge headlong into the night, I supposed. But it would be just so convenient for the creature—it must be a wolf, no other animal would make that kind of noise this late at night—to stalk over here. Then Benjamin and I could subdue it together and make out over a job well done. *This is a pretty great plan.*

"I'm positive," Benjamin said, firmly pressing me back down to the trampoline. "Not even a monster would try to come near this brightly lit area in the middle of the night."

"If you believe in monsters, do you think there's something like the wendigo in the woods here?" I asked him.

He shook his head, jostling the trampoline. "Nah, we'd have noticed by now."

"Haven't seen any evidence? No girls getting mauled to death?" I said sarcastically.

He shrugged. "You mean that Katherine girl? My dad said it was a bear."

"Yeah, that's what I keep hearing. But that's just it... I don't think it was a bear, Benjamin."

He furrowed his brows. "My dad usually knows what he's talking about when it comes to animals. It could have been some other species of rogue bear that wandered down from Canada?" he offered.

I shook my head. "No, the bite marks are just *wrong*. Besides, this entire area is only home to black bears. Plus, that sound just now—" I wanted to push the matter, but he waved his hand dismissively.

"There's no need to get into all that. I believe you. But I believe my dad, too. What about— I don't know, a mutant bear or something?"

I raised my eyebrows at him. "A mutant? This isn't the X-Men."

He smiled but shook his head, very fast. Almost panicked. "No, I mean, some animals are just born *different*, you know?"

"I suppose." But I didn't. My gut was telling me I was right. It was telling me to *get off this thing and go find that creature right now*. Nighttime and lack of weapons be damned. It was out there, waiting. But the other part of me, the one weighed down by the unrelenting handsome man (and a tiny voice of reason), knew I had to let it go. *For now.* Whatever it was would be back, of that I was sure.

A cold wind whispered across the roof, blowing the matter out of my mind. I pulled the blankets tighter around myself and snuggled in against Benjamin. He raised his arm, wrapping it around me and pulling me closer to his side. My head fit perfectly into the crook of his arm just below his shoulder, like we were made to go together. It *was* cold outside, and I was grateful both for Benjamin's warm body and for the excuse to get closer to it.

"Ready for the light show?" he asked.

"Yes?"

He pulled the small remote out of the basket, now almost empty, and clicked a wide button in the middle. The string lights went dark, and I jumped.

He felt my jolt and chuckled in the black of the night. "Your eyes will adjust in just a sec."

Sure enough, after a few moments of darkness, my light-blind eyes adjusted. They promptly widened at the carpet of stars that blanketed the sky above us.

I gasped in appreciation. "I've never seen so many stars before."

He chuckled beside me. "Yeah, it's impossible to get a view like this in a city. There's just too much light pollution. It's one of my favorite things about being out here."

My eyes drank in the twinkling lights of the stars, and I cuddled closer to Benjamin. "It's funny to think that this is the same night sky I see at home. I mean, I can only see the major constellations there, if I'm lucky. Like, *Look, Mom, the star is out!* But here, there's literally an entire universe of shimmer. It's like someone threw glitter across the sky." I smiled in the darkness.

"It's fun to think that there can be hidden secrets in something that you look at almost every day," Benjamin said musingly.

Hidden secrets in the everyday. How whimsical. I closed my eyes. A brisk fall breeze gently kissed my cheeks and filled my nose with the smells of pine and fresh night air. Part of my brain heard Benjamin say something about shooting stars, and whisper, "Make a wish, Jericho," but the other part was already falling asleep in the comfort of his arms.

The next day, we woke together at sunrise, still bundled warmly in the blankets on the rooftop. I laughed at how we'd fallen asleep on a trampoline. Benjamin just smiled and put one finger to his lips, like that had been his plan all along and now it was our secret.

After breakfast I made a point of going down to the library, this time armed with my notes and the police report from my pack in my—Benjamin's—room. I'm a professional, dammit. I refused to be beaten by bad dreams and errant books.

Benjamin also needed to start some process in the lab (which he tried to describe to me, but I zoned out as I got caught up in his gaze), and we agreed he'd come collect me in the library for lunch.

The now-familiar blue wendigo book was waiting on the floor beside the couch when I entered, just as it had been last night when it first fell. In the light of the day, though, it was just a book. I picked it up, turning it over in my hand as I reached to replace it on the shelf. Nothing ominous happened. It was still an ordinary book. *Not today, Wendigo.* I gave it a friendly pat as I slid it into place, when its neighboring book caught my eye. Another thick hardcover tome, but this one's gilded title read *Werewolves.* What had Benjamin said? "Every culture has a werewolf story." Did he really believe in them? I pulled it out on impulse then sat down with my notes beside the two wildlife books I'd been reading yesterday, both of which lay abandoned on the couch from my hurried exit the previous night. I stacked the books neatly beside me, putting the werewolf one on the bottom.

THE MIDNIGHT PACK

I started with the animal books again, but this time in the sections on wolves. Wolves had frequented this area long ago but had become almost nonexistent in recent years. But the Palmyra story was no doubt the work of real wolves, or coyotes, if anything. I'd learned that coyotes are found in every state but Hawaii, and wolves really only frequent a handful. *But wasn't it a wolf howl I heard on the roof? I was so positive last night.* Wolves were also too small to match the bite marks found on Katherine's body, though, which I'd already known from the police report. But frankly, from what I was reading the general jaw shape was *much* closer to her wounds than a bear's.

Interesting. Find and verify.

I got up and scanned the zoology section again, replacing the first two books where I'd marked their slots with the colored paper. I chose another that was mostly about bears, as well as two more that focused on wolves. The Grey family library had no shortage on the subject. And the more I read about both animals, the more certain I was that it couldn't have been either.

I put the books away and sat down on the couch, which was now thoroughly strewn with my case notes, both old and new. There were a handful of photos from the police report, including the one from Katherine's MISSING poster. She wore the same deep-blue sweater emblazoned with UTC from my dream. I frowned. There was something about that...I set about collecting the photographs into a pile as I thought, when my eyes fell on a small paper with the bed-and-breakfast letterhead. I'd simply written "Dire wolves," followed by an elaborate question mark. Dire wolves had existed, once upon a time. *What if . . . ?* My thoughts trailed off as I set the stack of notes beside me. My fingers brushed one last forgotten book that had slid under a pillow on the couch.

I pulled it out. *Werewolves.* The book felt heavy in my hands. *If you don't find answers where you should, maybe you'll find them where you shouldn't?* I opened the book and scanned the pages. Aside from a variety of strange and rather too-detailed illustrations, it was filled with Standard Hollywood Stuff, meaning junk and fluff. I skimmed a few sentences here and there.

> *Believed to have originated in Europe.*
> *Compelled to transform during a full moon.*
> *The strongest can make the Change anytime.*
> *Notoriously hard to kill due to rapid healing.*
> *Known methods include decapitation, cardiectomy, and of course, the infamous silver bullet.*

Cardiectomy—complete removal of the heart? *Gross.* I shut the book and sighed again. *If I'm going to waste my time, it might as well be on a book I want to read.* I stood carefully so as not to disturb my notes, then slid *Werewolves* into its place beside *Wendigo.* I stepped back to search for the science-fiction section of the library when I noticed where *Werewolves* and *Wendigo* were shelved: history.

Weird. I wondered how two decidedly *non*-history books made their way into the history section as I walked across the room. *Maybe they were mis-shelved?* My fingers fluttered over the sci-fi books, looking for the one I wanted. *One of the brothers was probably playing a joke on Kermit.* He seemed like the kind of guy who has a place for everything and everything in its place, so a fantasy book in the history section would surely get his goat. I pulled out a thick novel about a young man who finds out he is prophesied to save an alien planet. *Poor dude, that's a lot to put on one person.* I brought it back to the couch and sat, still thinking about the other books. Last night Benjamin said that he thought the wendigo myth was rooted in fact. *What did he say about werewolves?*

"I don't know, what *did* I say about werewolves?" asked Benjamin from the doorway.

CHAPTER 10

Benjamin leaned against one side of the library doorway, the thick wooden beams framing him like a photograph. I jumped at his voice (how the hell was this hulking man so silent?), brushing off my tights as I stood.

"I didn't realize I said that out loud." *Or that you were standing there, creeping like a creeper.* He was lucky he was hot.

Benjamin's lips curved upward in a sly grin, and he stepped into the library. "Some lighter reading this time, Jericho?"

I thought he was talking about the ironically heavy book in my hands, but he gestured behind me to the couch. *Werewolves* sat on the cushion I'd occupied only moments before.

Goose bumps prickled uncomfortably, snaking up my arms even as an icy wave chilled my blood. I dropped the sci-fi book with an almost inaudible *eep*, frantically rubbing my arms. If the goose bumps went away, maybe the book would, too. *Did I hallucinate putting it back on the shelf?* No way. *But that means...*

"I need to get out of here right now," I said, more breathlessly than intended. Benjamin frowned but didn't protest. He simply scooped up my crutches, handing them to me as we headed to the door.

I didn't want to look back when we reached the doorway, but I didn't want to get beaten by a book, either. I turned to glance. From the corner of my eye, I saw the light shift on the couch. Like a shadow from an occupant who wasn't there. *Nope.* I didn't need to see more to know that I *really* didn't want to be in the room. I trained my eyes forward and practically ran down the darkened hallway, crutches and all.

"Is your ankle feeling better?" Benjamin called from behind me.

"Nope!"

But I didn't care. I didn't stop until the hall opened up into the living room, where friendly sunlight poured in through the large bay windows. Light filled the room like a vase. My eyes teared as they struggled to adjust, so I simply closed them, finally leaning on my crutches. The handles dug into my armpits, but that was only a minor tragedy. I'd seen *something* in the library.

The crutches fell to the ground with a clatter as my overwhelmed body decided it was better to sit than to stand. Too bad it hadn't consulted my brain first. I followed the crutches down, landing hard on the tile.

"Jericho—"

Benjamin helped me up and we walked (limped) to a pool of sunlight near the window. He gently held my face in his hands, angling it upward to his own. His blue eyes scanned over me, as if running a diagnostic. I wasn't sure what he found, but he bent over and wrapped me in an almost vicious bear hug. My body stiffened for a moment, then relaxed into his embrace. I didn't have my crutches, but between putting my weight on my other leg and leaning into Benjamin, I didn't need them. I closed my eyes and breathed in deeply, allowing his scent to fill my lungs.

He angled me to the couch beside the (unlit) fireplace, where we sank together into the plush cushions. "You want to tell me what's wrong?" he asked gently.

I shook my head. What would I say? That I saw a *ghost* in the library?

He bent, edging his face closer to mine. I could feel his breath, warm and inviting as it spilled across my cheeks like hot spiced tea on a snowy day. Or a fall day in the Maine woods. "You don't have to talk, if you don't want to," he whispered. "But I'm here for you, if you do."

I shot him a half grin, which was the most I could muster at the moment. "Thanks. I guess I just thought I saw something from the corner of my eye. And, well, coupled with everything else, it freaked me out." I braced myself for a scoff, or laughter. But instead he simply nodded.

"You know, peripheral vision is made for detecting light changes. You can't see color as well, but there is more light sensitivity. A lot more. It's not a surprise you saw something from the corner of your eye in the library. I have before, too, but it's just a trick of the light. It must reflect weirdly off all the books."

I'd certainly like to believe that. Like to, but don't.

I chewed my lower lip. "There's something else. The werewolf book on the couch... I didn't put it there."

He cocked his head to the side, bearing an uncanny resemblance to a golden retriever. "You never touched it at all?"

I shook my head. "No. I mean I *did* have it out, but I put it away."

"Are you sure?" He raised his eyebrows imploringly.

"Yes, I'm sure." Annoyance tinged my voice, but I didn't care. "When I say something, I mean it, Benjamin."

He held up his hands, palms facing me. "Sorry, I didn't mean anything by it." His throat bobbed. "Why did you have the werewolf book out, then?"

I shook my head, my hair swishing across my shoulders with the movement. "You said every culture has a werewolf story. I wanted to see for myself."

"Did you learn anything?"

I tilted my eyes up, locking on his. "How to kill them."

Benjamin ran a hand through his hair, further ruffling his already scruffy locks. He looked like he wanted to say something, so I slid my hands into my pockets and leaned back on the couch, giving him the space to speak.

But my fingers connected with something small, something fabric, at the bottom of my pocket.

My eyes widened as I shot up. *How did you forget about that, Jericho? Find and verify.*

I turned to Benjamin, who raised an eyebrow at me over his lake-blue eyes. "Do the letters *TC* mean anything to you?" He shook his head, so I continued. "What about to Seth? Did he have a girlfriend with those initials?"

Benjamin shook his head again. "No. Seth's never actually had a girlfriend. We moved here so long ago, there was just never time for him to meet someone."

"And Theo?"

Benjamin crossed his arms. "No, he broke up with her before we moved, and anyway her initials were *MB*." He leaned closer to me, uncrossing his arms and resting his elbows on his knees.

"What about colleges?" I continued. "Did anybody go to, say, University of Tennessee in Chattanooga?"

Benjamin shook his head. "No, we did not. And these questions are awfully pointed, Jericho. What's going on?"

The lanyard piece was from UTC, I was sure now. What else could it be? I chewed my lower lip again and looked out the window behind Benjamin. The trees stood like silent sentinels, forming a wall of greens, yellows, and reds. "I just can't shake the feeling that I'm missing something obvious about Katherine."

Outside a sudden wind picked up, whipping through the trees as colorful leaves were torn from their limbs and flung into the sky.

Benjamin glanced at the forest scene behind him before turning back to me. "Whatever it was isn't inside this house."

But what if it is?

I closed my eyes and rubbed my forehead, exhaling heavily. A murder accusation is a serious charge, and not something I was prepared to level without more proof than a single scrap of fabric. A single scrap could just be coincidence. But, as my favorite author famously said, any coincidence is worth noting. Still, I needed more evidence. I needed...

My train of thought derailed as Benjamin's hands joined

mine, his thumbs rubbing gentle circles over my temples. "Oh, that's nice," I whispered.

"Good." His voice was low and rumbling as his hands made their way to my neck, massaging the tense muscles there. I groaned in pleasure, tilting my head downward to give him better access. His strong hands worked at my weary muscles, and I found myself wishing this was a full-body massage.

Then to my disappointment, Benjamin pulled away. I looked up, eyebrows raised. He kept his hands on my shoulders, but his eyes were back on my face, searching again for something, though I still didn't know what.

My amber eyes met his blue ones. I pressed my hand to his cheek. He closed his eyes, leaning into my palm. His unshaven scruffiness matched his hair, and made my heart feel fluttery in my chest. I wanted to let him know how I badly I wanted him. Wanted to tell him how unbearably sexy he was and how it was driving me wild. But the words caught in my throat.

So I kissed him instead.

Did you know that at their most basic level, atoms can't touch each other? It's true. Atoms can get infinitesimally close to one another, but they never actually touch. I can hear the questions now: But what about when I pick up my coffee mug? Or pet my cat? Or hug my friends? The atoms in each of these have electric fields that overlap and push each other apart. The sensation that we register as touch is simply how our brains translate these overlapping electric fields. So anytime you touch someone, you're essentially registering his or her electrical field.

Well, kissing Benjamin was like kissing lightning. A jolt ran through my body, shocking my senses as if they were coming to life for the first time. Everything about him was more intense. There was more pressure, more moisture, more heat. *Dear God, the heat.* I sank into this kiss, so exquisite, so deep that I could have let myself drown in it. And just when I thought that I would, Benjamin pulled back eyes wide and flooded with terror.

"Wha-what's wrong?" I stumbled out.

He held on tight to my shoulders, scanning my mouth and breathing heavily.

"I'm afraid that if we keep going, I won't be able to stop."

Well, duh, that's the plan, I thought. "I don't want you to stop." My voice was suddenly husky with emotion. *Please don't stop.*

He was still staring at my lips, so I licked them slowly as I settled my hips farther down on his lap. Even through his jeans I could very much tell that we both wanted the same thing. I edged my fingers down his chest, toward the waist of his pants.

"I just...I don't think you know what you'd be getting into." His brow creased even more, though his eyes locked onto mine.

My hands stopped before they reached their destination. I frowned. "Benjamin, I'm not a virgin if that's what you're implying."

"No," he said hurriedly, "I didn't think you were. I mean, I didn't think you weren't. Uh, I mean, what I'm trying to say is—"

He was drowning, and I was debating whether to throw him a lifeboat or just sit back and watch when something dawned on me. "Wait, are *you*—er, have you done this before?" He looked around my age, late twenties...maybe early thirties. But it's not like he lived in a bustling metropolis full of available singles.

Benjamin looked grateful for my interruption, though he blushed again. It occurred to me that "this" was somewhat vague and could mean any number of things in the context of our situation. Had he done *what* before? Sat in what's probably his dad's favorite spot on the couch with a woman he barely knows astride his lap? Had he ever—*what's the female equivalent of getting cock-blocked?*—someone?

Had he ever made love?

My eyes searched his face, as if I could read the answers somewhere hidden in the lines of his skin. Spoiler alert, I couldn't, or maybe I was just looking in the wrong places. He finally opened his mouth to respond but closed it again and tilted his head thoughtfully. He released my shoulders, and his hands trailed down my sides, tracing the lines of my hips. His blue eyes were unfocused, though, and stared beyond me into the living room and hallway. He was lost in silent contemplation.

And I was annoyed. Benjamin needed a lesson on the appropriate length of pause-time in conversation. Just when I thought he'd forgotten my original question, he turned back toward me, his eyes again focused on mine.

"Welcome back," I said. Only somewhat sarcastically.

He gave me a small half smile in return. "I did have a

girlfriend, before we moved out here. We were young but we were pretty serious..." He trailed off as his hands came to a rest on his thighs behind me. He looked down. "No, we were very serious."

I kept my face still but something inside me was suddenly and surprisingly jealous, and maybe a little bit sad. Part of me had wanted to be the only one. *Come on, Jericho, you've only known him for like five seconds and you're both grown adults. You've had other boyfriends. You can't be upset that he was with someone else before he even met you.*

Benjamin hadn't noticed my internal struggle, or if he did, he ignored it, continuing. "Her name was Lisa. We met in college and immediately started dating. I had never been so happy before. And then... she died. In a car crash. She was only twenty."

My sadness swelled, but this time it was for Benjamin and not myself. His eyes shone brightly, as if tears threatened behind them. "Oh, Benjamin," I whispered.

"That's why I didn't care when we moved out to the woods and away from the world. Seth and Theo were upset about missing their friends, possible girlfriends, pizza delivery, movie theaters, and general normal-life-stuff. But I thought I'd already lost everything that I could. Then we finally got into a groove here, and five years later my mom died, too." Benjamin's shoulders heaved as he drew in a long and heavy breath. "And I was helpless, both times. It terrifies me."

Silence hung in the air between us, not oppressive but soft, like a silk scarf. Benjamin looked at me with a mix of tenderness and worry as I thought about how I wanted to respond.

"Well, I guess you're right, and we could be scared," I said. "Or we could be lucky. Lucky to have something together, in this moment." I shrugged and met his eyes. "I choose lucky."

He smiled. "I want to be lucky with you, too," he said softly.

"Oh, Benjamin," I whispered breathlessly.

I leaned in for another kiss.

A loud banging shook the house, startling us apart. I fell across the couch cushions and Benjamin stood up. My eyes widened several degrees. I looked at Benjamin in alarm. His own eyes were narrowed, and he shifted uneasily, staring down the hallway in the direction of the door slam. It came from the front porch. His muscles were tensed, and every fiber of his being looked ready to pounce at the first sign of danger. A moment passed, marked by my tired heartbeats, and his muscles relaxed. As far as I could tell nothing had changed, though his eyes were still trained in the direction of the front door.

"It's my family," he said absently. "Something isn't right." Benjamin turned to me, looking into my eyes. Worry was written in the lines of his face. "Stay here."

But the guys said they'd be gone for a few days, not one night. Before I could respond he was already leaving the living room, striding away in hurried steps.

He'd said "stay here," but I was never one to stay still in a crisis. So I crept toward the front hallway, hoping I could figure out for myself what was going on. Kermit's commanding voice was easy to hear, even with the front door closed. "Something is wrong with Theo. Take the girl upstairs."

Benjamin muttered something indistinct, but Kermit's

deep tones resonated clearly. "He wouldn't change..." He trailed off, leaving the rest unintelligible.

Wouldn't change what? *His mind? His clothes? Speak up, Kermit!* I stayed in the hall, straining to hear more, but the only sounds were a door closing and footsteps quickly approaching. Benjamin rounded the corner, and if he was surprised to see me standing there, he didn't show it.

"Come with me, I'm going to take you upstairs while we sort some things out."

I thought about protesting, but the concern in his eyes stopped me. "Okay," I agreed.

We made our way quickly, for someone on crutches at least, up the large staircase to the upper level. There was no sign of Kermit or the other men. We approached Benjamin's bedroom door and I went to open it, but he continued past.

"This way," he called over his shoulder. "We're going all the way up."

We reached the sharp wooden staircase at the end of the hall, and like the night before, Benjamin took my crutches and gave me a boost. When I was safely on the attic floor, he passed the crutches up to me.

"Aren't you coming, too?" I asked.

"Uh, not yet." He glanced down the hall, then back to me. "Jericho, listen to me, I'm not really sure what's going on, but I want you to stay up here until I figure it out."

He turned his head away sharply, as if he'd heard a noise; I strained my ears but heard nothing. He looked up to me again. "They're coming now," he said hurriedly. "There should be a door on the floor beside you."

I was on my hands and knees on the floor, and from my vantage point I quickly saw the attic door. I nodded down at Benjamin in confirmation.

"Good. Close it, and don't open it again until I come for you."

I had been calm throughout this strange exchange until Benjamin said he wasn't going to be with me. Adrenaline had started edging into my veins, but with the new urgency in Benjamin's voice it surged through my body.

"Benjamin," I stammered, "should I be scared?"

He scaled the staircase in a few long strides and brought his head level with mine. His worried eyes locked with mine, and he kissed me briskly but gently.

"I'll come for you," he said. He disappeared back down the staircase, and his footsteps receded down the hallway.

That wasn't a no.

My heart pounded violently in my chest. *What in the darkest crack of hell is going on?* I put my hand on my chest, trying to calm my poor heart. I pulled on the attic door to close it. Benjamin had said before that the attic was rarely utilized except as storage and a walk-through to their ninja course, but the hinges were smooth, like they'd been freshly oiled. The door made no sound at all as it rested into place. I found a hooked latch, also smooth and gleaming as if it had seen its fair share of use. I guided it through a thick metal loop to secure the door.

I sat with my back against the wall and shut my eyes, taking deep breaths in an attempt to calm my frayed nerves. My yoga teacher would be proud. Minutes passed and I could hear the buzz of human activity in the home below, but nothing sounded out of place. My heart rate was getting back to normal, and the adrenaline had left me. No voices raised. No doors slammed. The lilting tones of regular conversation drifted upward to me, and though I couldn't make out any words it was clear they weren't arguing. *Maybe Kermit was just overreacting?*

And Benjamin along with him.

I chewed my lower lip then opened my eyes, taking stock of my surroundings. When we'd walked through the small room the previous night, I hadn't really paid attention to what was in it. Now I noticed details in the piles of bric-a-brac. An old, dusty, and clearly well-loved rocking horse leaned haphazardly against a box labeled BOYS: BABY STUFF. I smiled to think of Benjamin as a baby, playing with his brothers. I looked over at the photo of the boys as children that I'd found last night. They smiled up at me from under a layer of dust. Something about the photo was still familiar, but I decided it was déjà vu from seeing it briefly before.

There was a sudden slam as a door closed—the front door, it sounded like. I strained my ears again, but there was only silence from the house below. I waited for a heartbeat, then another. Nothing. They must have left. I stood up, wincing as I accidentally leaned on my ankle.

Regardless of what Benjamin had said, I'd never been a person who was content to wait around. I eased open the attic door, laying my crutches beside the opening. I tucked them under my arms haphazardly (but successfully) and made my way down the ladder to the hallway below.

THE MIDNIGHT PACK

The crutches clattered against the wood, but the house was otherwise silent. Who knows where the men had gone to, but they weren't inside anymore. And that's all the opportunity I needed.

Because I was sure that the *TC* on the fabric piece I'd found was part of *UTC*: University of Tennessee at Chattanooga.

And it had belonged to Katherine.

I walked down the hallway as silently as I could on the crutches, stopping briefly at Benjamin's room to retrieve my knife and gun. My face scrunched in a wince as I picked my way down the main staircase. Between the run from the library and the subsequent stairs, ladder, and stairs again, my ankle was feeling worse for wear. *Grin and bear it, Jericho.*

I paused at the bottom, listening for any sound, any indication, any*thing* at all to tell me where the men were. Silence. Propping the crutches under my arms, I took a deep breath and headed to Seth's room.

The room was exactly the same as it had been during my earlier snoop. I narrowed my eyes at the video games. Scratch that, the titles had changed order in the pile as Seth had clearly been playing. *But what else had he been doing?*

My eyes trailed across the room and back to the desk where I'd found the fabric scrap. The desk chair scraped across the floor when I moved it and I paused, wincing at the noise. I held my breath, listening for signs that the men had returned.

Silence.

Okay. I pulled open the desk drawers again, this time not bothering to hide what I'd moved. Trading cards, pens, a crumpled photo of his mom. Nothing else. I looked in the other drawer, the one I hadn't gotten to last time. It was empty.

Standing, I went to his closet, pushing aside hangers filled with hoodies and T-shirts. The metal hangers scraped against the bar and clattered together.

Green eyes flashed at me from behind the clothing I'd moved.

I dropped my crutches with a yelp before I realized it was just a poster. My throat bobbed as I swallowed hard, trying to still my now-thundering heart. I stood on only slightly shaking legs and shoved the clothing the rest of the way to the side. *Just a poster, Jericho.*

But it wasn't just any poster. It was one of my favorite actors: Corbin Cruz, star of the thrilling hit action series *Running with Thunder*. Here, he was tanned, shirtless, and smiling slyly, a thirst trap image to promote the third film in the series, though that had come out quite a few years ago. If I had been Seth's age and still living at home, I might have even had the same poster in my bedroom. I raised my eyebrows in approval. It seemed that Seth and I had similar taste in men. Then I looked at the floor around me, noticing a more worn area right where I was standing, and I imagined what had gone on in front of this poster. *Aaand that's your cue to leave.*

Back in the hallway between the brothers' rooms, I paused again, straining for any sounds around the house. Still nothing. *Good, because I need time to pick this lock again.* I've said before that my favorite accessories were my knife and my gun, but the two bobby pins I always wore in my hair were a close second.

Lock picked, the door swung open in relative silence. Which matched the rest of the home and *what the hell are they doing out there?* I supposed it didn't matter, as long as the men stayed out there while I was in here: Theo's room.

Even though I was familiar with the carnage of what used to be his bedspread, it was still shocking to see again. I scanned the room, from the quilt-littered floor, to the shredded portrait, to the completely empty closet. Clothes lay in piles in the various corners of the room. What a hellhole. The desk was the only thing seemingly untouched.

I paused to listen for signs of life in the house around me, but everything was still silent. I picked my way across the debris to the desk. A wooden chair—twin to the ones in Seth's and Benjamin's rooms—sat neatly before it, as if waiting for me. Leaning my crutches against the desk, I sat gingerly on the chair and opened the first drawer.

My eyes narrowed when I saw what it was filled with, because it was not at all what I was expecting.

Letters. Typed, handwritten, cursive, scrawled…all addressed to Theo. I rifled through the paper pile quickly. I'd been lucky so far, but wouldn't you know it if the men came in right as I found something good. That's what always happens in the movies. I scanned the words, eyes darting as I searched for Katherine's name among the black and white.

All of the typed correspondence seemed to be from the mysterious benefactor Benjamin mentioned, the Council.

All referring to the men's progress in the lab. The dates on those went years back... all the way up until... *Oh my God.* I gasped, bringing a hand to my mouth even as my other hand lifted the paper for a closer inspection of the date.

It was the day before I came to the woods. The day before that fateful hike that led me here, to this home. *What the hell?* There's no way a postman had made deliveries to their house when nobody in town knew about the brothers. Kermit hadn't been in town that day, either. I would have known. A PO box, then?

I frowned, reading the rest of the letter. The Council was apparently pleased with Theo's progress and were coming out to see "the Serum," whatever that was.

A noise from the front of the house made me pause. The deep tenor of men's voices broke the stillness. They hadn't entered the house yet, but I was quickly running out of time. I replaced the letters in a hurry, trying to stack the papers as they were when I found them. I removed the entire stack to straighten it when I saw something small and blue at the back of the drawer. It looked like a ball of ribbon. Why would Theo, of all people, have ribbon balled up and hidden? Unless it wasn't ribbon.

The front door opened with a creak.

I grabbed the mystery item and shoved the papers into place, no longer caring what the stack looked like. Jamming the ribbon ball into my pocket, I grabbed my crutches and hurried out of the room, locking the door behind me.

Men's voices continued speaking, but they hadn't actually entered the house yet. I said a silent thank-you to anyone who might be watching out for me as I tucked the crutches under my arm and made for the stairs.

Footsteps echoed down the front hallway and a door slam rattled through the house just as I reached the landing on the top floor. I pressed my back against the stucco wall and slid down until I sat on the carpeted floor. My heart thudded a rapid drumbeat in my chest and in my head. *Fuck, that was close.*

The men chatted in low voices as their footsteps carried from the direction of the kitchen. My legs were still feeling shaky from the near-run-in, and my ankle throbbed. I knew I should hold off on further inspection of the thing from Theo's desk until I was back in the attic, or at least in relative privacy of Benjamin's room.

But I couldn't wait.

I pulled it out, really looking at the bundle. It was navy-blue fabric, not ribbon. The same shade of blue as the scrap I'd found in Seth's room. And it was wrapped around something flat and hard. I unraveled it, staring.

It was a lanyard, embroidered with mustard-yellow thread. One side was cut and simply read U, then, after the gap, MOCS. The other side said UNIVERSITY OF TENNESSEE CHATTANOOGA. A student ID card was attached, dangling from the lanyard clip. The back of the card was facing me, but I already knew what the front would say.

Knew it, but didn't believe it.

I believe what I see. *I needed to see.*

The footsteps and voices sounded closer than they had been, but I didn't care. It was hard to care about anything over my thundering heart. I flipped the card over in my palm, and Katherine Waller smiled up at me.

Dread draped over my shoulders and down my back like an icy blanket. It lodged in my core until I was shivering. Teeth now chattering, I pulled the scrap from Seth's room out of my other pocket, holding it up to the lanyard. A perfect match. And now I knew.

Someone in this house killed Katherine Waller.

CHAPTER 11

As if the house was suddenly aware of my discovery, a bout of yelling echoed through the walls. Despite Benjamin's warnings, I edged down the hall toward the overlook.

Benjamin was confronting his brothers and father in the kitchen. I couldn't see any of the men from my perch near the railing, but I could hear them speaking. Their strong tones steadily grew in volume and agitation.

One angry and defensive voice erupted above the rest. *"That fucking girl needs to go!* She heard me, she went into my fucking room!"

I had been in both brothers' rooms.

I couldn't hear Benjamin's response, but I could easily guess what he said when Rage Voice replied, *"I'll kill her!"* Fury absolutely dripped from every syllable, and an icy sensation flooded my veins for what seemed like the umpteenth time that day.

I'd like to think that I can hold my own against a supposed "bad guy," but I'd never had that much pure, raw hatred directed at me before. There was no doubt in my mind that the first moment he could, the raging brother really would kill me.

Just like he murdered Katherine.

Panic held me frozen while I considered my fight-or-flight response. Then the adrenaline kicked in and I rushed, as quickly as my ankle allowed, back up the stairs to the attic. *Flight, please, one ticket for Jericho James.* I reached the attic and slammed the door behind me, scrambling anxiously to lock it. The metal latch seemed small and flimsy in the face of so much anger.

I heaved a pile of haphazardly stacked boxes on top of the trapdoor. Maybe the extra weight would stall the men? *And maybe I'll get a unicorn for Christmas.* I rushed through the small room to the thin doorway on the other side. I opened it and paused. A cacophony of voices poured after me as they drew nearer.

"She's getting away!" said Kermit.

"She'll lead them right to us—" Seth whined.

"So stop her!" yelled Kermit. Or was that Theo?

"*I'll kill her!*" the Rage Voice returned. I still couldn't tell who it was, but I wasn't about to stick around to find out.

The trapdoor slammed open easily, as if the lock and boxes were nothing more than so much dust. I gasped and scurried onto the roof, wheeling my head around just in time to see Benjamin.

"Jericho, wait!" he called.

I didn't wait.

I clambered across the roof as fast as I dared on my ankle.

I scrambled up and over a wooden ramp on the ninja course, putting my injury to the test. Every step shot pain like a lightning bolt up my leg, but my ankle was usable. *Thank heaven for small favors.*

But Benjamin was closer behind than I thought. He climbed onto the roof just as I dropped to the other side of the ramp, to the further dismay of my ankle. *Does he see me?* I didn't dare to move from my hiding place at the base of the ramp to check. I noticed a slit in the wood and peered through it. I had a clear view of Benjamin, and he wasn't chasing me. In fact, it looked like he wasn't doing much of anything. Then he began to swivel his head back and forth. *What?* It looked like he was... sniffing the air.

I held my breath and continued watching through the crack in the wood. He immediately turned and faced exactly where I was hiding. I hadn't so much as shifted a muscle, but his eyes somehow locked onto mine through the tiny wooden gap.

I sprang up and hurried toward the side of the house that faced the woods.

Benjamin cleared about half of the distance between us, then stopped and held out a hand imploringly. "Wait! I'm not going to hurt you!"

I scanned the side of the roof for a way down. *Keep him talking.* "Right," I scoffed, "like you guys didn't hurt Katherine." I kept searching the roof discreetly, not wanting Benjamin to know my plan.

"Jericho, that wasn't me, that was—" He shook his head and ran his fingers through his hair in exasperation. "Look, just come inside and I can explain everything."

Explain me to death, maybe. "Aha!" I'd spotted what I was looking for: a wooden ladder, carved directly into the side of the house. It went from the roof to the ground near the woods. It was farther away than I was hoping, but I'd take what I could get.

"What did you say?" Benjamin asked.

"Uh-huh," I called back. I edged closer to my escape.

An angry, bestial roar erupted from the attic, making the hairs on my arms stand up. *That was not human.* Benjamin turned to face the sound, then whipped his head back to me.

"Run!" he yelled, but I wasn't sure if it was really directed at me or if he was telling himself. His calm face had contorted with worry.

I was still several heart-stopping feet from the ladder, but I ran as best I could on my ankle. Benjamin sprinted toward me, easily clearing the ramps and assorted training equipment by leaps and bounds. He reached the top of the ladder by the time I was just a few rungs down.

I glanced up at him—*how?* But my poor tired brain didn't have time to process his speed. *Maybe I'm slower than I thought I was.* To my credit, I didn't stop but redoubled my efforts at descending. It was hard to get a grip on the hand-carved wooden rungs, which were less like actual ladder rungs and more like crevices dug into the exterior of the house. My fingers were filled with splinters at the effort. *Why couldn't this have been near the front door where the distance to the ground is shorter? Nothing worthwhile is ever easy.*

I was still about eight feet from the ground when Benjamin reached me on the rungs, but before I could decide what to do about it, he pushed himself *off* the ladder. He neatly jumped over me and landed gracefully on the uneven ground below.

What.

The.

He held his arms up to me. "Jump! I'll catch you!" he yelled.

Fuck. "Are you crazy?!"

Just then a horrific roar exploded from directly above me. I threw a furtive look upward and saw a hulking silhouette at the top of the ladder, followed by two more trying to hold him back.

"On second thought, okay!" I called down to Benjamin. I squeezed my eyes shut and let go, falling backward into open space. He grabbed me from the air as easily as I might catch a softball.

"You okay?" he asked.

"Okay," I replied shakily, fully aware that it was a non-answer. My head was splitting, and my heart felt like it was about to pound right out of my body. *Keep it together, Jericho.* I decided I didn't want to see whatever was going to happen next, so I closed my eyes and leaned against his chest. His heart rate was only slightly elevated, and Benjamin wasn't even out of breath from his race across the rooftop. But before I had time to think about it, he clutched me tighter and started to run.

I lost track of time during the frenetic race. It could have been minutes, but it felt like hours. After a while, we reached a small clearing in the forest and paused. It was much smaller than Katherine's clearing. The ground was covered in a myriad of roots, broken stumps, and other forest debris. Benjamin gently set me down in a relatively clear spot. I straightened my back and stretched gratefully as he heaved himself against a tree and squeezed his eyes shut.

"Shit, shit, shit," he muttered to himself.

That's not good. I stood up. "You need to tell me what the hell is going on. *Now.*"

He rubbed his face with both hands, suddenly looking exhausted. He sank down to the ground, still leaning against the tree, then looked up at me.

Lines of concern were etched across his face, but he didn't speak.

"What is happening, Ben?" I whispered.

His blue eyes, full of fear and worry, met mine, and I softened. He wasn't the murderer, and he hadn't known about it before. The truth rang as clearly in my head as if someone had spoken the words to me. Whatever we were facing, whatever was going on, I decided we would face it together. And we would be okay. *Everything is going to be okay.* As if he could read my mind, a corner of his mouth twitched into what wanted to become a smile. But it twisted grotesquely as his face abruptly contorted into a mask of shock and outrage.

He sprang to his feet and lunged at something behind me, but he was a heartbeat too late. An animal roar split the stillness of the clearing, and a searing pain spread across my back as I was shoved roughly to the ground. I fell flat on my chest and hit something sharp and hard. *Shit!* It felt like I'd been punched in the heart.

THE MIDNIGHT PACK

I gasped in pain and shock and tried to roll over. But I didn't have the strength to move. It felt like I was stuck to the ground, and my back and my chest were both on fire. *I'm burning*, I wanted to say, but I couldn't find the energy to speak.

Cool hands pressed through the flames against my sides—*Benjamin*. I heard a sharp snap and felt myself rolling onto my back as the burning pain receded into the background. It became a dull and distant feeling, like somehow my body and mind had become disconnected in the fall.

Benjamin's horrified face hung over mine. "Jericho!" It looked like he was yelling, but his voice sounded wavy and distorted, like I was listening to him from underwater.

"Ow," I whispered. I looked down to see a jagged wooden spike jutting out from my rib cage. I should have been scared, but it seemed far away, like I was watching through someone else's eyes, or looking at someone else's body.

And I thought the splinters in my fingers were bad, I thought woozily. I watched my blood quickly soak through my white shirt, until it resembled a crimson rose blossoming around a thorn.

My heart beat once. Then twice, laboriously.

"Jericho! Stay with me, Jericho!" Benjamin was still yelling, but it was so very far away. His form grew fuzzier as my vision faded. And then fuzzier still, until a growling wolf stood over me, blue eyes piercing my soul.

My heart stopped.

Well, damn.

That's when I died.

PART II

BENJAMIN

CHAPTER 12

Benjamin believed in werewolves. No, not just believed—he *knew*, for a fact, that they were real.

Because he was one.

His brothers and father were, too, a secret he was desperate to keep from Jericho. She knew there was something different about him, but she didn't know what. He could sense the questions lingering on her, clinging like a sultry perfume. He wanted to tell her. He had come close, in the living room.

The virus my dad has? The one we are working to cure? I have it, too. It's called lycanthropy...

But he was terrified of how she'd respond. Her brilliant eyes shone with a passionate fire whenever she looked at him. Nobody had looked at him that way since Lisa. It sped up his heart and ignited his desire. If he burned in the heat of her gaze, he'd die happy. He couldn't bear to see that fire quenched with a smoldering, sickly fear. Because of him. So instead, he'd told her that he was afraid, and it was true. *Coward*, he'd cursed at himself.

Coward. The word stung with truth. He hadn't even confronted Theo when he realized his older brother had been sneaking out of the house. Their father had a curfew for the brothers, even though they were all grown men. The restriction chafed like an ill-fitting shirt, but they all understood why it was important to comply. At least, Benjamin had thought they all understood. Their lab work was a secret—so secret that the Council didn't want anyone to know where they lived or that they even existed. And they were paid handsomely to keep it that way.

Very handsomely.

The nearest town knew about Kermit—an arrangement he'd worked out with the Council, it simply wasn't feasible for the *entire* family to stay hidden—but he propagated the belief that he was antisocial and craved solitude. Benjamin knew this hurt his father, a gregarious extrovert by nature, but if *he* could tolerate it, then so could they.

Besides, it wouldn't last forever. They were all passionate about the Cure, and the sooner they found it, the sooner they would be free to live their lives. The money they would be paid was enough that none of the men would have to work again. Ever. It was worth the wait.

But apparently, Theo couldn't wait. Theo was sneaking out. Benjamin sometimes wondered if his older brother had a secret lover.

When their family had packed up, trading a bustling city for a secluded part of the 100-Mile Wilderness in Maine, Theo objected but didn't really seem to mind. Benjamin had done so with a broken heart and was glad to throw himself into his research and work. Seth was bitter about it all, and rightly so, Benjamin supposed. But Theo *should have* cared more, and he didn't.

Why didn't Theo mind, unless he wasn't planning on following the rules?

A girlfriend would make sense, he mused. Theo had always seemed to have one before they moved.

Theo appeared content in their solitary forest life, though, which Benjamin supposed should have been a red flag. Theo was only content when he was leading something: They had been butting heads since puberty, when the lycanthropy virus kicked into high gear. Benjamin always won the rights of second-in-command as the stronger child, and Kermit never let Theo forget it. In fact, Theo even tried to take the lead in the lab, but Kermit made it clear that he was *not* in charge of the family's research.

So he was sneaking out, taking control of things for himself. And Benjamin didn't confront him about it. *Coward.* He had pushed the voice down and instead convinced Seth to track their brother.

"Why can't we just tell Dad about it?" Seth had groaned.

"Dude, you know he prefers that we handle disagreements on our own."

"Yeah, yeah. *You can settle it man-to-man.*" Seth's voice dropped as he parodied their father. "But this is different! If you really think he's breaking Dad's rules, and he's been doing it for a while, then we could all be in trouble." Seth shifted uneasily. "Also, I feel weird sneaking around behind Theo's back."

Benjamin tactfully didn't point out that Theo was the one doing the sneaking. "We're just going for a walk in the woods, and we'll see what we find. Maybe nothing, maybe something. But don't think of it as sneaking, Seth! We're just two brothers taking a little fall stroll," Benjamin said, falsely cheerful.

"Yeah, yeah. Whatever you say." Seth waived his hand dismissively but fell in line behind Benjamin when he walked out the door. Benjamin knew that his brother would follow him if he asked. Not because Benjamin was older, or even because Seth believed him, but because he was bigger. Benjamin hated pulling that card, though. He'd rather that Seth trusted him.

It was the wolf in them clashing with the man. One more reason why they had to find the Cure.

With Seth taking the lead, the two men picked their way through the woods.

"Seth, are you sure this is right? It looks like we're getting close to that path to town."

Seth rolled his eyes. "Come on, man. This is what I do, it's like the one thing I'm great at. He was here. His scent is all over the clearing up ahead." Seth gestured toward the bushes in front of them.

"Would he actually have gone into town?" Benjamin mused, watching Seth shrug in response. Seth bent down to pick something up. A tattered scrap of what looked like navy-blue ribbon. He sniffed it and frowned, pocketing the small slip of blue.

Benjamin stopped walking to ask what it was when

something dawned on him. "Wait, is this the same place they found that dead girl?"

His scent is all over the clearing... Seth was silent, but the growing unease Benjamin sensed from his brother was answer enough.

Where is Theo sneaking off to? Benjamin wondered for what felt like the thousandth time as they approached the clearing. The question plagued him ever worse the more he thought about it.

But that was before.

Before he smelled something so tantalizing, it demanded his entire focus, forcing all other thoughts from his brain. *That scent...*

"There's someone here," Seth whispered frantically as the brothers crouched low behind the thick foliage.

A lone woman stood in the clearing, with caramel-blonde hair that shone golden in the fading afternoon sun. She tilted her head upward toward the sky, and the motion blew her scent toward him. Benjamin closed his eyes and inhaled deeply. He opened his eyes again, wishing he could get closer. She wore a knife strapped to one leg and a gun strapped to the other. The bulkiness of the weapons sat in stark contrast with the tights and tank top on her slender form. *Badass.* Benjamin was completely and utterly captivated. He wondered what color her eyes were, and silently willed her to turn toward the bushes so he could see.

Keep it together, Ben. Benjamin raised his head for a better view of the woman. She was looking at the sky in dismay. *Why?* Benjamin's heart wrenched, and he was struck with the thought that he didn't want to see her sad. He started to get up, to ask her if she was all right.

"Benjamin. Get. *Down*," Seth growled, pulling his brother toward the ground. The woman's eyes flashed over the bushes, and the brothers hastily shifted into their wolf forms.

Benjamin silently cursed himself for making so much noise. A rookie mistake. Seth's wolf eyes flashed darkly and his voice chimed in Benjamin's head.

"What the fuck is wrong with you?"

But before Benjamin could further collect his thoughts, the woman shot her hand toward her gun, training her eyes on the bushes that surrounded the clearing. Benjamin froze, absolutely floored by the ballsiness of this mystery woman.

That's it. Benjamin would shift back to human, apologize for scaring her, and offer to walk her back to town. The idea gained traction as he flowed into his human form. *It would be almost like... a date.* A date. He hadn't had one of those in a decade. And... *Oh, that furry little motherfucker.*

Seth, still in wolf form, turned tail to chase the woman back to town. *Of course.* That plan backfired spectacularly as she ended up deducing (correctly) where he and Seth were positioned around the clearing. She darted between the brothers instead, and unwittingly toward their home. Seth lurched forward to continue the chase as she sprinted away, but Benjamin grabbed him by the scruff of his neck and yanked him back.

"What are you doing? We have to stop her!" Seth's whine rang as words in Benjamin's mind, and Benjamin shook his head.

"Stop her, maybe, but not chase her down. I've got this one." Benjamin tried to sound calm, but he positively *itched* to follow the woman. He wanted it in his bones. It *ached*. He'd never wanted anything more. It was as if an invisible force tugged at his core, pulling him toward her like a magnet to iron. He grabbed his clothes from where they'd fallen behind the bush and slipped them back on. Seth shifted back and did the same.

Seth's eyes widened as he pulled up his pants. "Oh. My. Dear. Lord. You just want to get close to her," he accused. "Your scent changed the moment you set eyes on her, you can't deny that. You also can't let her see you, Ben. And you know I'm right." Seth's tone wasn't sharp, but the words stung Benjamin nonetheless. Seth *was* right, and yet…

"Yup. Yes. You're right, Seth. Yup." Benjamin patted his brother's back reassuringly. He felt his brother's muscles relax under his pam. Then he shoved the smaller man down. "I just need to make sure she's okay!" Benjamin yelled as he sprinted after the woman. He heard Seth's grunt of annoyance from behind him as the other man got up and tailed him in close pursuit.

Following this mystery woman had completely consumed Benjamin, to the point that he didn't realize they were headed toward the ravine until it was too late. When she fell, Benjamin felt her pain. His soul burned as something broke within him. Out of the cracks, a protective instinct flamed to life: He wanted nothing more than to hold her close and comfort her. *Hell, I didn't realize a heart could ache so much for a stranger,* he thought. And that was even before she looked at him with those piercing eyes—*those devastating, mesmerizing eyes.* Eyes that took his breath away and made him forget everything he was trying to say. The ramifications of that terrified him. He was ruined after Lisa's death. Could he survive it if he ever lost someone else? Even someone he'd never met before. But the way she smelled...

Even if he wouldn't admit it, he knew with a certainty that he would never be able to get her scent or her eyes out of his mind, not for as long as he lived. And miraculously, she seemed to feel the same way, even though he became a stammering fool around her. He couldn't help himself. And he still couldn't believe his luck.

But that was before.

When Benjamin had woken up this morning, he felt like he was on top of the world. The crisp scent of the woods carried across the roof with every breeze, and the birds sang loudly in the cold morning air. That autumn air chilled Benjamin's face, but he couldn't imagine a more comfortable place to be. He turned his head to admire Jericho's sleeping form next to him. He had to admit that he'd orchestrated the night on the roof under the stars in the hope that they'd end up exactly as they were: wrapped under a sea of blankets in each other's arms. He closed his eyes and breathed in deeply, his chest expanding with the scent of her, until it buried itself in his core. *She's simply intoxicating, in every way imaginable.*

As if she sensed his thoughts, Jericho sighed in her sleep and curled in closer, her contentment palpable. Benjamin grinned, impossibly happy.

He'd known when he found Jericho in the clearing that something was different. She smelled like warmth, wind, and, well, freedom. The mixture sparkled around her like sunshine on a lake. It swamped Benjamin's mind until it was filled with nothing but her. It began the moment he picked up her unique scent in the woods, and the feeling only grew deeper whenever he experienced the various flavors of her moods.

He couldn't imagine living without the ability to detect feelings and moods in the air. It wasn't really *moods*, per se, just pheromones. Countless other animals could sense pheromones, too, but humans couldn't. Werewolves could.

Benjamin often thought that the world must be so two-dimensional to a regular human. He didn't have many memories from before his lycan cells activated, but he knew that life was so full, so much *more* as a werewolf that it would be impossible to give it all up in their quest to be fully human. So, while Kermit and Seth were focused on curing their disease, Benjamin and Theo had also begun work on something else. They called it the Serum.

It wasn't a literal serum in the medical sense, but his father had liked the word because it sounded "dramatic," and his other brothers agreed. Making it had been Theo's idea, and Benjamin was the brains of the operation, per usual. He was the one who had figured out how to use the inactive parts of the lycanthropy virus they'd isolated in a way that *should* grant all the ancillary benefits, or side effects, as it were, of the virus, without the actual *sickness*.

Ever since he'd met Jericho, though, thinking about the virus made Benjamin feel queasy and on edge.

Just tell her, you coward.

Benjamin despised being a werewolf most of the time, but he couldn't ignore its benefits. In human form, werewolves were naturally fast and strong, and possessed an unprecedented ability to heal. Benjamin appreciated the precision hearing as well, but his favorite thing was the consummate sense of smell. It's common knowledge that wolves have a heightened sense of smell. But to *know* is quite different than to *experience*.

Benjamin could smell fear, anger...love. *Lust*. He had sampled plenty of emotions over the years.

They all paled in comparison with Jericho's.

Everything Jericho felt was fresher and brighter to Benjamin, as if she were experiencing each feeling for the first time. As a result, it was like he was experiencing them for the first time, too. It was addicting—*she* was addicting. He was completely drawn to her, like your eyes to a bright spot in the dark. And miraculously, she seemed equally attracted to him. Whenever she caught Benjamin looking at her, there was a sweet shift in the air. It became warm and inviting, like apple cider on a cool fall day. Which of course only heightened his desire to look.

He would lose all of that if they cured the virus, and frankly the trade-off would still be worthwhile, but the Serum was supposed to be the key to unlocking the best of both worlds. *And why not keep the good parts, if they could?* Once they rid themselves of lycanthropy, the inactivated bits that he sequenced for the Serum would (should) retain their amplified senses without the dreaded *Change*. At least that was the plan, and the Serum was the hope.

But that was before.

Before he saw Jericho's slender, crumpled form at the bottom of a ravine and knew he would do anything to keep her from hurting again.

But he had failed.

Now Benjamin knelt beside a broken Jericho *again*, with his heart pounding and a cold sweat on his brow. She wasn't breathing. Panic caught in his throat as he frantically checked for a pulse.

Nothing.

He tasted bile in the back of his mouth. *No, no, no. Please, no.* His hands hovered over the spike jutting out of her chest: the impossibly sharp remains of some dried-up sapling's trunk. Jericho must have fallen in just the wrong place at just the wrong force. It was probably a one-in-a-million chance that this could happen. *Fuck.*

Tears threatened in the corners of his eyes, but Benjamin blinked the stinging away. Maybe he could still do something, he thought, but fear held him paralyzed. *Coward.* And yet what could he do? He was reluctant to pull the spike of wood from her chest; *what if it's keeping her from bleeding out?* He decided to leave it, and silently prayed to anyone who was listening that he was making the right decision.

Benjamin desperately felt her neck and her limp wrists again, already growing cool to the touch. "C'mon, Jericho, give me a heartbeat," he pleaded. Nobody answered. "Please, Jericho, please." The ragged words tore from his throat as he cradled her gently, careful to avoid the wooden spike.

"Please," he begged again in a whisper. He bent his head

toward hers and kissed her once on her soft lips. They were like ice.

She was dead.

Benjamin's panic redoubled until it burned white-hot inside of him, giving him tunnel vision. Just when he thought he couldn't bear it anymore, the heat extinguished in a fountain of grief that gushed forth like water from a broken dam.

Benjamin howled. He howled for Jericho, for his mother, for Lisa, for himself. Every time he felt something for a woman, *she died.*

"What the *fuck* have you done, Seth!?" Benjamin sprang up and flung his younger brother back in one fluid motion. "What have you done!" Benjamin's scream of rage reverberated through the forest, startling a flock of nearby crows into flight. "WHAT HAVE YOU DONE!"

Seth pushed himself up on wobbly legs. "It's not my fault!" he whined. "I wasn't trying to kill her! I didn't know she'd fall on that stump-stick-thing. I just wanted to stop—"

Benjamin didn't let him finish before punching his brother in the middle of his chest, sending the smaller man flying. Seth didn't get far before his back cracked against a neighboring tree with a sickening *thunk*, and he collapsed to the ground in a heap. Benjamin closed the distance between them in a few furious strides until he towered over his brother, his broad-shouldered shadow completely engulfing Seth's slender frame. Seth's own shoulders heaved up and down with each pained breath. He was alive, but otherwise motionless. Benjamin didn't care, he knew his brother would heal shortly. He wanted to hurt him more. He stared unblinking at Seth's crumpled form, but his mind whirled around one thing and one thing only: Jericho.

What had Jericho said? *"I choose lucky."*

Movement at the base of the tree pulled Benjamin's gaze: Seth was stirring. Benjamin raised a fist as he glared down at his brother.

"Ben, wait," Seth panted quickly.

"You killed her," Benjamin growled flatly. His arm was still poised above the smaller man, but he paused.

Seth held his hands up in front of his face, as if to placate Benjamin or protect himself from being beaten. Maybe both.

"You can try to turn her! Then she could heal," Seth offered quickly.

"You know I can't, not when she's already dead," Benjamin spat. "We've both heard the stories." Dark, spine-chilling stories about werewolves turned after death. Victims became nothing more than monstrous, blood-craving creatures, like the wendigo.

Their father had instilled this from a young age with every campfire tale, and even the occasional bedtime story. Other kids were scared of the dark; Benjamin and his brothers feared the creatures born from turning the dead. It's exactly what had happened in Palmyra, years ago. A werewolf and five of his monsters surrounded a farmhouse, attacking the home and the family inside. The Council apprehended the Were responsible and put down the pack he created. They paid handsomely to keep the event out of the news, but you can't keep everything off the gossip sites.

Benjamin shuddered, but nevertheless he considered it.

Jericho had been stabbed directly through the heart, but she hadn't been gone for long, so maybe it would be different, *maybe*... He lowered his arm, and Seth exhaled and slumped against the tree.

"I can try it if you don't want to, Ben," Seth offered, meekly but gently.

"No. You will *not* touch her *ever again*," Benjamin growled forcefully. He knew Seth would listen to him. Pack rules were clear on following brawn.

"Ben, it's so close. It's been, what, seconds? A minute? That barely counts as dead. I bet you can do it."

"Barely counts?" Benjamin was incandescent with fury. "There's no such thing as *partially* dead, Seth! She's gone," he snapped. Though a small voice inside his head whispered, *What if Seth is right...?*

But turning someone could be violent in the best of times, and this was the worst of times. It couldn't be a clean turning, either. She had to be willing and *living* for that. She was barely gone, but... His heart pounded in his ears, and he tasted bile again. Benjamin wondered if he could do it. If he could risk her living a half life as a monster.

Would she even choose a "normal" werewolf life over death, though? We're just another breed of monster. Can I make that choice for her? he asked himself, torn. *Is there any other way?* He had to hold on to hope, he told himself. *Hope... the Serum.*

THE SERUM.

Benjamin glared down at Seth, still whimpering by the tree, then he ripped off a ragged swath of Jericho's blood-soaked shirt and shoved it at the younger man. "Take this and run with it back toward town. Be generous with the blood, rub it everywhere. I want a strong trail."

Seth stared up at his brother, clearly confused. "But where are you—"

Benjamin didn't let him finish. "Don't let them find you, Seth. Be quick. If they see you, tell them that we went south toward the next town where she wouldn't be recognized, and I asked you to find some help."

Seth gaped at Benjamin, his brown eyes flashing. "You want me to *lie*, Ben? They'll know immediately. You know what Dad will do to me if he thinks I'm lying."

Benjamin's mouth shaped into a thin, hard smile. "Then you'd better run fast, Seth."

Seth stayed frozen against the tree, staring at the bloodied shirt that Benjamin had jammed in his hand as if he were holding a rattlesnake.

"*Run, now!*" Benjamin roared at his brother.

Seth whimpered but jolted up and away. As the smallest of the family, he was also the quickest. Benjamin hoped that coupled with a head start, Seth would have no problem leading the other men off his trail.

He didn't want anyone to know where he was going next.

Benjamin gently scooped up Jericho's limp body in his arms and doubled back around toward the house, careful to go wide around the first path he took into the woods. Kermit and Theo were likely tracking them along that very path right now. He knew from years of childhood hide-and-seek with his brothers that they could tell exactly where and even *when* someone had passed by, if they were going by scent and not sight. Giving the other men two scent trails to follow should buy them some time. He was forced to take a longer way home, but if he ran into them now, then this was all for naught.

He looked down at Jericho's lifeless form hanging in his arms. The blood from her chest had completely saturated her midriff, dyeing the torn edges of her once white shirt a stark, deep red. *Her heart's blood*, he thought to himself as the icy sensation of fear rushed through his veins. His vision blurred, but he blinked the tears away. *No time for that*, he thought, *you can cry later if this doesn't work.* His blood still ran cold, but the fear was replaced by grim determination. He knew what to do; he just had to get there in time. He grunted and ran faster.

Benjamin would later remember that as the fastest and most terrifying run of his life. He managed to avoid the rest of his family but was poised for a fight the entire time. His frayed nerves jangled as he ran around the back of the house and sprinted through the patio doors, barely blinking in the blast of air that hammered him on entrance. He shoved the shining door to the lab with his shoulder, forcing it open with the sound of glass on metal.

In his hurry he ignored the handwashing station, running past the boxes of gloves and masks as he pressed into the belly of the lab.

His heart pounded violently against his chest, but his hands were gentle as he set Jericho down on the white tile floor. He cleared the distance between himself and a small fridge in two purposeful strides, rattling the vials inside as he tugged the door open.

He didn't need to reach far. The bright cerulean blue of the Serum gleamed back at him from the front of the shelf. He pulled the tray out with shaking hands, suddenly nervous.

What if it doesn't work? What if it turns her into something else? He shook his head angrily, dispelling the thought as soon as it entered his brain. *No. Be brave. It* has *to work*, he told himself.

His fingers danced over the vials, selecting one from the back to fit with a syringe. He growled: It was empty. Icy uncertainty froze his hand. The two on either side were drained as well, with nothing but bright-blue dregs staining the bottom of their barrels. He squinted. There was an empty space in the back row: a vial completely missing. *Fuck.* Four doses gone.

If Seth or Theo has gotten into this... They had a finite and potentially unstable supply of the Serum and had only hypothesized its effects. It was a strong hypothesis, sure, but his brothers had agreed they wouldn't try anything before working out a test case together. And that certainly didn't involve testing on themselves! They'd disputed dosage and testing methodology, but they all agreed that the Serum would unequivocally cause an overload of virus. An overload that could have myriad unintended consequences. Including irreversible mutation.

And if one of them had used all four of the vials...

"I don't have time for this!" he yelled, slamming the empty vials back into the case. The empty hole glared up at him. He grabbed a vial from the front, clearly full of gleaming liquid, then hastily replaced the case before turning back to Jericho.

No room for error now. He pulled open the drawer of syringes, tearing the plastic packaging off one of them with his teeth. Though his heart raced, his hands were steady as he uncapped the Serum vial, exposing the rubber seal beneath. He pulled the stopper on the syringe back as far as it would go, then uncapped the needle and inserted it through the rubber, careful not to touch the sides of the vial. Expelling the air into the vial made withdrawal easier. With that done, he flipped the vial upside down and again pulled the stopper on the syringe back, this time sucking all the precious blue liquid inside.

The clock ticked on the wall behind him, a brutal reminder of the time he took, but it was necessary. He tapped the barrel of the syringe twice, then carefully extracted it from the vial. He angled the needle upward, inches from his face, so he could clearly see when a single drop of cerulean blue blossomed from the needle tip. No air there. Even if—*when*—the Serum revived her, if Benjamin accidentally injected air into Jericho's veins, she would die. Again.

The clock ticked. He exhaled once. Then he removed the wooden stake from her chest and plunged the needle into her heart.

PART III

JERICHO

CHAPTER 13

I gasped, violently sucking air into my reluctant lungs. They burned as they expanded with oxygen, and the burning traveled down and out. It radiated through the rest of my body, filling every particle until it felt like I was on fire. I opened my eyes to a searing white light, and I screamed as I burned, and the world went black again. Either seconds or a lifetime passed.

I heaved. My body convulsed in shock as my blood abruptly turned ice cold, then intensely hot, and continued alternating between frigid chills and flame. The harsh chill of marble tile pressed against my face, and I opened my eyes again. I was in the lab, on the floor, and I was burning.

I sensed without seeing that Benjamin was in the room with me. My body ached with too much pain to wonder how I could feel him, so some part of my brain simply accepted it and moved on.

"What did you do to me?" I gasped, my body still heaving with each mutinous breath. I shakily sat up on my hands and knees and angled my eyes upward to Benjamin, glaring at him under my brow.

He sat stock-still against the far wall with a syringe in hand. The remnants of a blue liquid stained the sides of the barrel.

"What did you do to me?" My convulsions had dulled into violent shudders. My voice was steadier now and gaining volume.

He didn't move. Without thinking, I flung myself off the table, charging toward him. I roared and lifted him up—somehow I held him aloft and pressed him against the wall, with only fistfuls of his shirt gripped in both of my shaking hands. I didn't stop to think about how I got across the room so quickly, how my ankle didn't hurt anymore, or how I was able to lift Benjamin with only a modicum of effort. If I had paused, I would have marveled at any of those things, but I didn't stop. I couldn't stop. I was simply too angry, and pained, and brimming over with furious flames.

"What. Did. You. Do. To. Me." I hissed each word slowly through clenched teeth. Benjamin dropped the syringe to the floor, and his eyes followed it down to where it landed with a small tinkle.

A low growl from the back of my throat brought his eyes back to mine. "WHAT DID YOU DO TO ME, BENJAMIN!" I screamed out my pain.

Benjamin didn't flinch, even as I yelled in his face. Instead, he held my gaze, unblinking. Was that fear I saw? Or sadness? Maybe both.

"The only thing I could do. I'm so sorry, Jericho."

I pinned him harder against the wall, and a piercing shriek

reverberated around the room. I realized it came from me, and I shrieked again as I flexed. I heard my bones crack and pop in sickening concert. It sounded familiar, like, *like Mikey's fucking monster.*

I gasped and dropped Benjamin. He slid to the floor with a dull thud, and I backed into the opposite corner of the room, rattling the empty rat cages as I went. I saw him looking at me and turned hastily to the side, unable to meet the pity in his eyes. Instead I found a reflection in the gleaming metal table beside me. A pair of shining eyes glinted back at me. Eyes that pulsed with a vibrant golden fire, and burned from a smooth face framed in a halo of shimmering silver-white hair. The image was striking, but wavy and unreal in the metal's sheen and the harsh light of the lab. I gasped and touched my cheek; the girl in the reflection did the same. I looked away, hiding from my own gaze. I touched my hair in disbelief as I sank down to the ground and hugged my knees against myself, afraid. Afraid of him. Afraid of me.

Tears sprang to my eyes unbidden, and the fire and rage in my veins was replaced by grief. I began sobbing as I remembered what had happened.

I *died.*

I gasped again as I remembered the pain of being slashed across the back and stabbed in the heart, and gently touched my chest. No gaping wound. No wound of any kind. I ran my fingers furtively up and down my body, searching for the gash that had to be there, but found only smooth curves and newly taut muscle. A glance downward showed that my bloodied shirt had been ripped away just below my breasts, exposing a silvery scar in the vague shape of a star. I traced the outline, tearfully.

I should be dead. And yet I was somehow still alive. My lungs burned and ached with each deep breath. Maybe they were reluctant to work again after their deathly respite, which made me cry even harder. But the fact remained that I was breathing. *How? What the hell happened to me?*

I sat there, rocking with my forehead pressed against my knees for what felt like an eternity. My burning flames were as weary as my body, and they petered out until all I felt was cold. Cold and alone, and so very tired. Then a warm arm wrapped around me, and another body joined me in my solitude, like a candle flame in the darkness.

Benjamin hugged me close, and I leaned my head against his chest. I still fit perfectly, and he still smelled of pine and cinnamon, but also something new: pain.

"I'm so sorry, Jericho," he whispered.

A last lone tear welled up in my eye and trailed down my face. Benjamin caught it halfway with a gentle thumb, stroking my cheek as he drew his finger back.

He kissed the top of my head, and I took a deep shuddering breath in.

"Benjamin," I started.

"Yeah?"

"What did you do to me?" I whispered.

CHAPTER 14

"Are you saying I'm a *werewolf*?"

We sat together against the wall in the lab while Benjamin went through everything that had happened in excruciating detail, patiently answering all my questions.

"The Serum I gave you *should* only magnify senses that you already have. Faster healing, faster running, better sight, better smell, and, well, maybe some other things, too, but, um, I mean, it's the best option we had...well, it's the *only* real option we had, and we've never tested it before—"

"Benjamin, what the *fuck*?" I interrupted. I thought I'd thoroughly depleted my ability to feel shock for the rest of the day, but apparently not.

He hung his head and raked his hand through his scruffy brown hair. "I'm saying..." He trailed off, thinking. Finally, he sighed. "I'm saying you're *probably* not a werewolf, but we won't know for sure until the next full moon."

The last full moon had just passed, I knew. The moon was waning into its C shape, *como Cristo who died for our sins*, said a familiar voice in a faraway memory. I had died, too, because of a werewolf.

Werewolves are the missing puzzle piece. Werewolves are real. Benjamin is a werewolf, like his brothers and father. One of them killed Katherine. And I might be one, too . . . I hugged my knees to myself again as I rocked back and forth, trying to make sense of everything Benjamin was telling me. I probably looked like a crazy person, but I didn't care. The thought was somehow both terrifying and ridiculous, and I giggled at the absurdity of it all.

Benjamin's brows furrowed, and he *smelled* concerned. It was a fruity, almost peachy scent, which made me laugh all the harder. My laughter peeled through the lab, and I imagined it bouncing off medical instruments until we were surrounded by ricocheting hysterics.

Benjamin's concern heightened to alarm. "Jericho!" I felt his arms around me as he tried to calm me down, then a warm hand over my mouth attempting to stifle my laughter. "Jericho," he said sternly, "you have to stop. Seth may have bought us some time, but I don't know when the guys will be back. And they can't know you are here yet, do you understand? Not until we have a plan."

Some distant part of my brain said, *He's right! Get it together, Jericho!* But it was far away and easy to ignore. Benjamin was beside me, though, and much less ignorable.

He held me close with his other arm and leaned his head toward mine. "I've got you, Jericho, and everything is going to be okay," he said gently. I felt myself relaxing.

"I've got you," he said again. He whispered it softly, as if to himself, though I heard each word clearly.

I felt a warmth spread through me, like the fire from earlier, but instead of burning it simply caressed in a comforting way. The internal fern I'd imagined before was back, stretching into every nook and cranny that could contain it, and bringing warmth with every tendril. I let out a long, deep breath against Benjamin's palm, which he'd kept pressed to my mouth. Reasonably certain that I wasn't going to lapse into continued hysterics, he pulled his hand away from my face. He placed it around my shoulders instead, wrapping me to his chest.

I leaned into him, fitting my head into the crook of his neck and his shoulder, like I had so many times before. I may have changed with the Serum that Benjamin used to save me, but I think, at least, that I was still me.

Benjamin pulled away and examined my eyes, as if reading a medical chart. "I'm okay," I responded, and as I said it, I realized it was true. I felt slightly ill, tired, and in need of a long, hot bath, but I was alert and alive.

He didn't blink but nodded. "Good, and—" He paused and cocked his head to the side, frowning. "Damn, they're here already. Jericho, get ready." He exhaled heavily, then stood and pulled me up with him.

I leaned into Benjamin's chest as I stood, then closed my eyes and listened. I could hear his heart beating, steady and firm if a little faster than normal. I concentrated, and heard a tiny, gentle whooshing that could only be his blood flowing through his body. Then I listened for things farther away. The wind. A crow cawing outside. There it was: three men speaking in low voices, walking purposefully through the home.

Wide-eyed, I looked at Benjamin. "But you said we needed a plan first. Do you have a plan?"

His mouth was set in a grim line, but it softened as he sighed. "No. But I have you. And you have me. And we're going to go out there and face them, together." He took my hand in his and gave it a squeeze.

"Together." I nodded, and we stepped out of the lab.

Theo confronted us by the main living room, in the open space between the couch and the kitchen. He was flanked by Seth and Kermit. The latter two looked tense, but Theo was positively enraged. Even though he wasn't the tallest of the group, his presence was looming in its anger. He stood before us slightly hunched and with his arms out to the sides, poised to grab me should I try to run.

"Step aside, Theo," Benjamin said in a steady voice.

"I'm going to do what's best for the family, just like I've always done. If nobody else will help me, so be it," Theo growled as he shot me a menacing glare.

Benjamin nudged me back and planted himself squarely between me and Theo. He crossed his arms and widened his stance. "And what would that be, brother?" His tone was firm and unwavering.

"You shouldn't have to ask me that question. *Brother.*" Theo spit the last word toward Benjamin like a curse, then turned his hateful glare on me. "I liked you, you know. I would have done it quickly. You wouldn't have even known what was happening. But... now I think we might drag things out a bit." He bared his teeth in a wicked grin.

Seth and Kermit both eyed Theo warily, like a rabid dog, and they slowly edged to either side of him. I'd thought that the other men were acting as his backup, but I realized they were getting ready to pin him down.

A deep growl ushered from Theo's throat, and he glared daggers at his brother before him. "Step aside, Benny boy. I'm going to take care of this right now. She's seen too much, just like that hiking girl, Katherine. Katherine ran into me after I Changed, unluckily for her. But unlike that girl who was just in the wrong place at the wrong time, this one also *knows* too much. Just like... What was her name again? Oh yeah. *Lisa*. And your little infatuation isn't going to keep Jericho any safer than it kept your last pet."

I could literally taste the tension in the air, the bitter, tamarind-like flavor making me want to retch. *So fucking gross.*

Benjamin's face darkened, and he radiated anger like a storm. "You—"

Theo smiled viciously and gave Benjamin a mocking bow. "Me. Lisa swerved so she wouldn't hit a wolf in the road. She hit a tree instead. Don't worry, she died on impact. I checked. Just in case I needed to finish the job."

Fury and pain billowed out of Benjamin like smoke from a fire. Before he could do anything, Kermit sidled up to Theo with his hands raised in placation. "Now, Theo, my boy. This isn't how we do things. This isn't how to take care of this situation. This—"

Theo cut his father off with a yell. "Of course it's how we

do things! You've just been content to turn a blind eye every time it needs to be done! It always falls to me to keep this family safe! With this girl—"

He jerked his hand toward me at that, saying "girl" like you might say *cat vomit*.

"With Mom, with Lisa, with the hiker chick... I'm always the only one doing what's best for us! *Me!*"

Seth and Benjamin exchanged a confused look, and a veritable thundercloud passed over Kermit's face. Kermit closed the distance between himself and Theo in one large step and grabbed his eldest son by his shirt collar.

"What did you say about your mother?" Kermit's rough whisper was barely audible, but I managed to hear it clearly from my position behind Benjamin.

Theo glared back at his father in silence and scorn.

"What did you say about your mother?"

I swear the hair on the back of Kermit's head rose up, like an animal ready to attack. The tension in the room was heady and oppressive.

Theo sneered in Kermit's face. "Did you really think she was happy, Dad? She *hated* it here. She hated what we are, and she wanted to end it. But she didn't have the guts to do it herself, so I took her to the roof, and I *helped* her."

The silence that followed was so absolute, I thought I could hear autumn leaves falling gently on the earth outside. After a moment, I exhaled. I hadn't realized I was holding my breath.

A cold look of realization and intense fury crossed Kermit's face. "She didn't jump. You pushed her." His voice was ice and iron, and Benjamin and Seth joined their father, forming a thick wall of wolf-laden testosterone in front of Theo.

Theo crossed his arms and kept talking, either oblivious or indifferent to the threatening looks from the rest of his family. "She wanted me to do it. She just wouldn't admit it! The Council may have sanctioned our work and agreed to foot the bill, but you know as well as I do that she was the only reason you dragged us into finding this so-called Cure!" He uncrossed his arms and gestured wildly in the air. "But *she* was the one that needed to be cured, can't you see that? We were given superior powers to use, not to eradicate like some disease!"

Kermit's eyes widened at this, and he let go of his son as he opened his mouth to respond. Theo was faster. He jabbed an accusatory finger at his father's chest, pushing the larger man off balance. "No, Dad. You're growing soft in your old age. I can see now that you lack the vision needed to propel this family forward."

Theo stepped backward toward the living room, smirking. "There are some on the Council who agree with me, I'll have you know. And others who want to weaponize the Cure, did you know that? They want to use it as a threat!" Theo sneered. "To keep those of us who push the boundaries *in line*. I'm keeping us on the right side of the line: the side with all the power. That's why I created this, to bring us to the next stage of evolution." He pulled something from his pocket, and I recognized the blue-liquid-filled syringe, a twin to the one that Benjamin had injected me with in the lab. A strangled sound escaped Benjamin's throat, a mix of shock and outrage.

Theo looked at Benjamin then and clicked his tongue,

shaking his head. "Oh, little brother. Don't look so betrayed. You helped me succeed. I wouldn't have figured out the key to isolating and disabling the retrovirus without you." He shot Benjamin an oily smile that didn't reach his eyes.

Benjamin broke his silence. "The Serum isn't meant for anyone who's already infected, and you know it. You have no idea what it'll amplify. After the Cure... we can have all the benefits, all the 'superior powers,' as you said, without the Change. We can have our cake and eat it, too."

Theo laughed maliciously and shook his head. "I'm talking about expanding our potential, and you're talking about *cake*? I guess Father isn't the only one who lacks vision."

He held the syringe up to his face with the needle pointed toward the ceiling. He gave the barrel a quick tap, then squeezed the plunger to let out any bubbles.

Eyes wide, Benjamin held up a hand to his brother. "Wait, Theo, stop! You don't know how it will react with the virus you already have. Your body will be overloaded, you could mutate—don't do this!"

For a moment everyone froze like a Renaissance tableau. Benjamin stood near the dining room table with an arm outstretched in Theo's direction. Theo was closer to the living room, still delicately holding the syringe aloft. Seth and Kermit stood between them. The sun shone brightly through the bay windows, glinting off the cerulean-blue liquid that gleamed in the syringe. Theo's mouth twitched, and for a moment, I thought he might surrender.

Then a wicked smile split his face maliciously, sending icy shards of fear through my body.

"Oh, Benny boy. But I've already done it." Theo let the full syringe fall from his hands, unused. He collapsed to the ground with a thud as the glass vial shattered on the tile.

"Oh my God, the empty vials—" said Benjamin. His face twisted in horror as he stared transfixed at his brother.

At first, I thought that Theo had simply fallen and was reaching to Benjamin for help back up. But his form kept on stretching and growing. Bones cracked and sinews snapped in jarring dissonance. I scurried backward and under the dining room table as I watched the nightmare unfolding in front of me.

The thing that used to be Theo howled, a loud and twisted sound. The same one that I'd heard the night before, the same one from little Mikey's recording. This was it.

This was the monster.

Thick, jet-black hair sprouted over every inch of his body, covering him in a coarse, dark mat. Vertebrae extended from his back with a series of sudden pops that made me jump and cover my ears. Pitch-black skin stretched over the bones as they grew, until they stuck above his jet fur like jagged, black, flesh-covered mountains. His monstrous spine had barely finished popping when his hands and feet deformed into paws the size of dinner plates. Shiny black claws squeezed forth with a revolting squelch as they sliced through muscle. His evil smile contorted sickeningly as his face stretched into a long snout. Finally, the wretched muzzle split open, revealing jet-black teeth.

Chaos erupted as everything exploded into action at once.

The three remaining men transformed fluidly, in stark

contrast with the horror show Theo had just put on. It was one thing to see it on TV in any number of werewolf movies, another to have Benjamin explain it to me, and *quite* a different thing to watch it happen with my own eyes. The men didn't reshape so much as *melt* into their wolf forms. One second there was Benjamin, then like some viscous liquid he simply *flowed* into the shape of a wolf. Any other time and it would have been mesmerizing, even graceful to watch. As it was, panic gripped my throat as the three new wolves leapt at Theo. They were easy to tell apart, so I had no trouble keeping my eyes locked on Benjamin. His wolf sported thick, shiny chestnut fur. The brawny white wolf could only be Kermit. And the last, a lean and wiry black wolf, was Seth.

They were much bigger than ordinary wolves. Even someone who'd never seen a wolf before would know that these were something different, something special. I could only hope that combined they would be a match for Theo's beast, which towered over them all.

The wolf trio landed as one atop the monster's body, each sinking into the dark mass with a flurry of claws and teeth. My heart surged. *They're doing it!* The scene before me was not unlike those wild-animal shows where wolves work together to bring down an elk. But Theo wasn't an elk. He was a monstrous, unholy terror who turned and ripped each wolf off with a roar, as easily as a human flicking at flies. In seconds the smaller wolves crashed to the floor around Theo as my heart skipped a beat; then they sprang up again just as quickly. The battle ebbed and flowed in a similar series of exchanges, each ending with the three wolves battered to the ground as the monster fought them off. To my dismay, the wolves' rebounds were getting noticeably slower each time, and the beast seemed indifferent to each blow they landed on him.

This isn't working... I clenched my fists so tightly I heard my knuckles pop. I had never been the sit-back-and-watch type of girl. I needed to do something. I crawled out from under the table, hoping a plan would come to me.

But my mind went completely blank when I saw what Benjamin was about to do.

While Kermit and Seth continued circling Theo like sharks looking for an opening to attack, Benjamin growled with unbridled ferocity and leapt at the beast, going directly for his face.

I felt like I was watching a movie in slow motion. Benjamin's wolf flew toward the monster's jaws. Theo's vast mouth spread into a vitriolic grin, then split into a gaping maw of flashing teeth and bitter evil as his brother drew nearer.

"Benjamin, *no!*" I shouted as I ran toward the monster that was once Theo, but I was flung back by his muscled, brutish black arm. My head went foggy as I slammed into the wall and I sat for a moment, shaking it off. My eyes were glued to the fight even as I planned my next move.

It was a raucous tumble of fur, claws, and blood. The howls and roars reverberating through the open room were enough to give anyone a lifetime of nightmares, but the thing that chilled my blood and stilled my heart was Benjamin's wolf. His face was badly mauled and bleeding as he charged shakily toward the black beast. Seth and Kermit were also bloodied and flagging, but still standing. Theo had more wounds than all of them, with thick oily blood matting his fur until his body gleamed eerily in the light, yet he didn't seem to be affected at all. If anything, the giant beast grew more emboldened and vicious the longer he fought.

The three smaller wolves still circled Theo, no longer with the frenzied energy of blood-maddened sharks but instead with exhausted caution. Theo's eyes were wild as his black jaws split into a grin and he barked out a—*oh dear God, was that a laugh?* I choked back vomit.

I had to help them somehow, but what could I do? What did I have that three huge wolf-men didn't? *Think, Jericho.* Opposable thumbs. My knife, with the silver handle. My newfound strength. My speed.

Run! Katherine's scream echoed in my head. She'd been trying to warn me, to prepare me. A lifetime of lacing up sneakers and running down pavement, trails, and racecourses flashed through my mind. *Run.*

That's it. They were all bigger than me, but I'd be damned if I wasn't just as fast as any of them, and more maneuverable besides.

I sprang up, and I ran. I leapt over fallen furniture. I dodged as Kermit's snowy wolf was thrown into the cabinet just in front of me, bringing it crashing to the ground in a rain of shattering plates. I grabbed a thick piece of broken hardwood as I dashed into the thick of the fight, watching Benjamin and Seth circling Theo's beast like a storm. Clutching the wood I leapt wildly, using one of the wolves' backs as a springboard to get farther ahead. I landed on Theo's neck, clenching him with my thighs for purchase. Before he could react, I rammed the wooden stake into his neck, roughly forcing the wood through his vertebrae with both of my hands and all my strength.

Theo howled and reared up, throwing me from his back. I crashed down hard on the floor as Theo careened down the hall. The sharp tinkling sound of shattering glass and a *whoosh* of air told us that he'd slammed through the glass doors that led to the patio by the lab. I sprang up and whipped down the hall to follow, not noticing or caring if the wolves were with me.

I paused at the exit. There was no sign of Theo near the lab or the patio outside, but the ground was littered with shards of glass from his passing. I made to step around the wreckage of glass, but a now-human—and fully naked, but there was no time to ogle—Benjamin grabbed my arm. I looked back at him, confused.

"Jericho, he's still too dangerous. We'll go alone. You should stay here."

My eyes hardened. "No way."

"But—" He paused, his blue eyes looking directly into my golden ones. "—I want you to be safe. Please, Jericho."

"I want you to be safe, too." I smiled at Benjamin, a welcome respite amid the insanity. "You saved my life."

Benjamin smiled warmly but creased his brow and opened his mouth as if he was about to protest further. Whatever musings he had were interrupted, however, when a now-human Kermit charged into the hallway and almost bowled us over. "Would you two quit mooning and *get him?*" he roared.

"But I stabbed him through the neck," I said. I pointed

to blood splatters that intermingled with the shattered glass on the floor like a gruesome Jackson Pollock. "He can't have gone far."

Kermit shook his head, clearly frustrated. "Yes, yes, and he'll *heal*. And only God knows how quickly with however much Serum he took."

I blinked, confused, then I realized none of the men were as beat-up as they had been mere moments before. As I stared at Benjamin's face, a cut above his eyelid sealed neatly. The only evidence of injury was a faint smear of blood where the cut had been. I wiped the blood away with a finger, astonished. If they heal this quickly without the Serum, then with it... *Duh, Jericho, of course.* That was how I'd literally been brought back *from the dead.* I shivered. I knew firsthand how powerful the Serum was.

Kermit paid me no mind and continued. "Come on, we'll track him. Seth." He turned to Seth's wolf, who had entered the hallway shortly after Kermit. "You're with me. We'll follow his trail." The black wolf nodded in a very un-wolf-like fashion and sat back on his haunches. "Benjamin, go the opposite way, in case Theo doubles back."

"What about me?" I asked, annoyed at being left out.

"Uh, Jericho, why don't you go to the roof to be the lookout?" Benjamin suggested.

It felt an awful lot like Benjamin was trying to get me out of the way, which of course I immediately moved to protest. But Kermit quickly agreed that it was a good idea to have some eyes from above.

"Okay, let's go," Kermit said, and I turned away as he

melted back into his wolf form and bounded out the door with Seth at his heels.

"Stay safe, okay?" I said to Benjamin, my voice tight.

He nodded and raised a hand to my face, like he wanted to straighten an errant hair or maybe caress my cheek, but pulled away. "I'm coming back, Jericho. I promise," he said. He turned and leapt out the ruined door, and when he landed on the other side it was as a wolf.

I watched him lope away until he disappeared in the woods beyond the house. Then I took a few deep, slow breaths to calm my body and my nerves, shook my head to clear it, and ran upstairs.

It was obvious that the men didn't expect me to find Theo on the roof. I mean, he clearly ran outside, right? I heard the air-blast *whoosh*; Benjamin heard it. We all heard it. All I anticipated finding upstairs was resentment at being excluded. I pushed the attic door open with the frustrated sigh of someone feeling left out. We all knew Theo was in the woods somewhere.

We were all wrong.

CHAPTER 15

The only thing I had going for me—*the only thing*—was that Theo clearly wasn't expecting me, either.

I stepped into the sunlight on the roof of the house and stared in shock at the hulking black form of Theo's beast licking his wounds at the base of the nearest ramp.

His head shot up as he stared at me with the same surprise. For a single, perfect heartbeat, neither of us moved.

Run! Katherine's scream somehow echoed in my ear once more, startling me into motion. I was about two seconds quicker than Theo—thank you, Katherine. I hurtled toward the training course as he sprang at me.

The open course seemed like a better option than going back into the tiny attic. Outmaneuvering him in the jungle of ramps, ladders, and ropes wasn't much of an actual plan, but it was at least *something* to buy myself some time. *Think, Jericho, think!*

Theo's angry roar rattled my eardrums as I bolted over the first wooden ramp and swung across a rope to the next structure. I was feeling cautiously optimistic. The ramps varied in size, but they were clearly constructed with humans in mind. These were a good twenty feet high. In his current form, Theo was going to struggle with the rope for sure.

I mentally patted myself on the back.

A loud crash and the sound of wood cracking into splinters split the air behind me, shattering my optimism. *Damn!* It sounded like the first ramp had exploded.

Don't look, just keep going!

I looked.

The beast had fully destroyed the first ramp, and as I turned my head he locked his flashing, menacing eyes on me. Every ounce of him oozed malice (and believe me, there were a lot of ounces in the thing-that-was-once-Theo). I could *smell* his malevolence. I could *taste* it. It was acidic and burned my new senses. The raw hatred threatened to consume me down to my last breath. My panicked brain wanted to freeze on the spot, but thankfully my legs didn't get the memo and had already started running.

I looked away just in time to register his dark mass leaping out of the corner of my eye. The platform shuddered and creaked dangerously as he slammed into the wooden side about halfway up, digging his steak-knife-size claws into the wood. I reached the end of the platform atop the ramp just as the bulky black monster heaved itself onto the other side. We jumped at the same time. As he hurtled toward me, I leapt into space.

I was aiming for the rungs of a ladder suspended horizontally between this ramp and the next. My plan formed as I jumped: I would grab hold of the ladder and monkey-bar it over to the other side. The old Jericho, pre-Serum boost, never would have succeeded in that jump. She would have missed the ladder entirely and fallen twenty feet to the rooftop below.

The new Jericho, though.

The new Jericho also fell.

I squeezed my eyes shut, but I didn't have long to contemplate my plummet before I hit the bottom and *didn't die.* Instead, the ground sank beneath me before rebounding upward. My leg muscles coiled and sprang on autopilot as I felt my body being pushed back up, into the sky above.

The trampoline.

I had landed on the trampoline! The thrill of being alive shot through me as I hurtled upward faster and higher than I thought possible. I opened my eyes just in time to see the ladder again and stretched out a desperate hand to grab it. My fingertips connected with worn wood, and I held on tight. *I did it!* My body swung precariously as I lifted my other arm and clutched at the rungs with both hands.

Theo shrieked, enraged. *Shriek* doesn't do this heinous sound justice, though. It was indescribably painful to hear. A veritable army of goose bumps prickled up at the noise, and I turned my head as far as I could from my hanging perch, straining to see what was happening on the platform behind me. Theo was no longer looking in my direction. Instead, his eyes seemed trained on something on the ground, in the woods. *Could it be Benjamin?* My heart fluttered with hope.

The hope-flutter quickly turned into an am-I-about-to-die-flutter when Theo whipped his head back toward me. He growled, pacing on his monstrous black paws, but didn't try to follow me across the ladder. *He must know he's too heavy to come across*, I thought.

Just then a howl pierced the air from below, like a clarion bell cutting through the autumn sky. Two more answered it from the other side of the house. *The cavalry is closing in.* I turned to see the hair on Theo's back bristle angrily. Thick muscles rippled beneath his black, leathery skin. And something else: His cuts had stopped bleeding. The deep wounds that had crisscrossed his body were almost completely healed. Theo's beast turned back toward me and smiled wickedly. He smelled...*excited*? Was that excitement? The sparkling Champagne taste that radiated from the creature was normally something I would have loved, but this was laced with the acrid poison of Theo's malevolence. I gagged, my sweaty palms still gripping the ladder rungs.

He continued smiling at me—an awful, hideous perverted thing. I knew then that no matter how much damage he took, no matter how much pain we inflicted, he would come back again and again, seeking vengeance or death.

We had no option but to answer in kind. We had to finish him.

But how do you kill a creature like that? A passage I read in the werewolf book replayed itself in my mind:

Known methods include decapitation, cardiectomy, and of course, the infamous silver bullet.

I didn't have a silver bullet, but I *did* have my silver-and-abalone-handled knife strapped to my side. The blade itself wasn't silver, though, just simple stainless steel. *But if he ate it, would the handle be enough?* I wasn't sure how far the silver aversion went, and I didn't want to bet my life on convincing him that it was snack time. But it was looking like I might not have a choice. Even if it was far-fetched, I'd rather go down fighting than not.

Theo was still pacing, as if considering his next move. I was still dangling from the ladder rungs. Old Jericho wouldn't have been able to hold on for this long, but my newfound strength flowed through my body and I could feel my muscles accommodating the strain and literally *growing stronger*. Maybe I wasn't out of time just yet.

Think, Jericho. What else? Decapitation. I looked around furtively from my aerial view. I didn't see anything on the roof that would do the trick, and I didn't suppose Theo would hold still long enough for me to hack his beastly head off with my small blade. *Nope.*

What's left? Cardiectomy. Complete removal of the heart. I thought of my little knife again. *Fat chance.* But something glinted out of the corner of my eye. I craned my neck, searching for the source. The glinty-thing sparked in the sunlight as I twisted to get a better look. It was coming from the garden side of the house. *What?* A single point of sunlight twinkled back in answer. *The horrifying black sculpture!* The realization hit me, and my eyes widened as my tired brain formed the beginnings of a real plan.

Yessss, Katherine's voice whispered in my ear. Or was it the wind? Either way, I gasped, drawing Theo's attention back to me.

I almost froze under the weight of his glare, but the not-quite-a-plan slammed itself to the front of my thoughts. My hands let go of the wooden bars before my brain caught on to what was happening, and I began to fall toward the trampoline. Theo growled horribly. His muscles tightened as he backed onto his haunches, preparing to spring toward me. I had exactly enough time to register what was going on—Theo was going to leap out and snatch me from the air, like some kind of fly-by dining—and think, *Shiiiiiiit.*

I tensed as I fell, 100 percent expecting to feel Theo's weight slam into me as he plucked me from the sky. Then all hell broke loose.

Theo leapt, and a cacophony of growls and roars erupted from the attic doorway. The frenzied commotion broke Theo's gaze away from me as his eyes were drawn to the action behind him. He whipped around in midair in time to see three huge wolves burst through the doorway and onto the roof in a tumultuous sprint toward us. Theo's beastly form jerked his head back to me, but the rapid pivots were too much for his momentum, throwing him off course. He flung his monstrous arms at me anyway, swiping at my face in vain. I felt the air from his long, black claws as they streaked past my nose, neatly shearing off a lock of silver-white hair that had been floating there only milliseconds before.

Benjamin and the others were coming closer but were still too far to get between Theo and me. I hit the trampoline and started sinking downward as my non-plan congealed into a somewhat mushy plan. I pivoted my body to spring out and *off* the trampoline instead of back *up*, amazed that I could alter my trajectory. I flew over the woven mesh and the bars, then hit the rough concrete of the rooftop and rolled smoothly into a tense crouching position like some kind of superhero. *Oh my God, I am so cool right now.*

Theo hadn't expected me to leap off, so he had scrambled to stay on the trampoline for his next attack. He struggled for his footing on the bouncy surface, which was decidedly not made for four-legged creatures. He roared in frustration and slashed at the trampoline's woven mat, quickly reducing it to threads with his wicked claws. Seconds later, he fell through the now-wrecked bottom and immediately slunk angrily in my direction: a dark, lumpy mass of teeth and claws. If malfeasance and toxic hatred congealed together into a solid form, this would be it. I shivered at the sight.

The guys had nearly reached us, and part of me wanted to stand back, to hide somewhere, and let them fight while I simply watched. They wouldn't mind, and nobody would call me a coward, I knew. It was their fight, after all: wolf versus wolf, brother versus brother. Years of wrongs set for atonement.

I could just come out when it was done. Benjamin would carry me off into the sunset.

Unless Benjamin was hurt too badly. Unless Benjamin died.

My heart skipped a beat. *No.* I couldn't think about that, and I couldn't just stand by and let something happen to him. Jericho James had never been the stand-by type before, and I wasn't about to start now.

Benjamin's wolf barked at me as he drew nearer. To my ears it sounded no different from a dog, but my brain somehow translated it as *"Go, now!"*

THE MIDNIGHT PACK

"No!" I shouted, then concentrated on thinking *I have a plan, trust me!* I imagined the words echoing out of my mind and soaking into Benjamin, like water into a sponge. *Did it work? But if it did, could Theo hear me, too?* At that moment, Theo growled. Whether it was connected or coincidental I don't know, but I decided to examine my animal communication methodology later, as there were more pressing things at hand. Like my impending doom.

Theo's attention had shifted to Benjamin when his younger brother barked, but now the older wolf only had eyes for me. Flashing, menacing eyes that spelled *death for Jericho* if I stared at them too long. I straightened up but stayed slightly crouched, ready to run. Timing was everything if my plan was going to work. If nothing else, I'd go out with a bang, I supposed. *Oh well.* At least it would buy the others more time to catch up to the monster.

Theo's muscles tensed, and I *smelled* his malice and determination. It was overwhelmingly sulfuric, like a noxious gas that slowly scorched my brain, threatening to erode my thoughts and reason. *Not today.* I locked eyes with that darkness and met it with all my pent-up rage: rage for my death, rage for doubting myself, rage for Katherine.

We sprang forward at the same time. Theo toward me, and me toward the side of the roof. I sensed Benjamin following behind, and he was *not* close enough to catch up. But that was okay. "*I'm here!*" I yelled, mostly to myself. I spied my target in the gardens below and stopped running. I stood on the razor's edge of the roof, with my heels kissing the empty space behind me.

When Theo had chased me through the training course, I thought my heart was going to burst out of my chest. Now, though, in this make-or-break, winner-take-all-and-loser-*die* situation, I was strangely calm. It felt like I was watching myself from far away, like I was playing a Jericho James video game and had just reached the boss level. From this detached space, I witnessed the horror rushing toward me. But I was at peace. If Theo was a raging hurricane, then I was the eye of the storm. I took a deep breath, enjoying the sensation of air filling my lungs in case it was my last.

I exhaled slowly as the beast charged.

"*No!*" a now-human Benjamin exclaimed.

Seth and Kermit howled.

I saw Theo's muscles flex as he leapt toward my face. He would reach me at the bottom of my exhale, I knew. As the last of my breath left my lips, I flung myself down, pressing my body flat against the rooftop. I was so close to the edge that my left arm dangled completely off the roof, and Theo almost grabbed it as he careened over me, flailing desperately, almost in slow motion from my viewpoint, into the empty space below.

There was a sickening *sheeenk* as the beast's body hit the black spire statue, and a pained, guttural roar reverberated through the air.

The black marble horn had completely impaled the beast that was once Benjamin's brother. A torrent of blood covered the abhorrent statue. *So much blood.* I watched him slide down, desperately clawing at the dark sculpture even as it split the center of his chest. Miraculously, he'd hit directly on his chest, and the tip of the spire pierced his heart and pushed it out of his body as he slid down the sculpture, still clawing wildly. The beast now lay at the bottom of the statue, and the spire erupted from his chest, slick and shiny with blood, like an unctuous skeletal tree growing from a black and bloody field. At the top, his black heart stayed put, coated in dark blood that reflected the afternoon sunlight, shining like a grotesque mockery of a Christmas tree star.

Complete cardiectomy.

I leaned my head over the roof and threw up.

Benjamin appeared by my side and knelt, gently rubbing my back with a warm hand. "It's over, Jericho. You did it," he said softly, with both pride and sorrow in his voice.

Kermit and Seth, still in wolf form, flanked him. Together the three men stared down at Theo. Kermit howled. The beast below abruptly shuddered. Kermit and Seth exchanged a worried look, and I thought I heard something in my head about "making sure." They disappeared across the roof, presumably to the ladder I knew was there, but I barely registered their absence.

Benjamin had said it was over. *It has to be over, right? Not even a werewolf can survive that.* But the weight of the day caught up to me and I was suddenly exhausted. No, I was beyond exhausted. I felt completely empty, like the last drop of whatever-makes-me-*me* had dripped out onto the roof and evaporated in the autumn sun. I hadn't even felt this empty when I died.

I closed my eyes, wondering if death was really all that bad if it came with sleep. What did Shakespeare say? *For in that sleep of death what dreams may come?*

I didn't hear Benjamin's frantic worry when I became suddenly and completely unresponsive. I also didn't see the other men below, examining Theo's body. I didn't notice when Theo's wolf body melted back into his human form, a sign that he was well and truly deceased. I even didn't feel it when Benjamin lifted me from the roof, gently wiping concrete pebbles and dust from my face, and carried me back into the house.

I blacked out.

And I dreamed.

I walked down the now-familiar path in the woods. It was so much more than just a path. I could see that now. It was a gateway: to answers, to my death, and to my future. This time I felt a shift in the air as I entered the clearing. Like walking into a new room in an old house. I stood in the center of it all and closed my eyes, breathing in deeply. The autumn sun was warm on my back, even dappled as it was through the trees. The smell of pine and loamy earth was everywhere. I smiled, remembering the nature Zen I'd felt when I first entered the woods.

When I opened my eyes again, Katherine was in front of me. She smiled, too. She was herself again, her face intact, clothes untorn. She looked like she did on the MISSING poster I'd seen in town when I first arrived.

"It's bad luck to stand where the dead have lain," she chided—though her smile never faltered, and her eyes twinkled with mirth.

"I've heard. I'm not sure I believe it now, though," I said.

"Really? Haven't you experienced any hauntings recently?"

"Yes, but—" I paused.

Katherine raised a slender eyebrow at me, silently imploring me to continue. "But...?" she asked.

"But, if the ghost is a friend, would we call it a haunting?" I responded.

Her smile spread across her face, and she opened her arms. She wrapped me in a tight hug, which I returned.

"Thank you, Jericho James," she whispered, beaming. We stepped apart, and she held my hands as we stood together in the clearing.

She really was beaming. I smiled back at her and wondered how her smile was so dazzling. Then I realized she was simply growing brighter all over. The light became intense. So intense that I had to let go of her hands and shield my eyes to look at her. It was like she'd become a ray of sunlight incarnate. Finally, I couldn't take it any longer and blinked. When I opened my eyes again, I was alone. My only company was a handful of dust motes that floated lazily in the sunlit space that Katherine had occupied moments before.

"Katherine?" I asked, tentatively.

"Goodbye, Jericho," her voice echoed from the treetops. Or was it the wind?

CHAPTER 16

The afternoon sun was warm on my eyes when I opened them. It poured through big, friendly windows and filled the room with a golden glow. I sat up in a familiar bed filled with blankets and a well-worn, mustard-colored quilt, enjoying the stillness of the moment. *I've been here before.* When had I first arrived at this strange house in the woods—four days ago, five? A week? In another lifetime. Was that even me? *Was my old life even real?* Looking back, it felt like a practice session for whatever this was.

I didn't have to turn my head to know that Benjamin was sitting on the wooden chair next to the bed. I simply *knew*, the way you know where your left hand is even if you're not looking at it. I rolled on my side to face him. His arms were crossed over his broad chest, and his head was tilted backward in what looked like an uncomfortable sleep. He snored. I smiled to myself. I wouldn't wake him, not just yet. Instead I stretched, taking stock of my injuries after the hard-won battle. *I've been here before, too.* To my shock, this time I felt fine. I felt better than fine, I felt amazing. Strong. My muscles were a little sore, but in an I-just-had-a-great-workout-and-feel-all-the-better-for-it kind of way.

I silently slipped out of the bed and padded over to the bathroom. Last time I'd looked in the mirror here, it was to a bruised and battered face under a tangled mess of caramel-blonde hair. This time I didn't recognize the person looking back at me. She—I mean, *I*—was dazzling.

My hair had turned a sleek white, and it shone like spun silver when it caught the sunlight. My face, for all that it should have been damaged beyond recognition, was as smooth as porcelain. I touched my cheeks in disbelief. My tan complexion hadn't paled, but it had softened somehow. And staring out at me were bright, golden eyes, shining like burnished metal. They were like, like... *like wolf eyes*. I shivered, hugging my arms to myself.

What if I'm a werewolf? A cold wave washed over me as if a cloud had passed over the sun, yet nothing had dimmed the bright light in the room. The enormity of everything that happened yesterday hadn't sunk in yet. All my attention had been focused on simply staying alive. But now...

Werewolves are real. One killed Katherine. I killed one. I might be one. The knowledge settled on my body like an overweighted blanket, threatening to suffocate me. I came gasping out of the bathroom, forgetting I didn't want to wake Benjamin. He shot up in alarm, hearing my pained breaths.

"Jericho!" He was by my side in an instant, his hands warm on my shoulders. "Are you okay?"

I looked up at him with wide eyes, unable to answer, but

Benjamin seemed to understand. "It's okay," he said gently. "Just breathe with me." He inhaled deeply and exhaled slowly. I rested my head on his chest as my breathing gradually matched his. I closed my eyes, feeling his chest rise and fall with each breath in a soothing rhythm. I felt a new weight on my back: his arms, wrapping me close. The suffocating feeling was gone, replaced by a comforting warmth.

He pulled away without breaking our embrace. "Better?" he asked.

"Yeah, actually."

He smiled. "Sometimes we need a hug to put the broken pieces back together."

"What if that's all I am? A collection of broken pieces?" I asked in a whisper.

He shook his head and took my hands as he guided me back to the bed, where we sat side by side. The mattress pressed down with his weight, sliding me closer to him.

"We are not defined by our broken parts, but rather how we put those pieces back together. It takes strength. And Jericho, you're, like, the strongest woman I've ever met." He held my hand, and I leaned my head against his broad shoulder.

We sat there in silence and sunlight, he and I. We were surrounded by warmth and comfort, but my mind still slipped back to nagging worry. A nightmarish image of Theo's transformation popped into my head as I pictured my bones stretching and my mouth splitting open into a wolf's muzzle. I shuddered.

"Benjamin—" I hesitated. I didn't want him to think I was weak after he'd just finished telling me how strong I was.

Then again, he'd told me that he was afraid when we were in the living room. That must have taken more bravery than I realized.

He angled his body toward mine, raising an eyebrow expectantly.

"I'm scared," I finally said in a soft voice. "I don't think I want to be a werewolf."

He shook his head sadly, and he spoke in a gentle rumble. "Frankly, I'd be worried if you weren't scared. It's a big change..." He paused as he felt me stiffen beside him. "But it's not insurmountable. And it might not even happen. It *shouldn't* happen. But if it does, you won't be alone."

I closed my eyes. *I won't be alone.* His words resonated in my mind. *You can do this, Jericho.* "Thanks. I guess I just need... hrmm, I need—"

"You need to get some fresh air. Let's take a walk outside."

I nodded and accepted his hand as he pulled me to a stand with him.

I shortly found myself back on the front porch, surrounded by the intricately carved pillars Benjamin had shown me in my previous life. We walked slowly, hand in hand, and I once again ran my fingers over the wooden animals as we passed. I had thought the wolves looked so life-like last time I was here, as if they could leap from their wooden prison and make a dash for the forest.

"*My mom always said her favorite thing about the forest were the creatures living in it,*" Benjamin had said. It made so much *sense* now. I mentally kicked myself for not connecting the series of dots I could see now in hindsight, but I stopped. *There's no way you could have guessed it was werewolves.* I nodded in agreement.

Benjamin shot me a quizzical look but didn't say anything. I laughed. "I was just thinking to myself. My dad used to catch me doing it and tease me." I stopped walking and looked up at Benjamin, my expression serious. "I informed him that I only talk to myself when I need to consult an expert's opinion."

This time it was Benjamin's turn to laugh. "I don't doubt it," he said with a smile.

We reached the stairs that led to the garden, but I froze as I remembered what had happened there. What I'd be forced to relive if I saw it again.

"Whoa," said Benjamin. "Are you okay?"

"No." An image came unbidden into my mind: Theo's monstrous black beast impaled on the spiral sculpture in the garden. *So much blood.* "I can't, Benjamin. I can't go down there. I'm already going to replay that scene in my nightmares for as long as I live. I don't need to see it again in person." *I'd like to commence blocking this from my memory ASAP, thank-you-very-much.*

"Oh, ah." He ran his long fingers through his hair. "I understand. But there's something I want to show you, and I think you're going to like it. I mean, I think it could be worth your while." He looked at me hopefully, but I didn't move. *So. Much. Blood.*

He squeezed my hand gently. "For what it's worth, we cleaned up the spire. You won't see anything. But, um, you don't have to look, either."

"Okay. I'm not going to look." *Where is the body?* I vaguely wondered, then decided I didn't want to know.

He nodded, and we continued down the stairs to the garden path, where I studiously ignored the dark, swirling spire to my left. I stared intently toward the other side of the garden, where clouds of wildflowers were still billowing across the terrace, like last time. As we drew nearer, I noticed the butterflies were still there, again like last time. I'd learned since then that a group of butterflies is called a kaleidoscope. Staring at the fluttering tangle of color, I could see why. The constant swirl of shifting hues mimicked the rainbow patterns of my favorite childhood toy.

We were well within the heart of the garden now, and Benjamin was staring at me intently. I ignored him, still a little miffed that he'd brought me out here after what had happened just *yesterday*. Was he *trying* to give me more nightmares? What could possibly be "worth my while" that I hadn't seen before? I sighed, focusing on the brilliant butterfly kaleidoscope before me as I studiously tuned out my darker thoughts.

The fluttering colors did serve as an effective distraction, I decided grudgingly. I saw brilliant blues, vivid oranges, iridescent greens, tiny, pointed faces, and delicate hands and feet, each with fragile little fingers and toes.

What in the actual fuck.

Next to me I sensed the bubbling of Benjamin's joy and

amusement, like sparkling Champagne overflowing from its bottle, with a light hint of pear. "Benjamin," I said, somewhat breathlessly. "Are these...?"

Benjamin chuckled, smiling beside me. "I told you it would be worthwhile."

I was still in shock. "They're *fairies*," I whispered. *There's no such thing as fairies*, said my brain. *There's no such thing as ghosts, or werewolves, either, and yet here we are*, I reminded myself. I exhaled, realizing I'd been holding my breath. "But how...?" I trailed off, but Benjamin understood what I was asking.

"I was wondering if you'd be able to see them now." He paused as an ebony fairy with velvety black wings alighted on his shoulder. She opened and closed her wings slowly as recognition dawned on me. *The butterfly from before!* She winked knowingly in my direction, then came fluttering to rest on my shoulder. She lifted a delicate arm and stroked a single strand of my silvery hair, flashing me a bright-white smile before taking off again.

Benjamin chuckled. "I told you she likes you." I watched her rejoin the blur of swirling colors and felt Benjamin's warm hand in mine, drawing me farther down the path.

Distracted by the fairies around us (real fairies!), I paid no attention to where my feet were taking me. I was surprised when the ground beneath them suddenly changed from sunny gravel to shadowed brick. My eyes shifted from the splendor in the garden to the source of the shadow. We'd reached the gazebo.

Benjamin gestured to the wooden love-seat-size swing hanging from the center of the gazebo. We sat together, swinging in a contented silence, until my brain stopped marveling at the fairies long enough to form a coherent sentence.

"So how can I see these fairies now? Or are these new? Were there actually butterflies here the last time we came out?"

I sensed Benjamin's amusement as he grinned beside me. "You can see them because of the Serum. You'll recall it enhances your senses—and I now believe it may spark chemical changes that stimulate some typically underutilized parts of your brain."

"Chemicals in my brain? I'm not hallucinating, am I?" I asked doubtfully.

Benjamin laughed. "Not at all. Think of it as opening your mind. You're finally seeing clearly. The world is much, much bigger than ordinary humans can perceive. But uh..."

"I'm not an ordinary human anymore?" I offered.

"Right. And yes, to answer your other question, these are the same fairies that were here when we came to the garden before. They're here every year, in fact, though they migrate south when it gets too cold."

I imagined a group of colorful fairies sipping tropical drinks on a beach and questioned the nature of my new reality. *But that's just it, isn't it? Perception* is *reality, and we all see the world a little differently.* It would take some adjustment to think that while I see a fairy, someone else is seeing a butterfly, though. "Wait, do butterflies even exist?"

Benjamin laughed again. "Yes, they do. Fairies just mimic them as a sort of camouflage. And of course, human eyes generally see what they expect to see." He shrugged.

My focus was back on the colorful wings dancing in the breeze. *If fairies have been hiding in plain sight, could that also mean...* "Benjamin, what about unicorns?"

"What about them?"

"You know what I mean," I said with a pointed glance in his direction. "Are they real?" I didn't think the answer to this question would matter to me that much, but my heart beat faster as I waited for his response. Child-me would have flat-out fainted from anticipation.

"Well, uh, I haven't seen one personally, but I've talked to others who say they have."

"Others, like humans?"

"Like werewolves," he responded in a mocking sort of tone that I gathered was supposed to sound like me.

"Oh," I said intelligently. It hadn't really occurred to me that there would be other werewolves, *but that's silly, of course there are.* "Do you see other werewolves often?"

He shrugged again, his face blank. "Not really. We generally keep to our own pack, but we've run into other packs before. And there's the Werewolf Council."

"This is the same Council that funds your research, isn't it?" Benjamin nodded before I continued. "They sound fancy."

He shrugged. "I guess so. They're kind of like the governing body for the werewolf groups in North America." He looked at me with a half smile. "Too much power, too much money, but not too exciting."

"What about the US president?" I asked.

"Oh, totally real."

I shoved Benjamin's shoulder playfully, laughing, as we

continued to rock back and forth on the gazebo swing. Benjamin smiled at me and reached over to tuck a silvery lock of stray hair behind my ear. "The president governs human laws, and the Council takes care of werewolf-specific things."

How mysterious. "Like what?" I asked.

"Just stuff." He shrugged nonchalantly. "Mostly about not being discovered, and some pack-loyalty issues."

I wondered what "pack-loyalty issues" meant, but I didn't push Benjamin for an answer. His clear blue eyes were turned back in the direction of the garden but focused far away, like he was looking at something unseen (at least by me) beyond the sea of flowers and fairy wings.

I cleared my throat, bringing his attention back to me. "Okay, have you ever met a vampire?"

He turned with his eyebrows raised and scoffed. *He scoffed at me?* "Vampires aren't real," he said, in a tone that suggested this question aggrieved him.

I returned his look with my best are-you-actually-shitting-me-right-now face. But a werewolf telling you there are no such things as vampires is about the same as the monster under your bed telling you there's no such thing as a monster under *his* bed.

"Really, Benjamin?"

He blushed under my glare and shrugged. "Well, my dad said they don't exist—"

"Yeah, your same dad that said Katherine was *clearly* mauled by a bear," I interrupted.

Benjamin frowned, and the air took on a new scent that my senses read as *"I'm offended."* "Well, I just think that if they did exist, I would have seen one by now. I mean, don't you think?"

"Ugh, Benjamin, have you not seen *Twilight*?" The perplexed look on his face told me that no, he had not. "Vampires and werewolves hate each other. It is known."

"So...?" He raised an eyebrow.

"So, you wouldn't necessarily have seen one. Ever. In fact, if they were around, I bet they'd probably avoid you." I coughed. "Er, us."

"Are you saying that they must exist purely because I have never seen any sign that they do?" he asked.

"Hrmm. Yes."

He laughed. "That's some fuzzy logic right there."

I shrugged, gesturing to myself. "Stranger things have happened, it turns out."

"The only strange thing about you is how you can be so completely and utterly mesmerizing. You're...bewitching," he murmured as he gently brushed a silky strand of silvery hair behind my ear.

My hand caught his as he pulled away. His palm was wide and warm. I absentmindedly traced the lines in his palm and wondered what I'd learn if I could read them. I bet a witch could do it, speaking of bewitching. *Are witches real?* Two weeks ago, I would have told you that palm-reading was for charlatans and fools, and there could no sooner be witches than werewolves. But the latter had been proven unequivocally true. *What's even true anymore?* Now that I was living in my own personal fairy tale (in which I might be a monster), I questioned the reality I was once so certain of.

Maybe monsters can be the heroes sometimes.

Benjamin spoke, interrupting my reverie as if he could read my mind. "Everything else can be explained by science," he said confidently.

Our night by the fireplace came to mind, along with Benjamin's tales of the wendigo and the evolution of viruses. I still wasn't sold. "*Fairies* can be explained by science?"

A group of three fairies had broken away from the garden to flutter around the gazebo. At my question, their fluttering grew more erratic and downright bouncy, like they were laughing at my sarcasm. They danced out of the gazebo on silent wings, and Benjamin gestured at their passing.

"Well, they're essentially tiny humans with butterfly wings. Humans exist. Butterflies exist. It makes sense. And take unicorns. They're similar enough to horses, it also makes sense. Other animals have horns or tusklike horns. I mean, look at the narwhal. Dragon stories were surely born from the discovery of dinosaur bones. Werewolves, well, when we Change, we're similar enough to normal wolves. From the way the lycanthropy virus evolved, it also makes sense."

My raised eyebrows said, *Not to me*, but I stayed silent, even as he gave me a wilted look.

"But vampires? The undead? They have no heartbeat. There's nothing powering them. That's just not possible."

He sounded certain, but my skepticism remained. "Do you believe in ghosts, then?" I asked him. *Talk about no heartbeat...*

"Nah, they don't seem likely."

Have I got some news for you. "Okay, what about the wendigo book. You saw it on the ground after my dream—how do you explain that?"

He shrugged. "Like I said before, coincidence and a slippery bookshelf."

"You actually believed your own story that night?"

He shrugged again. "Even in a world full of werewolves and fairies, the simplest explanation is usually the right one. Plus, you said it yourself: Stranger things have happened."

"Benjamin," I started, wondering if I should tell him about Katherine. *Will he believe me?*

"Besides," he interrupted, "I wouldn't want to think about all the restless spirits there would be if that were true." His suddenly serious blue eyes glanced almost imperceptibly toward the dark spire at the other end of the garden, but I noticed his attention shift and could guess exactly whose "restless spirits" he meant.

"What's even true anymore?" I whispered softly, barely audible though I knew he'd be able to hear me. My mind had become swamped with images of Theo's beast, chasing me, desperately clawing at me, and finally falling to his death. If ever there was a restless spirit, it would be that one. *Hopefully Hell snapped him up quicker than he could squirm his way out. Who knows, maybe there really is such a place. What's even true anymore?*

Benjamin either sensed my mood change or could read the shadows on my face. His eyebrows suddenly bunched in concern, and before I fully registered what was happening, he was apologizing. "Ah, I'm sorry, Jericho. I didn't mean to bring up, um..." He trailed off as he put an arm around my back.

I pressed my face against him and sighed into his chest. My heart hurt and my head was spinning.

"It's okay. I mean, I'm okay. It's just a lot, you know?" I said.

"I know." He sighed. "I really, *really* know. I'm sorry." The sudden bitterness in the air around us betrayed his unease.

"You don't need to be sorry. I—"

He interrupted before I could finish. "No, this is all my fault. All of it."

What does he mean? "What?" I asked, cleverly.

His eyes were tight, and his heartbeat sped up audibly. "I'm the one who chased you. In the woods." The bitter taste of his nervousness seeped into me, until anxiety pressed against my heart like an intruder at the gates.

"What." The word came out like a command, but I'd had enough unanswered questions in the last week to last a lifetime.

"It wasn't malicious. It was just... Seth and I were out, and I saw you in the clearing, and you looked so badass. And gorgeous. And so *sad* about something. And God, you smelled *so good*. Every cell in my body was screaming to get closer to you. Then you ran, and I wanted to make sure you were all right." His words came out in a jumble, and his voice was oddly tight. "I *needed* to make sure. I was trying to help."

He thought I was gorgeous even then? And he looks so cute when he's distressed.

My brain was having a hard time processing what he was saying. The creature that chased me in the forest *was* him. That was how he'd gotten to the ravine so quickly. It made sense now, and I could feel an invisible puzzle piece fall into place with a satisfying click in my brain.

Benjamin hung his head. "I just wanted to help, but I messed everything up. I'm so sorry, Jericho."

"What?" I was starting to feel like a broken record. "You didn't mess anything up." He raised his eyebrows hopefully.

"Well," I added, "you should never chase a woman through the woods. That's just a no-no, Benjamin. Like, rule number one of trying to communicate with a woman is *Don't chase her through the woods*. You could've—I don't know, called out to ask if I was okay."

He opened his mouth to respond, but I held up a hand and continued before he could start. "Wait, I could have *shot* you, you know. I could have *killed* you. What were you thinking?"

"Actually, I find it awfully hard to think when I'm around you," he said softly. Then he shook his head ruefully. "I'm trying to apologize for hurting you, and you're worried about *me*?"

"You didn't hurt me, Ben. A fall into a ravine hurt me, your brothers hurt me, that stupid wooden stake in my heart hurt me, but you... You took care of me. You saved me. You literally brought me back from the dead! And"—I blushed, looking up at him shyly—"I really like you. And you like me, I think. You don't need to apologize for that."

A breeze filtered through the gazebo, and the same three fairies who'd laughed at me before floated lazily above our heads. *Probably enjoying the show*, I thought.

Benjamin shook his head. *Men are so stubborn!* "But if I hadn't chased you—"

"Then we never would have met," I interrupted. "Benjamin, I'm so incredibly happy that I met you. I could never regret anything that led me to you."

Relief rolled off him in cool waves, refreshing and clean, and I couldn't help but smile. His blue eyes shone overbrightly. Had he been close to tears before? Now they were filled with warmth. The kind of deep, wanting warmth that kindled an answering flame of desire within me. The air between us changed, becoming both sweeter and spicier, and somehow more pure. Benjamin's thumb found its way under my chin and gently angled my face up, tracing the lines of my cheekbones as he slid his hand behind my head and swept me up in a kiss. *And oh my God, what a kiss.*

My hands trailed behind his head and I wound my fingers in his hair, even as his hands did the same in mine, pulling me closer. His full lips were warm and wanting. They invited me to kiss him deeper and longer, until I didn't know where his breath ended and mine began. Benjamin made a profoundly contented sound and slowly traced the lines of my cheekbone with his thumb, leaving a pleasant tingling in his wake. He broke our kiss to look at me. His blue eyes held my golden ones like sunshine on a lake, and I was drowning blissfully.

I sank into stillness in Benjamin's arms, trying to preserve our moment together. The fairies above us had grown in number. They tittered on colored wings and threatened to disturb said moment, but I studiously ignored them. I focused all my attention on the man who held me and my heart. It was clear from the intense look in Benjamin's eyes that he was doing the same. Nothing existed but us. With warm fingers,

Benjamin continued tracing the lines of my body, down my neck to my collarbone, then up to my shoulder before gliding gently down the curve of my waist. *Yesss.* I edged closer to him as best I could on the swing seat. I wanted to feel the heat of his body on mine, I wanted to—

A man's gruff cough beside us shook me out of my thoughts and almost off the swing.

CHAPTER 17

Benjamin turned and glared at the entrance to the gazebo, which darkened with Kermit's towering figure. Seth stood a few feet behind him.

"We need to get ready. The Council is coming," Kermit said. His tone didn't betray any emotion, though the tightness in his eyes suggested he was concerned.

I gaped openly at the men as I leaned forward in the swing.

Benjamin stood and walked toward his father. "But why now? Do they know?" he asked.

Kermit shook his head. "It is not for us to question the Council, Ben." He sighed and rubbed his temples. "But yes, they do know something happened, and two of them are on their way. Theo had apparently been in communication with them, and they're wondering why he stopped. I found notes, in his room. No names. He told them about the Serum. He—" Kermit's voice broke, and he abruptly pivoted and punched the side of the gazebo with a loud *crack*. The gazebo shook, startling our fairy audience back into the garden.

None of us said anything as the older man hunched over in the entryway. His only movements were his shoulders, which heaved with each breath. Finally, Kermit straightened and cleared his throat. When he spoke, his voice was heated.

"The things he was doing in *my* house, under *my* roof... things we didn't even know about!" He ran his fingers through his hair and sighed deeply. "But I still remember holding him when he was first born. The way he'd fall asleep on my chest as a baby." His voice cracked. "And now he's gone."

Benjamin had been edging closer to Kermit and finally reached him, putting his arm around his father's shoulders. Seth left his position outside of the gazebo and joined in, hugging his father from the side.

I looked away, blushing. I somehow felt like an intruder in a private moment. *And now he's gone.* Kermit's words echoed in my head. Theo was gone because of *me. Yeah, but he was also a homicidal, monstrous maniac,* I reasoned.

Forgetting I was among three men who could acutely sense emotions, I was surprised when Kermit broke away from his sons and walked toward me.

"Now there, Jericho, don't feel too bad about it. It's a heavy thing, an impossible burden—taking another person's life." He paused and sighed. "But in this case, it was necessary. I should be thanking you. If you hadn't done it, I would have had to," he said in a soft and rumbling voice. "I wish Theo hadn't done the things he did. But the fact is he did, and now we need to deal with the consequences."

Kermit turned back toward his sons. "The Council emailed. They're sending a pair. We have to assume it's the same two from Theo's notes, his associates, since their arrival dates match. They will be here in three days' time. We have from now until then to decide what to do with the remainder of the Serum." He paused and rubbed his temples. "And with our Cure."

Seth and Benjamin stared at their father, and the air filled with a mixture of anxiety and outrage.

"I know," said Kermit. "But from what I found, it seems that Theo was telling the truth about the Council using it as a weapon or a threat... We may have some control over that."

Benjamin's eyes widened, but he nodded in agreement. My eyes widened as well. *Did he just say "email"?* And did Kermit mean they could control who has access to the Cure? Or that they would destroy it? *But they worked so hard for it!*

Kermit continued. "All right, let's reconvene in ten minutes in the dining room to discuss and prepare.

"Jericho." My attention had shifted to Benjamin (I had questions for him), but on hearing my name, I looked back to Kermit. "Like it or not, you're involved in this now. You'd better come, too."

I nodded.

Kermit tapped Seth on the shoulder, and the two men stepped out of the shady gazebo and into the bright, billowing clouds of wildflowers and fairies.

Benjamin stood in the center of the gazebo, running his hands through his hair.

I coughed, breaking the silence. "Email, huh? In this house with no Wi-Fi?" My tone wasn't unkind, but I was deciding how mad I wanted to be about Benjamin's lie.

"Oh," Benjamin said distractedly. He took his place beside me on the swing. "We *don't* have Wi-Fi. We have the old-fashioned internet. It was put in with the phone line. Kermit's room only." He smiled weakly. "Sorry I didn't tell you. The computer is off-limits, but that seemed like the easier thing to say, rather than explain why."

I nodded thoughtfully. *Fine.* "Next time, just tell me the truth, okay?"

"I promise," he said seriously.

"Good. So, about the Werewolf Council..."

Benjamin nodded, then hung his head. "I told you they're the ones funding all our research. Did I mention they create and enforce our laws, too? This is where pack loyalty comes in."

"Oh." *That's probably not a good sign.*

He looked at me. "Yeah...hence all the secrecy and so on. We need to follow their orders exactly. They didn't want other packs to know what we were doing. Didn't want to 'worry' them. And, well, we thought our interests were aligned, so we didn't mind. Though now it seems at least some of them want to use it to control the packs and 'cure' anyone who doesn't agree with them." He ran his hands through his hair dejectedly.

"Well, shit," I said, recalling the notes I'd found in Theo's desk. "What do you think people like that would do with the Serum?"

"Probably the same thing Theo did," Benjamin said. He hunched his shoulders as he buried his face in his hands. I patted him on the back in what I hoped was a comforting way. He inhaled deeply and stood up.

"My dad will know what to do," he said. *Was he trying to reassure me or himself?*

"I guess we should go down now." He reached a hand toward me, which I accepted, and he pulled me up from the swing.

The other men were already there when we arrived. Seth sat at the dining room table with one leg tapping the ground nervously, while Kermit stood in the kitchen, slowly cutting cheeses and various salamis for a big charcuterie board. For all of Kermit's calm demeanor, the tension was thick and oppressive.

Benjamin and I sat side by side at the big table, and Kermit joined with the charcuterie. Benjamin opened his mouth to speak, but Kermit beat him to it.

"We have to destroy it," he said in a low voice.

Both of his sons widened their eyes simultaneously. Seth stood up, slapping his palms on the tabletop as he spoke. "You can't be serious, Dad!"

"Dad, we worked so hard on this. We are so. Damn. Close. I mean, we're there! Please don't do this," Benjamin said, his voice shaking with emotion. "Mom would want us to keep it."

Kermit wore his sadness like a mantle. When he spoke, he enunciated each word slowly and clearly, giving them a palpable weight. "Your mother would want us to stay safe. And she wanted the Cure to be a choice. She would never, *ever* advocate to have it forced on someone. Choice is always what matters." He locked eyes with each of us around the table. "If the Council is going to use it as a threat, we have to act." He selected a piece of cheese from the board and chewed it as he regarded his sons thoughtfully.

Frustration and fear rolled off Seth in noxious waves, and Benjamin radiated a slow and steady anger.

Yikes. I cleared my throat, and all the men turned to me at once. Even though I was closer to their equal now than ever before, I couldn't help but feel like a field mouse facing down a, *well, a pack of wolves,* under their intense stare. Benjamin blinked, noticing my discomfort, then held my hand and gave it a gentle squeeze.

"So, yeah. Destroy which one? The Serum or the Cure?" I asked, meekly. *Maybe we can focus on a bright side here.*

"Both," Kermit replied. *Well, there goes that idea.*

Benjamin's face reddened and Seth's glare could've cut ice, but Kermit continued, ignoring his sons. "A letter from the Council in Theo's room mentioned 'injecting the weapon of our creation.' The Cure is that weapon. We cannot in good conscience allow that, boys. Since Theo and the Council were in closer communication than I was aware of, it seems the Council knows about the Serum, too. With it, they could do the same thing Theo did and become virtually unstoppable, not to mention unstable." He shook his head and sighed heavily. "It's simply not a risk we can take."

Kermit paused and looked between his sons. "If you disagree with me, if you think we can chance this...and if you think we can challenge the Council without eliminating our work and *survive,* look me in the eye and tell me so right now."

Seth shifted uncomfortably in his seat, then slammed a fist on the table before burying his head in his hands. Benjamin shook his head and looked down, but neither of the men said a word.

"Right," said Kermit. "We destroy it, then. All of it."

A sad resignation hung over the table, as if the men were having a moment of silence for the loss of their work.

"Wait." The word was out of my mouth before I knew I was speaking, and three sets of eyes studied me intently. I coughed, attempting to shake off the unease I felt, and continued. "You won't destroy it all. I mean, I'm here, right?" Total silence filled the room as they waited for me to go on. "That Serum stuff, it's in my blood now, right?"

Benjamin nodded slowly, and Kermit had a faraway look in his eyes; a half smile began to form on his face. Seth was the only one who remained motionless, considering.

"Jericho, you're a genius," Benjamin said. His eyes filled with pride.

"Are you confident you can extract it, Benny, and make more?" asked Kermit. Benjamin nodded in response, and Seth looked between the two men with widening eyes.

"You mean you can produce a new Serum using only Jericho's blood?" Seth asked incredulously. "But it was so hard to make the first time."

Benjamin shrugged. "Yeah, but before I was starting from scratch. This time I'll have a little help." His eyes held mine with a potent mixture of pride and desire that radiated out like sunshine, warming me to my core and causing my face to flush.

Kermit grunted, bringing the attention at the table back to him. "I assume you could do the same with the Cure?" Benjamin nodded, and Kermit continued. "In that case, I'll inject myself today."

A spicy-hot scent of surprise tinged with—was that anxiety?—filled the air around the table, but I wasn't sure why. Kermit had said before that he was going to test it on himself, so the news wasn't shocking. *But they acted surprised then, too, Jericho.* I decided I wasn't going to press the issue, because, after all, it wasn't about me, and the answer wouldn't make a difference to me anyway. *So, bring it back to business—*

"Why is that so surprising?" I blurted out.

The astonishment level in the room rose by several more degrees as Seth and Kermit assessed me with eyebrows raised. Benjamin cleared his throat. "Oh yeah. I should tell you guys, the Serum does everything we thought it would."

Kermit nodded excitedly. "That is most excellent. Of course, I noticed that she has our healing abilities, speed, and overall strength. It's nice to know she can sense emotions in the same way as well. Can she—"

"*She* can speak for herself," I interrupted, more hotly than I'd intended.

Kermit inclined his head slightly in my direction. "Forgive me, Jericho, it wasn't my intent to leave you out. I've just grown accustomed to talking to the boys." I nodded once, and he went on. "Can you see anything, shall we say, differently, in the garden?"

"You mean the fairies?" I asked.

Kermit beamed. "Just so. Benny my boy, you've outdone

yourself with this Serum." Benjamin smiled, obviously pleased with his father's praise. "Jericho," Kermit continued, "I'm sure Ben has told you there's one aspect that we're unsure of here."

I swallowed hard and nodded. I'd managed to forget about the Change-with-a-capital-*C* between the discovery of fairies and the drama with the Council, but the fact that I might be a werewolf loomed over me like a shadow in the full moon.

Kermit frowned. "In a perfect world, you'd simply stay with us until the next full moon, and you'd have all of us here to protect you."

"From what?" I asked, confused.

"From yourself," Kermit replied, not unkindly. I shivered and felt Benjamin's warm arm wrap around my shoulders protectively. "But," Kermit continued, "this world is far from perfect, and frankly we can't risk the Council getting their hands on you."

"What are you saying, Dad?" asked Benjamin.

"Ben, until this business with the Council is finished, you need to take the girl and get out of here. Go somewhere far away."

I locked my wide eyes with Benjamin and saw that he was as taken aback as I was. A clatter rang out across the table as Seth dropped his fork, astonished. "But, Dad—"

"No buts, Seth. Listen, I know this isn't how we do things..." Kermit trailed off as he ran his hands through his white hair, with sadness and frustration rolling off him in alternating waves. The last time he'd said those words was to Theo, his eldest son, *whom I killed*. I swallowed hard. Luckily,

I didn't have time to fully resurrect my guilt before Seth spoke again.

"Dad, you said the pack always sticks together. Loyal to the last, to the pack and to the task, right?"

Kermit opened his mouth to reply, but to my surprise Benjamin beat him to it. "Jericho *is* pack, Seth." Benjamin took my hand (now somewhat cold and clammy with nerves) in his warm palm. "I gave her the Serum...and it changed her. Even if she's not a werewolf, she's closer to us than she is to humans now, and it's because of *me*. You don't have to like it, but you need to accept it." Benjamin held his brother's gaze rather like a hawk glaring at a rabbit, and the younger man wilted visibly before looking away.

"Seth," Kermit started, "Benjamin is right, she's one of ours now." The younger man glared at Kermit, but he continued. "Besides, as long as Jericho is safe, the Serum is safe."

Across the table Seth sighed heavily, then nodded. I wasn't sure how glad I should be when it seemed like he was more interested in my blood and what it carried than in my charming personality and, well, *life*, but I'd take whatever acceptance the surly brother offered at this point. Besides, it didn't sound like I'd be staying much longer.

Once upon a time my future had felt so secure. I'd found a niche for myself in my business. I considered myself a successful entrepreneur. I had a collection of nail polish and some dead plants. I was happy with my job and my life.

Then I took a walk in the woods.

And maybe going out into the woods alone was a dumb idea. Now when I thought about the future, the road that had once seemed so firmly paved was crumbling beneath my feet. But, to my surprise, I wasn't sad about it. Underneath the wreckage of my old future was a new path for me to explore, and a new future to define. The tingling excitement and flutter in my chest made me feel like a kid staring at a beautifully wrapped gift: An adventure awaited me.

"When should we leave?" I asked, drawing the men's eyes to me.

Kermit ran a hand through his hair again, then crossed his arms as he regarded his sons. "As soon as possible. I want a good bit of distance between you two and the Council before they arrive. However, I do need Benjamin's help in administering the Cure to myself before you go."

Surprise and anxiety filled the room again, hitting me like a slap. I furrowed my eyebrows as Kermit leaned in and explained his plan.

It was pretty straightforward, as far as plans go, if you ignored all the minutiae that could go wrong. Benjamin would inject Kermit with the Cure, then he and Seth would burn the lab and all its contents (including Theo's body, a cremation of sorts) to destroy the evidence. Seth would erase hard drives beforehand, to make sure nothing was recoverable. The burning would be pinned on Theo, who flew into a furious rage after we discovered he'd killed all those people, which was true. I would stay out of the way and be ready to leave with Benjamin when it was time.

Easy-peasy, lemon-squeezy.

Except that the Council might be able to pinpoint when exactly something was burned.

"All the more reason to do it now," said Kermit.

And none of the men knew exactly what would happen once they injected Kermit with the Cure.

"It might be unstable," Benjamin said with a frown that flowed from his face into his feelings.

And according to Kermit, by werewolf law the Council had the right to require that any deceased werewolf be, er, *replaced* by its pack. At this exciting legal refresher, Benjamin shifted uneasily, avoiding my eyes. *Would the Council ask Kermit to turn me, if I wasn't already?* I raised an eyebrow in Kermit's direction. As if reading my thoughts, Kermit looked away. *Shiiit.*

All the better that Benjamin and I were planning to leave. But we would need a believable reason why Benjamin and I would split off from the pack, because Seth was right about at least one thing: Werewolf packs do *not* split up. Loyal to the last, indeed.

Okay, more like hardy-tardy, screw this lemon.

"Well," I started, "I *do* have a job. I mean, I need to go back to town and let the sheriff know that..." *That I killed your son,* I thought guiltily as I looked at Kermit. "That Katherine's killer is gone."

Kermit left his place at the table and came to stand beside me, resting a large hand on my shoulder. I fought the urge to recoil from him. Last time he'd touched my arm, it was to threaten me with a push down the stairs to keep his sons' existence a secret. This time, however, he radiated a fatherly warmth along with something I'd come to associate with Benjamin: *pride.*

"You'll let him know that it was an animal that killed her.

A beast mutated beyond identification, and it was burned in a fire at my home," he said softly.

I nodded slowly. "Okay, yes. And...I realized I needed a partner." At this, I slipped a tentative look toward Benjamin. "I was lucky to meet Benjamin, who was visiting you, and we decided to work together?" My voice raised at the end, making it a question. *Please say yes.*

At the mention of his older brother, Benjamin's eyes had grown distant and sad, but his face transformed at my question. "That's perfect, partner." He grinned broadly. He said "partner" with a gentle warmth, like someone might say, *You're beautiful.* I blushed as my heart swelled with gratitude. Even if our partnership surely had a time limit. I glanced around the room at the other men. *Loyal to the last...* This was Benjamin's pack.

The laboratory burning would be less easy, as there was no way to disguise when it had been burned. If the Council could tell the timeline didn't match the family's story, well... Kermit said with a shrug, "Seth and I will cross that bridge when we come to it. The overwhelming smoke smell should fuzz their senses enough, but the sooner we can do it, the better off we will be."

That only left Kermit and the Cure.

There was one thing that could go right: It could eliminate the virus as intended, and Kermit would no longer be beholden to the moon and its sway. He could choose to be a regular human, keeping a promise he made to his late wife and fulfilling his own life's work. And crucially, it would mean that for the first time, werewolves would be able to make that choice for themselves. Unless the Council got their hands (er, paws) on it.

Of course, there was a lot more that could go wrong, and Benjamin made sure we knew it. Kermit's body could rebel as the Cure attacked the virus in his blood, potentially causing an "extreme immune system response" that could hurt or even kill him. It could make Kermit *smell* different, to the point that the Council would be able to deduce what he'd done if they had even half a brain between them.

Or it could cause Kermit to lose all his strength, leaving him and Seth vulnerable to the Council.

Or some combination of the troubles above, because you know what? Life's not easy.

I understood the brothers' surprise and anxiety now. It filled me, too. What seemed like a simple choice before had gotten a lot more complex, not to mention dangerous. If only the Council weren't coming.

Thank God I'll be long gone by then. A wave of guilt flooded my conscience as I thought about the Greys, sitting under a dark cloud with nothing but a series of hard choices facing them. *Life's not easy.*

I sighed heavily. We moved our discussion into the living room to finalize plans, and the men's raised voices echoed off the rafters in the open room as they argued over next steps. Kermit still wanted to inject the Cure right away ("I've waited long enough for this, I am not going to wait any longer!"). Benjamin was having second thoughts about him doing it at all ("It would be different if the Council weren't coming, Dad, but they are, and things have changed."). And Seth wanted

Kermit to take the Cure, but only if Benjamin agreed to stay with them instead of leaving with me.

"Losing progress in the lab aside, the Council will be furious that we don't have a replacement for Theo, Dad," argued Seth. "It'll come to a fight, and I can't fight them by myself. If you take the Cure, then Benjamin has to stay."

The men's voices fell away as I turned them out, and I focused my attention on a singular speck of dust floating languidly in the air before me, illuminated by a sharp sunbeam that streaked its way through the room like a saber. The light fell on a framed photograph of the brothers as children, hugging a woman that had to be their mother, all love and smiles. Beth's eyes crinkled behind a pair of round glasses, which reminded me of the ones a younger Theo wore in the photograph I'd seen in the attic. Theo was a little older in this picture, and the glasses were gone, but the mop of dark hair remained.

A mop of black hair and glasses.

A chilling blast of shock shot through me as sudden recognition hit. My mouth fell open, and I grabbed the photo with shaking hands.

Oh, Jericho James, you fresh idiot.

"Uh, guys?" I started, but my voice fell on deaf ears. Or more accurately, my voice fell on a family of male ears too wrapped up in the heat of their moment to hear me.

"But why can't Benjamin and Jericho just stay here?" Seth growled, with arms clenched at his sides.

"No way." Benjamin's voice was cut through with anger. "She needs to get as far away from the Council as possible. They absolutely *cannot* get their hands on her."

Seth scoffed, but Benjamin ignored him, continuing. "It takes one look to know something is special about her. Hell, even a blind person could see it. What if they figure out it's the Serum? What if they can smell it on her? What if—"

"What if Theo had a son?" I interrupted, loudly.

The sudden silence left a ringing in my ears. Every eye was on me, and I half expected my skin to curl and smolder under the burning heat of that stare.

The room was a bomb, and I had become the match. *Defuse, defuse, defuse.*

"What did you say, Jericho?" Kermit asked in a low, almost whispery rumble.

CHAPTER 18

Once upon a time, a little boy lived at the edge of the woods in the small town of Stillbridge, Maine. He had red shoes, glasses, and a mop of unruly black hair, but he didn't have a dad. Each month he heard shrieks and growls outside of the window that faced the forest. *His* window.

But he wasn't scared.

He knew the monster stayed in the woods.

CHAPTER 19

"Let me just get this straight. You're saying this kid has never met his dad, he regularly hears strange noises outside his home, and he's a dead ringer for Theo." Kermit paused, his eyes hard and eyebrows raised. "That doesn't make him Theo's son." The sour taste of skepticism stung my senses.

I nodded emphatically. "It may sound crazy, but l know I'm right."

"Do you have any idea what these 'strange noises' sound like?" Kermit asked, crossing his arms over his chest.

Like me when the Serum brought me back to life. And "Like Theo, when he changed," I said.

"About how often does this occur? Did the boy say?"

I thought for a moment, remembering Mikey's words. "Once a month, and the last time he heard it was Wednesday, during this past full moon."

Seth and Benjamin shared a deep and meaningful look. "Where was Theo sneaking off to?" Benjamin whispered.

Kermit turned toward his sons, his blue eyes piercing like a hawk's. "Did you know something about this?" His tone was calm, but he radiated a menacing heat, pushing at us like a barely contained blaze.

Benjamin ran his hands through his hair, as he did so often when he was thinking or stressed. "Yeah. I mean, no, but we suspected something was going on. It looked like he was sneaking out. That's how Seth and I found Jericho in the woods..."

Seth picked up where his brother trailed off. "We were tracking an old trail of Theo's, but we ran into her instead. It was hopeless after that! Ben got *completely* distracted." His eyes flashed with annoyance at Benjamin, and the older man blushed. Seth sighed. "Anyway, from what I found, it looked like he could have gone toward the town. But you always tell us to settle things among ourselves, so we thought you'd want us to handle it on our own."

Seth's words were met with complete silence. Kermit's internal fire had all but disappeared, leaving behind an extra brightness in his eyes. And Benjamin smelled... *ashamed*? The slightly musty scent itched my nose, and I rubbed it, confused.

Seth looked between us and sighed again. "Jericho," he started, "I'm sorry I've been... less than friendly toward you. Ben had a feeling that something was up with Theo for a long time, and he was dead set on figuring out what it was. Until he met *you*. It's like you gave him amnesia or something. *So annoying!*" He shook his head to himself. "It felt like you waltzed into our lives and messed everything up. But it's not your fault. And you didn't mess *everything* up. So..."

"Thanks," I said with a grin in his direction. Everything

was connected, and more pieces came together in my mind, *click, click, click* into place.

"So," I continued, "this is good news, right?"

The men glanced at one another in silence until Kermit finally spoke. "A new addition to the pack is always a reason to celebrate. And the Council will demand we replenish our numbers after Theo's death. And if my boy had a boy of his own..." Kermit's voice cracked as he paused, and a mix of emotions came rolling toward us in undulating waves. *Grief, love, hope.* Waves of clashing feelings big enough to drown in.

"Why do I feel like there's a *but* coming?" I asked.

Kermit cleared his throat. "But...I need to ascertain this boy's parentage before we announce him to the Council, so I must meet him."

And you can ascertain that, how? I thought. "Oh, but you already have met!" I said. All eyes turned to me in surprise, so I continued. "You said there was a little boy waiting by the edge of the woods when you went into town to get my things. That was him, that was Mikey."

Kermit's face blanched as his eyes widened. "Of course... oh, of course. I sensed it then. The boy had Theo's scent. But I had Theo on my mind that day, so I thought I was imagining things." He paused as he shook his head. "You even told me about the noises the boy was hearing." Kermit ran his hand through his hair, suddenly looking older and more tired than before. "I'm a bigger fool than I thought."

You're also a grandfather, I thought to myself. The wet shine in Kermit's eyes told me he was thinking the same thing.

"Fool or not, we need a plan," said Benjamin.

The men sat in a pensive silence, finally broken by Kermit's heavy sigh. "Okay, this is what we're going to do."

The three of us leaned in closer as Kermit laid out next steps. It was not what any of us were expecting. *But if we weren't expecting it, maybe the Council wouldn't be, either.*

"Just to recap, we're up against at least two powerful werewolves from your, erm, *government*, and they probably want to control the rest of the packs. So, objective number one is to keep the Cure and the Serum—erm, myself, I mean—out of their reach," I said, and the men nodded, so I continued.

"They will require a replacement werewolf because of..." I trailed off as my head suddenly swam with the image of Theo's beastly body impaled on the spike in the garden. *So. Much. Blood.* I shook my head, trying to dislodge the unpleasant thought. "Well, anyway, so objective number two is Mikey. And—"

"Objective number three: Keep ourselves in the Council's good graces so they don't murder the lot of us for treason, and hope that they will continue the funding of our research. We will rebuild the lab, replicate the Serum, and test the Cure." Kermit's voice was filled with all the fervor of a Southern pastor giving a sermon on Sunday. "Objective number four is to do the latter secretly. The Cure *must* be a choice, not a punishment."

The brothers beside me nodded solemnly.

"Okay, guys, let's do this," I said, with much more confidence than I felt.

The rest of the day passed in frenetic action as we scrambled to prepare. My thoughts were a whirlwind of tasks that needed to be done, frantic worrying, and lots of what-ifs.

My mom always told me not to borrow trouble, and she encouraged me to live in the moment. However, I'm a serial overthinker, and worrying comes easily to me. *If I plan for it, then it won't go wrong!* It had always worked for me in the past. This time, with everything that had to get done, everything that had to go right, and the dire consequences if we failed, my brain was churning at ludicrous speed. As a result, my recollection of the day was spotty, to say the least.

Instead of a clear idea of what happened, I was left with a jagged timeline and a handful of memories. Even those sharp moments struggled to find their place in the bigger picture. Instead they lay jumbled together in my mind, each memory haphazardly piling over another like a stack of old photographs.

Snap.

Brilliant, cerulean liquid poured onto the white floor of the lab, sitting in stark contrast with the pale tiles. It pooled like bright-blue blood. In another setting, it could have been artwork. The tinkling sounds of broken glass echoed in my head like Christmas bells as the men shattered every last syringe that contained the Serum. The only proof of its existence was me.

Snap.

The oppressive smell of gasoline swamped my senses as Seth thoroughly doused the laboratory. We'd all gathered to watch, and to say goodbye to the lab and the men's work. And to Theo, whose body lay on the white tile beside splashes of blue Serum. The acrid taste of bile rose in my throat when I thought about the monster I'd killed. *I killed someone.* Did that make me a monster, too? *Can monsters be heroes?*

Snap.

"This doesn't feel right, Dad," started Seth. "Just burning him, I mean."

In the living room, Kermit had just finished explaining his plan, and the brothers shifted uneasily.

"I sometimes forget you haven't seen everything I have." Kermit's voice was low and grumbly as he continued. "We burn our dead, we always have. Before medical advancements could ascertain death, it was the only sure way to know a werewolf was really gone. In the old days... Well, you know they couldn't always tell if someone had truly passed. Have you heard of the Bell System? Folks were sometimes buried with a string attached to their hands, and that string led to a bell. They could ring it if they were still alive." He paused for effect before continuing.

"But anyhow, nobody comes back from cremation. We continue cremating now for tradition, and to hide any evidence—yes, there are signs in the body, if you know where to look." This last part Kermit directed at me when my eyebrows rose in surprise. "It was started by the Vikings, with their funeral pyres, and passed down from there."

"The Vikings?" I asked, lost as my brain tried to comprehend what Kermit was implying.

"Of course. Where do you think the Berserkers came from?" Kermit replied.

"They were... *werewolves*? The Vikings?"

Benjamin's words echoed in my mind: *"Every culture has a werewolf story."*

Snap.

A perfect silence filled the hall as Kermit tossed a lit match into the lab. The sudden percussive *whomp* of ignition and animal-like roaring of the fire filled the soundless vacuum. The rush of noise pounded my eardrums painfully as the laboratory and its contents exploded in flame. Kermit's silent sorrow combined with his sons' as he overrode the sprinkler system in the lab, resigned to letting it burn.

Snap.

The harsh sting of smoke filled the corridor outside the lab, where a heavy-duty fan was fully engaged in blowing it outside. The four of us trudged back up the stairs to the living room with heavy footsteps, as if leaving a funeral. In a way, we were. *At least we don't have to set up a Bell System.*

Snap.

Night had fallen, gently tucking us into her dark embrace. Benjamin's lips pressed softly against mine, then harder. The adrenaline of the day hadn't yet worn off, and my heightened pulse wearily kicked back into gear as his kisses became more insistent, kindling my desire and need despite my fatigue. His lips heated me more than the fire in the lab ever could, down to my very core, until it felt like I was a flame made living.

Snap.

"Jericho, wake up."

CHAPTER 20

"Wake up," Benjamin's voice rumbled gently in my ear.

No thanks, I tried to say from somewhere inside the cocoon of blankets and Benjamin's arms, but all that came out was an unintelligible mumble accompanied by a deep yawn. A blast of cool air succeeded where Benjamin's prompting hadn't, as Benjamin rolled out of bed and yanked away my blanket-nest.

It was still a soft dark outside the window, as if sunrise was but a distant thought in the mind of the sky. Which meant it was earlier than I wanted to be awake. "Ugh, what time is it?" I groaned.

"Time to get going. We need to be as far away as possible when the Council gets here."

I nodded and followed Benjamin out of bed. So much had happened yesterday, it felt like the day had been a lifetime long. Kermit had suggested that we stay one last night and leave first thing today. He planned to accompany us to town to talk to Mikey together, and to corroborate the events in the story that I'd tell Sheriff Jackson. *Katherine was killed by a beast, but it was destroyed in a fire...*

It was a good thing we had a story of simple truths to tell the police, because the reality was just too... *unreal*. I still couldn't believe the sheer magnitude of the monster that Theo had become, or the fact that the men had willingly destroyed their life's work in the lab, or that Kermit had ultimately declined to take the Cure and instead let it all burn. Benjamin promised detailed notes for Seth and Kermit to work from later. I swallowed nervously. "It's the last thing the Council would expect," he'd said. It's certainly the last thing I expected.

I take that back, Mikey being werewolf-Theo's son was the last thing I expected. Actually, werewolves in general—you know, just existing—took the cake.

No, wait, *I* was the last thing I expected.

I got ready in the bathroom, still unaccustomed to the face that looked back at me in the mirror. My silver-white hair had a lustrous shine that contrasted sharply with my black tank top, making it appear even brighter. The gold eyes that stared out of the mirror also glowed like twin suns. I blinked. *Yikes.*

I stepped out to Benjamin's raised eyebrows. "We need to do something about, um—" he started, gesturing to *all of me*.

"Yeah, I know. Do you have a hat or something?"

Benjamin produced a worn, black baseball cap with a Boston Bruins logo on it, and I pulled my hair through the back in a hasty ponytail. "Better?" I asked.

"Hold on, use these, too." He grabbed a pair of aviator sunglasses from the dresser and handed them to me.

I put them on with my best Audrey Hepburn impression.

"How do I look?" The too-large sunglasses succeed in covering about half of my face, hiding my newly flawless skin and shining eyes.

"Like a movie star who's trying and failing to hide her beautiful self."

I blushed under the sunglasses as Benjamin turned and began to search his closet. "Last but not least," he said. He pulled something blue off a hanger and tossed it in my direction.

I caught it easily and unfolded the bundle, reading the words as I held it up. "Johns Hopkins University—did you go there, Benjamin?" He nodded. "That's, like, a really, really good school."

He shrugged. "Yeah, it is. My dad had some high expectations for our medical future."

"Well, clearly it worked," I responded, impressed.

"Anyway, this shade of blue," he said, "should help tone down your, um, self."

I removed the hat and sunglasses, then pulled the oversize hoodie over my head, checking my reflection in the sunglasses' lenses. My eyes didn't seem to blaze as much when they reflected the cool periwinkle of the sweater, and my hair didn't immediately stand out like it did against my black ensemble.

Benjamin regarded me with an eyebrow raised. "It's like trying to disguise a Monet by changing the frame, but it's the best we can do for now. Hopefully the folks in town won't notice anything too different about you.

"Aside from my lack of fashion sense," I added.

"Hey," he said with a face of mock pain, "the Blue Jays and Bruins are always in style."

We rendezvoused with Kermit and said our goodbyes to Seth, then stepped out into the cool fall morning.

Our feet crunched on the dead leaves that littered the path, but the woods were far from silent. Kermit went over our plan and its contingencies as we walked, pausing only to point out any animal or plant life of interest along the way. If I didn't know any better, we could have been taking a guided nature tour.

But I did know better.

A fluttery butterflies-in-my-stomach sensation (*fairies in my stomach* somehow sounded more macabre) began to build as he sprinkled his tour-guide spiel with critical Council-related information. My poor frayed nerves were getting whiplash as a result.

"See that yellow? That's an ash tree. The leaves will keep turning until they're a dark, almost purple-red color as winter approaches. And the Council should arrive the day after tomorrow if I'm estimating their travel correctly."

"They will certainly invoke the Replacement Law with Theo's death—there's a gray squirrel—but we'll head them off there by announcing Mikey. That will satisfy those old dogs."

A small part of my brain recognized that I should be amused by a squirrel distracting a werewolf, but I was too full of nervous energy to acknowledge it.

THE MIDNIGHT PACK

"I'll tell them that every vial of the Cure and the Serum in my possession was destroyed in the fire. Oh, see that over there? That's a red maple. Anyhow, that's the God's honest truth. They'll sense that, and they won't have a problem with it." *What if they do? What if they know better? What if they sniff out our plan? What if, what if—*

A heavy hand clapped me on the shoulder and shook me from my thoughts. We'd stopped moving. *When did that happen?*

I looked from my feet, in now-worse-for-wear black running shoes, to the feet opposite mine, wearing sturdy brown hiking boots. My eyes traveled up the steel-gray pants, taking in the pale-blue button-up flannel shirt, partially covered by an open black leather jacket. Kermit peered down at me through tired blue eyes, and I was suddenly swamped with his sympathy and determination. He positively *reeked* of it. It wasn't an unpleasant combination, per se, but the strength and dissonance of it all made me crinkle my nose.

"Jericho James. You've accomplished more in one week than some people do in a lifetime. You solved a murder, discovered that werewolves live among you, defeated a powerful creature, and became a—" Kermit paused here, and the silence said what he wouldn't: *potential werewolf.* "A supernatural being yourself." *Nice recovery.*

Kermit cleared his throat. "And you worked out that Theo had a son. That I have a *grandson*. That is nothing short of miraculous to me."

I shrugged. When he put it that way, I guess it did sound impressive. *All in a week's work, guys.* "Why are you telling me this?"

"It's clear that you're worried six ways from Sunday. Worrying means suffering, Jericho. What's going to happen will happen whether you worry about it or not. We'll face it when it does. Among the four of us, we can figure things out. Frankly, I am not worried, precisely because we *do* have one another in this scenario, and you're a force to be reckoned with."

Benjamin nodded appreciatively, and I blushed. That was high praise, especially coming from Kermit. I told him so, and he laughed.

"It's only God's honest truth," Kermit said. "Feeling better?"

I closed my eyes for a moment and felt the warm fall sun on my shoulders, which paled in comparison with the heat of Benjamin's hand still in mine. *We do have one another.* I took a deep breath before opening my eyes again. To my surprise, I did feel calmer. "Yeah, actually," I said.

Kermit nodded. "Good. Let's press on."

Our walk was silent after that, with Kermit in the lead and Benjamin and me right behind him, still holding hands. For someone who historically didn't get a lot of physical contact (I'm not counting snake wrestling), I relished it. The simple steadiness of Benjamin's hand around mine, his warm palm in the cool fall air, and even the rhythmic sway of our arms as we walked together all made me feel at peace. Even as we were marching out of our bubble in the woods and toward the real world, with the Werewolf Council to evade.

We stopped only for lunch, which consisted of a collection of sandwiches and granola that Kermit had thoughtfully wrapped in his backpack. We carefully packed away all our trash before continuing.

Too shortly after that, we reached the place I'd seen so many times in my dreams. By this point l knew every nook and cranny by heart. The bush-lined clearing where Katherine had been murdered waited for us in the shadows, like an all-too-familiar stranger. My feet stopped moving as if disconnected from the rest of my body, and it dawned on me that I'd been subconsciously dreading our arrival here. Benjamin took another step before stopping at the tug of my hand when I didn't follow.

"C'mon, Jericho, the quicker you walk through, the quicker it'll be behind us."

I sighed, because of course he was right.

I stepped into the clearing.

And nothing happened.

I exhaled, not realizing I'd been holding my breath. I looked at the spot on the ground where Katherine had been killed, then turned my gaze upward to where she had disappeared in a collection of shining lights in my dream. *Was it only a dream?*

Kermit marched through the center of the clearing, entirely unperturbed.

"It's bad luck to stand where the dead have lain," I muttered under my breath. I forgot, of course, that werewolves have perfect hearing.

"Nonsense," said Kermit. "Besides, this earth of ours is so old, the dead have likely lain just about anywhere you walk."

Well, damn.

At a gentle tug on my hand from Benjamin, I followed the men through and out of the clearing, and onto the path toward town. I turned around for one last look at the clearing and waved goodbye. Katherine had vanished in a blaze of light, but I wanted to show her I was thinking about her, just in case.

As my arm dropped back to my side, a fall breeze swept across the back of my neck like a whisper. Goose bumps immediately prickled up the length of my arms as the breeze washed its way through the forest, mimicking the sound of ocean waves as the sea of trees bobbed and swayed. *Just the wind.* The wind picked up and the trees rocked together in time with the rhythm of nature. The sound of the waves intensified until they beat upon my mind. If I closed my eyes and simply listened, I might have thought we were at a beach. *A beach that smells like pine needles and... someone's fear? Wait, what?*

"Hey, guys? I think there's someone up ahead," I said, pointing down the path toward town. As if on cue the wind stopped, and the flapping sound of tennis shoes hitting the dirt beat against the new silence.

There *was* someone. Running straight toward us.

My muscles tensed as my brain prepared for the worst and the men straightened their backs. My attention was divided between mentally tracking the mystery runner and monitoring the men's reactions to it. They smelled alert and aware but, to my surprise, not alarmed. I strained my new senses, trying to visualize the runner. When I glanced at the men, they both had their eyes closed and brows furrowed. I realized they were doing the same.

"Could it somehow be the Council?" I asked.

Kermit immediately shook his head. "No. Not the Council. This is only one person, and it's somebody—"

"Young," Benjamin finished for him.

Before I could wonder why a young person was running scared through the woods, there was a surprised yelp as a short blur of black hair and red sneakers dashed around the corner and slammed directly into Kermit.

Mikey tumbled backward, landing on the ground with a thud. His pale face was tear-streaked and flushed. His little eyes widened as he took in the men that he'd crashed into. The strong stench of fear swelled—a sickly, bitter smell, reminiscent of vomit.

I shook off the urge to dry-heave and stepped out from behind the men. "Mikey, are you okay?" I asked.

His brown eyes softened when they took me in, and he promptly burst into tears. I hesitated awkwardly as Benjamin and Kermit shot me a look of combined alarm and expectation. I shook my head at them and knelt beside Mikey.

"Hey, buddy," I started. Mikey wrapped his arms around me in a hug, burying his face in my shoulder, where he sobbed. I continued kneeling, but kept my hands awkwardly at my sides, unsure of what to do.

I'd never had anyone cry on me before. And I didn't really have any experience with kids, aside from being one myself long, long ago. I knew what to do with upset snakes, but... *This is why you struggle keeping friends, Jericho.* Kermit coughed behind me, and when I looked up at him he made a hugging motion with his arms.

I returned Mikey's hug, patting him on the back as the boy tightened his grip.

"Mikey, what happened?" I asked gently.

He pulled his face away from my sweater and looked at me with wet eyes and a runny nose. He took a deep shuddering breath in, and Benjamin nudged something small and white in my direction. I realized it was his handkerchief, and I slowly wiped Mikey's tears as the boy exhaled.

"My mom is dead." His voice cracked as he spoke, and tears threatened in the corners of his eyes once more.

"Oh no." I hugged him again and opened my mouth to say something reassuring.

"The monster killed her," he said in a rush. *That's not possible.* I shut my mouth with an audible click as my teeth trapped my words. I looked up into Benjamin's equally wide eyes.

"Tell me everything." I hadn't noticed Kermit kneeling beside us, and I jumped at the sound of his voice.

Mikey swallowed hard and spoke in a small, wavering voice. "I called the sheriff with Mom's cell phone when I found her. And he let me sleep over at his house last night, but he said I have to go live with a foster family now. That means with *strangers*! But I just want Mom. So I ran away to find you, Jericho." He looked at me hopefully. "I thought maybe you could help me?"

I patted his back. "You found me, and we'll figure everything out. But first can you tell us what exactly happened?"

He nodded and scuffed the dirt path with his red shoe. "I walked home from school yesterday, like I always do. And she was at work, like normal. But then, she didn't come home."

THE MIDNIGHT PACK

His voice broke, and I noticed Mikey's breath was beginning to shudder. I put my arm around him again and passed him the handkerchief. He clutched it in one grubby little hand like a lifeline, haphazardly wiping his nose before he continued. "We don't have a house phone, so I couldn't call her, but I got hungry, so I knew it was dinnertime. And she works a lot, but she never misses dinner. *Never.* It was mac-and-cheese night, so I tried to get out the things I knew she would need, you know, to help her."

Tears welled up in Mikey's eyes, and my throat felt strangely tight as he continued. "I climbed on the counter and reached for a macaroni box in the cupboard, but it was too high. I stretched my fingers as far as they could go and ended up knocking down all of the boxes."

I pictured Mikey reaching for a box of macaroni and cheese, hopeful to see his mom soon and trying to help her out, not knowing she wasn't coming home again. Ever. My arm tightened around his back protectively.

"That's when I heard the noise."

Kermit and Benjamin exchanged a meaningful look beside me.

"What noise, buddy?" I asked.

"It was like a growl and a thud, but I thought I imagined it because it happened at the same time as the boxes fell." He paused and hugged his legs into his body, burying his face in his knees. "If I'd gone out right away to look for her, maybe it would have been different." His sad voice was small and muffled as he spoke to the ground, but we heard him clearly.

"No, you can't think like that, Mikey. The only thing that

would have been different is that you could have gotten hurt, too. That is not what your mom would have wanted," Kermit said gently.

Mikey lifted his head and peered at Kermit over his knees. A spark of relief flared from the boy but was quickly overwhelmed by sadness as he put his head back down. The wind blew through the trees again, and a bevy of yellow leaves fell from their branches like golden rain, scattering around us. It was too pretty a place for such dark news.

I put my hand on Mikey's back. "What happened next, bud?"

He moved his shoulders in what might have been a shrug if he weren't still hugging his knees to himself. "Nothing. I filled a pot with water on the stove and set the table. My mom doesn't let me use the burners on the stove by myself, so I couldn't heat it up. I did everything I could do, and she still wasn't home, so I went to look outside."

I could hear Mikey's heart pounding hard and fast, and I steeled myself for what I knew must be coming next. "I opened the front door, and I saw...a hand."

He looked up at me, eyes wide as if he was taking in the grisly scene again. He continued in a rush. "Just...a hand! Then I looked past the hand, and there was the rest of Mom's body." The tears that had teased the corners of Mikey's eyes fell freely. Fat droplets rolled down his face and dripped off his chin. He buried his face again, rocking back and forth. "Something pulled her apart, Jericho. She's supposed to be together. But she was in pieces."

Mikey's cries rocked his body. He looked smaller than

before as he lay curled in a ball on the forest floor, surrounded by falling leaves and despair. I hugged the boy again and my heart ached as his sadness entwined with mine. *But how could this be? Theo was already dead...* I noticed that the men smelled alarmed. I looked up at them, my eyebrows furrowed.

Concern etched Kermit's face, but it was Benjamin who spoke. "Mikey, I'm sorry. I know how hard this is." Mikey lifted his head briefly to give him an accusatory look that said, *How could you possibly know?* Benjamin continued. "My mom died, too."

Mikey raised his eyebrows and wiped his face with the handkerchief. "Was it the monster?"

"It was, actually, though we didn't realize it until recently," Benjamin replied.

Mikey gazed at Benjamin with his eyebrows furrowed in thought. Then he turned to me. "I thought you were going to kill it, Jericho," Mikey said. The accusation in his voice hit me like a slap to my face.

"That's just it, Mikey, I did kill it. Two days ago," I said.

"But my mom died last night..." Confusion filled Mikey's voice as his face softened.

"There's another one," said Kermit.

"Shit," I whispered.

"Shit," Mikey said in agreement. I still wasn't sure what the rules were for kids and curse words, but I figured if your mom had just died and a monster was on the loose, we all get a pass.

"So... I should probably mention there were some vials of the Serum missing," Benjamin started. If this were a movie, this is the part where a loud record-scratch would stop the background music as we all gaped at Benjamin.

"What." Kermit managed to make it an accusation, rather than a question.

Benjamin turned his face aside, ashamed. "I just assumed Theo took them all."

Kermit stood up, and Benjamin straightened with his father. Kermit gave Benjamin a frigid stare. To his credit, Benjamin returned it evenly. He crossed his arms but didn't look away. The two men were matched in height and stood eye-to-eye. Kermit raised an eyebrow, silently demanding an explanation from his son. Mikey kept his head down and leaned into me, as if shielding himself from the iciness that emanated from the pair.

"That was a dangerous assumption. You should have told me," Kermit finally said.

Benjamin sighed heavily and shook his head. "There wasn't time, Dad. I'm telling you now."

"How many were missing?" Kermit's tone was harsh when he spoke.

"Um, four. Theo smashed a full one before the fight at the house. So there were three he could have taken."

Father and son glared at each other for another tense moment until Kermit sighed, too. "Or one we know he did take, and two he could have shared."

"And exactly two Council members are coming?" I asked in a whisper.

"These beasts are unstable, they're dangerous, and they need to be destroyed," Kermit said, ignoring my question. He looked through the trees, as if he was focused on something beyond them. I suspected he was imagining the creature that had been his eldest son. I didn't want to imagine anything worse than that. My nightmares were inventive enough already, thank-you-very-much.

"We'll figure this out," Kermit finally said. He put a hand on Benjamin's back. "I'm sorry, Benny, it's just been a lot."

Kermit wasn't talking to me, but I nodded in agreement. *Understatement of the year.*

Mikey sniffled, drawing our attention back to him. "But what does all that even mean? Can you help me?"

"Of course we can, buddy," I said. "Right, guys?"

The men quickly voiced their agreement, and Kermit returned to Mikey's side. The comforting scent radiating from Kermit also came from Benjamin, and from myself: protection.

"Mikey, you remind me of my eldest son," said Kermit. Mikey gazed up at the older man, widening his tear-brightened eyes. "It's true," continued Kermit. "And we *will* figure out your housing situation. In fact, I..." Kermit trailed off, but I was pretty sure I knew what he was going to say next. I silently willed him not to. Yet. It didn't seem like the time or place to drop that much news on Mikey. Kermit must have picked up on my thoughts, or simply came to the same conclusion on his own. "Well, you won't go to live at a random stranger's house, at any rate. This I can promise you," he continued.

Mikey nodded solemnly. "Thank you," he said.

Kermit hoisted both Mikey and me up from the forest

floor. My legs were cramped from maintaining my crouched position with Mikey, and I shook out the tingles as Kermit spoke.

"We need to track whomever Theo gave that Serum to. Likely it's the Council. At least one member must have arrived early."

"But how will you track them?" I asked. The task seemed rather daunting, considering we didn't know exactly who we were looking for, how many there were, or where they might be.

"Seth," said Benjamin simply.

I raised my eyebrow at him. Seth hadn't impressed me all that much during our time together, but Kermit was already nodding.

"Yes, if anyone can do it, it's Seth," he agreed. "I've never seen a tracker as good as him. I'll wager that since he now knows what to look for, Seth would be able to detect the Serum in a bloodstream," Kermit said. "I'll head back to the house to get him—no *buts*, Ben. I'll take the fast way." Benjamin had opened his mouth to argue with his father but shut it at Kermit's quick rebuttal.

I suspected that "the fast way" meant the furry, four-legged way. Which meant we needed to get moving with Mikey in the other direction.

"In that case, the three of us will continue on toward town to prepare," I said. *Prepare how?* my brain asked. I didn't have an answer yet.

"I'll meet you back in the town, at Mikey's house," said Kermit. Benjamin nodded. "Watch out for each other and stay safe, all right?" He hugged his son, then, to my surprise, put his arms around me and Mikey as well. "See you soon," he said. He turned around and began walking briskly back the way we came. I knew that as soon as we were out of sight he'd be running as a wolf.

I turned to find Benjamin and Mikey staring at each other. "Oh," I started, "Benjamin, this is my buddy Mikey. Mikey, this is my new, uh..." I paused. We'd never discussed this part. The attraction was there, of course. But we hadn't put a label on it. And I didn't necessarily want to. Was he my boyfriend? That word alone didn't seem to encapsulate all we'd been through together.

"I'm her new partner," Benjamin said. *My partner, exactly. I like the sound of that.* "In her private investigator business." *Oh.* "And, um, in other things." *Yesss.*

"Um...okay," said Mikey, scuffing his shoe along the packed dirt. "Should we go back now?"

I rolled up my sweater sleeves and nodded. "Yup, we need to get back as quickly as we can, and prep to find whoever killed your mom."

"Good," said Mikey, darkly. He picked up his pace to walk beside me. "What can I do?"

"You have the very important job of showing me and Benjamin around the town," I replied, gingerly stepping over a root in the path.

The boy's eyebrows furrowed as his face scrunched into a frown. "No, I mean, what can I do to find the bad guys?"

"You can stay hidden somewhere safe," I said.

"No!" The power behind Mikey's voice startled me, and I

felt Benjamin's surprise from behind us. "I want to get them, Jericho. They *killed* my mom."

I could sense the tears threatening again, so I stopped walking and put my hand on Mikey's shoulder. "I know. And you saw firsthand what they're capable of. And you're very, *very* brave. But your mom would never, *ever* forgive me if I put you in danger. She would want you to stay safe. You know that she would."

Mikey wiped his nose with his sleeve and nodded reluctantly. We started walking again and he stared glumly at his feet as we continued along the path. "So what do we need first?" Mikey looked up at me as he asked.

I thought about the ways to kill a werewolf from the book I'd read, but Benjamin answered instead as he walked along behind us. "We could use something very sharp, like an axe." *Decapitation.*

Mikey nodded, and the path widened, so Benjamin stepped up to walk in line with us. "Or something very sharp but also very pokey, like a machete," he continued. *Complete cardiectomy.* "Or even better, but probably not feasible, silver bullets."

Do they even make silver bullets anymore? It wasn't like we could just go down to the nearest blacksmith with a bar of silver. Or could we? *Do blacksmiths work with silver? Do blacksmiths even exist anymore?* Oh, the irony of wondering if blacksmiths existed while knowing for a fact that *werewolves* did. Another thought occurred to me.

"Does it have to be silver bullets? Can it be a silver, I don't know, sword or something? As long as it cuts deep enough?" I asked.

"Yup," Benjamin answered quickly. "It just needs to penetrate the heart or infiltrate the bloodstream, and a bullet is the easiest way to do that."

I thought about the silver-and-abalone-handled knife, and how I'd briefly considered jamming it down Theo's throat. *The worst that would have done is cause indigestion, probably.* I shuddered. He would have been digesting me after that. I tried to empty my mind before the next image could make its way into my head, of Theo impaled in the garden. *So much blood.* Mikey's voice snapped me back to the present.

"You guys are acting like this is a vampire."

Benjamin scoffed. "There are no such things as vampires."

"Fine then," replied Mikey. "A werewolf."

My heart skipped in a moment of panicked silence, and I burst out in nervous laughter. "Werewolf? We didn't say anything like that," I said as nonchalantly as possible.

Benjamin coughed but spoke in a cool and even tone. "What makes you say that?"

Mikey looked up at him, his small face fully serious. "I'm a kid, I'm not stupid. Of course I know about werewolves."

Benjamin glanced my way and shrugged, but I shook my head. *He's just a kid; he doesn't need to know the truth yet. Even if it is in his blood...*

"Well," I started, "some of this stuff would just be good to have, for safety."

"For safety," Benjamin echoed.

Mikey didn't respond after that, so I chanced a glance at him. He stared at his feet as we walked, kicking the occasional pebble or dirt clod. Benjamin shot me another questioning look, and I shrugged. We continued down the path, and I began to recognize places I'd passed by before, in my previous lifetime a week ago.

I noticed a particular log hanging halfway into the path that I remembered seeing near the beginning of my hike from the town. "Hey guys, I think we're only two miles away," I said. "Mikey, once we hit town, will you be able to lead us to the nearest hardware store?"

I realized that at some point in my life I had stopped paying attention to directions, or even where things were, because my phone did it all for me. The same phone that was now long gone, likely lying broken and buried somewhere under the detritus of the forest around us. I was a little disturbed to find how helpless I felt without it. *Note to self: Become sufficient without your phone. Ha, ha. Yeah, right.*

Mikey still hadn't answered me, so I tapped him gently on the shoulder. "Mikey?"

"That would explain it," he said.

"What?" Benjamin and I asked in unison.

Mikey looked up at us as if he'd been deep in thought and was startled to see we were still with him. "That would explain the noises I've been hearing. I'd been thinking Tote-Road Shagamaw, but now I know. The monster outside my window must be a werewolf." He said it matter-of-factly, like you might say, *I like pizza*, or *It's hot today*.

The group came to a halt, mostly because my feet had stopped moving in shock when Mikey correctly and calmly guessed the mystery creature. I coughed and told the guys that we needed to keep moving. We started again, with Mikey looking back and forth between Benjamin and me as if trying to discern the truth from our faces.

I was busy running through scenarios in my mind: What if we told Mikey the truth? What if we didn't? Did he still believe in Santa Claus? How is it that werewolves are real but Santa is not? That didn't seem very fair.

I had just about decided that we could tell Mikey the truth, at least most of it, when Benjamin spoke. "Well, *if* it was a werewolf, it would be dangerous. Very dangerous. And we would need to take precautions."

Mikey perked up so much at this, I could almost see him standing a little straighter as we walked. "What kind of precautions?"

"First, if it was a werewolf, we wouldn't tell anyone about it, because—"

"Because people would call us crazy?" Mikey interrupted.

"Yeah," said Benjamin with a knowing look, "and they definitely wouldn't believe us. So we're just going to keep this one between us, okay?" Mikey nodded earnestly, and Benjamin continued. "Next, if it was a werewolf, we would need both fighters and lookouts. Jericho and I are the fighters, but we don't have a lookout yet."

"Oh! I could be the lookout!" Mikey said excitedly.

"I don't know," Benjamin started. "It's a very important job. Do you think you're up for it?"

Mikey nodded. "Yes, yes, I am! Just tell me what to do."

I was thankful for Benjamin's distraction for Mikey. *At least this will keep his mind off his mom.* I was also glad the two seemed to be getting along so well. *Benjamin is surprisingly good with kids.* My thoughts occupied, I almost didn't notice when the trail beneath our feet became smoother. We abruptly left the shade of the trees and stepped onto a path near the school playground.

Last time I'd been here, the playground was full of laughing children. Now it was empty. *Everyone must be staying inside, with a murderer on the loose.* One swing moved eerily despite the lack of wind, creaking as it rocked. *That's not creepy at all.* I shivered.

"First thing's first, let's find a hardware store," said Benjamin.

CHAPTER 21

We couldn't have asked for a better guide than Mikey. He never once complained about being tired, even after he'd trekked through the woods and led us to the bed-and-breakfast on foot. After dropping off our packs at the B&B (where, to my immense amusement, Benjamin gave Cute Christopher several threatening glares), we piled into my VW Bug (thank goodness I had my keys!). From there Mikey directed us to the hardware store. It was housed in another old-timey whitewashed wood building, and I suspected it was the most adorable big-name hardware store I'd ever been in.

We could have asked for more luck in our shopping, however. The store had run out of axes (who runs out of axes?) and didn't carry machetes. Or anything silver that we could melt down for bullets (we hadn't really expected it to, and we didn't have a way to make bullets anyway, but if we had melted silver, we could at least dip *something* in it, like a machete or an axe, which the store didn't have). The clerk suggested we check out the jewelry store on Main Street instead, so we did.

But we struck out there as well when we learned that the silver that jewelry stores carry isn't 100 percent pure.

"Why don't you check with the Maine Blacksmith's Guild?" asked the jewelry store associate, a kindly looking older woman with short, graying hair. She wore a big smile and a gold-lined name tag that said CAROL.

"Excuse me?" I asked.

"Oh, well, it's just that I overheard you just now, talking about melting down the silver? And I thought, why not check with the Blacksmith's Guild?" she twittered eagerly.

Benjamin and I exchanged a look. "There's actually a Blacksmith's Guild?" The surprise was clear in my voice, and Carol laughed.

"Oh yes, of course, dear. My husband just joined himself! Something to keep him active in his retirement, you know? Life's too short not to try new things."

The blank looks on Mikey's and Benjamin's faces must have implied *No, we didn't know*, because she laughed again. "Well, why don't I just call him for you and ask?"

We nodded appreciatively, but Carol was already on her way to the counter, where she picked up her cell phone. She held her hand over the receiver, covering it as it rang, and asked, "What did you say you wanted to make again? Maybe dip a rose in it, to make an everlasting token of affection for a special someone?" She winked at Benjamin as she tilted her head in my direction.

"Um," he stammered. He was saved from replying when Carol's husband answered the phone.

"Gary, honey, I have a young couple and their son in the

store, asking about melting down silver to dip a rose into?" Carol said, then she paused, frowning.

"I'm telling you about it because you're in the Blacksmith's Guild." Another pause, then, "No, of course I didn't know that. How would I know blacksmiths don't work with silver?" Carol put one hand on her hip, listening intently to the phone.

"It's in the name? Well, of course I know that silver isn't black," she continued.

I sighed. I knew it had been too good to be true. Mikey's shoulders slumped, and I patted his back.

Carol again listened intently to the phone, and her posture relaxed as she smiled. "Oh, honey, you always have good ideas, don't you? I'll let them know. See you tonight. Kisses!" She hit a button on her cell phone and put it back on the counter.

"Gary said he doesn't work with silver, but he thinks he knows where you can find some pure silver to melt down!"

"Oh, that's great," I said halfheartedly. I fully expected to hear that a block of silver was readily available somewhere hours away. I glanced at the clock on the wall. We had about an hour before the sun set. About an hour before we were going to rendezvous with Kermit and Seth. About an hour before we prepared our offensive, since the men were confident that the Serum-enhanced Council member(s) wouldn't Change until nightfall, and equally confident that if we didn't find them tonight, they would kill again...

"Yes, well, he said the sports shop here in town had a handful of silver bullets last time he was there!"

Silver-fucking-bullets. Carol continued talking, but my brain had stopped listening. *No way.* I looked wide-eyed over at Benjamin and Mikey, both of whom were frozen in place with twin looks of surprise on their faces. *Good, I didn't hallucinate hearing that.*

"...there for a while, I guess, because who wants an ornamental bullet? That's what I want to know? I mean for how much they cost! Nobody in their right mind would use them to shoot with."

"Mikey, do you know where that is?" Benjamin whispered, as Carol continued talking. The boy nodded. I made a circular motion with my arm and pointed to the door. *Let's go!*

"...so happy to hear that it'll be used for something nice, you know? Melting down a bullet for something lovely, what a great story. I can't wait to tell my knitting group!"

Oh, if the knitting group only knew.

"Will you come back in later, to show me what you've done with it?" she asked, hopefully.

I plastered a smile on my face. "Oh, that would be fun. Thanks so much, Carol! Thank Gary for us, too! Bye!"

The three of us rushed out the door as Carol waved happily from the store window.

The sun was beginning its lofty descent when we pulled into the parking lot at the sporting goods store, where we were the only car in the lot with fifteen minutes before closing time. My hands were shaking when I released the steering wheel, and I realized I was more nervous now than I had been facing

Theo. *What if this is a dead end, too?* We'd exhausted all our time and options.

"Well, this is it," said Benjamin.

Mikey opened the back door and stepped into the parking lot. "What are you waiting for, guys?"

The ammo case was easy to find. And miraculously, there shining on a shelf in the center of the case sat precisely three silver bullets. They gleamed in the fluorescent lights of the store, nestled in a small box lined with black velvet. Not only that, but I could tell from where I was standing that they were .45-caliber, the same as my gun.

We had to tell the pimply-faced clerk twice that we wanted to buy them. His shock was palpable as he explained that the bullets had been in the inventory since the store opened. When he brought the velvet-lined box down for us, I could understand why. The price for the three bullets was over half of what I'd paid for my gun. While I was still working out the mental math, Benjamin pulled out his credit card to make the purchase.

"Thanks," I said to him as we left the store.

He laughed. "Don't thank me, that was our business card. The Council is footing the bill for these. I guess if all goes according to plan, we'll be delivering them personally."

I laughed at that as well. A long, slightly maniacal laugh. The kind you have when your subconscious knows it might be the last laugh you'll have in a while, because you're about to do something very dangerous.

I hope you never find out what I mean, but if you do, enjoy the moment.

The soft light of fall's early dusk had begun to settle on us in the car, so I finally took off Benjamin's aviator sunglasses and hat as we got in. I watched Mikey fasten his seat belt in the rearview mirror but looked away quickly when his eyes met mine in the reflection. *Maybe he hasn't noticed anything different?* His mouth fell open, forming a small O. *He's noticed.*

"Uh, Jericho?" he asked. "What's wrong with your eyes?"

"What do you mean?"

"They're glowing," he said flatly.

"Oh, that," I said. "Uh—"

"Jericho got hurt, in the woods," Benjamin started. "I gave her a medicine that helped, but that was a side effect."

Mikey thought about this in silence for a moment, then shrugged. "Well, that's okay, then. You shouldn't hide it, though, Jericho. It looks cool."

I looked at him again in the rearview mirror and smiled. "Thanks, Mikey."

We'd agreed to meet with Kermit and Seth at Mikey's house, because that's where the scent of the attacker would be strongest. The idea was that Seth would pick up the scent of the Serum, then we would track the mutants. We'd decided on nighttime because Seth could track best after he Changed, and it was easier for him after dark. With the police involvement after the attack, night was also a better time to, er, *dispense vigilante justice* unnoticed.

Kermit also wondered if we'd need to track them at all, or if the combined scent of our group would be enough to draw the Serum mutants out. Old Jericho would have shuddered at the thought. Even the Jericho of this morning would have had second thoughts about the whole thing. But now I was feeling pretty good about it all. Finding the silver bullets seemed like a sign that things were going in the right direction, and it gave me hope. Benjamin rested his hand on my leg as we drove, and I smiled at his touch.

If you ever find a glimmer of hope in a hopeless situation, enjoy that moment, too, while you can. *You never know when it will end.*

I knew how to get back into the center of town, and Mikey directed us to his house from there. Mikey had once told me that his house was the closest to the woods, and sure enough it was the only one on the forested side of the street. And conveniently, we were the only car on the block. When we drew closer, I noticed an old blue Volvo sitting in the driveway.

"Oh!" I said, surprised.

Mikey's glum voice answered me from the back seat. "It's my mom's car."

"Oh." I hadn't thought about how hard this was going to be for Mikey. I peeked at him in the mirror. He was hunched over in the back seat, looking particularly pale in the fading light.

I stopped the car on the side of the street in front of Mikey's home. "Mikey, is there somewhere we can drop you off? You don't have to come with us," I offered gently.

"No! I'm going to help you. You said I could be the lookout!" His voice trembled as he spoke, but the force behind his words was unmistakable.

"Nobody's saying you can't," Benjamin interjected. "But you should know you have another option."

Mikey crossed his arms as Benjamin and I both turned around in our front seats to look at him. "I don't want another option. I'm coming to get whoever killed my mom."

Mikey began to unbuckle his seat belt, and Benjamin and I turned toward each other. "Tell him," I said softly. I began the process of loading the silver bullets into my gun.

"Tell me what?" Mikey asked, the heat still evident in his voice.

"We need you inside the house, to look out through the windows. That way, you'll be able to spot anyone coming from behind that we won't see from where we're waiting at the front," Benjamin started.

I opened the black velvet case, and the three silver bullets gleamed back at me, somehow shining extra bright in the fading light.

"Okay..." Mikey said.

"And, um, you might see some things that surprise you, or even scare you," Benjamin continued.

I opened the gun's magazine, still empty from my stay at Benjamin's house.

Mikey was listening in rapt silence now as Benjamin spoke in slow, even tones. "The important thing for you to remember—"

I slid the first bullet into the magazine.

"—is that no matter what you see—"

I added the second bullet.

"—and no matter what you hear—"

THE MIDNIGHT PACK

The last bullet seated into place.

"—we are the good guys, and we are on your side."

I inserted the magazine and carefully holstered the gun.

It was fully dark now. Mikey nodded solemnly, and together we stepped out of the car and into the night.

CHAPTER 22

Yellow caution tape fluttered gently in the breeze from where it surrounded Mikey's driveway, closing off the entire front of the house. We stepped under it, beside a dark stain that splashed across the pavement. Did you know red is the first color to fade to black in the dark? I shuddered, momentarily glad that his home wasn't better illuminated—the only light came from the waning moon and a dim lamppost across the street. We carefully sidestepped the stain and made our way to the front door.

We paused on the front steps. "I guess my dad and Seth aren't here yet," Benjamin said. "I don't sense them anywhere nearby, either."

If Mikey wondered what Benjamin meant, he didn't ask, instead looking at me expectantly as I ripped the caution tape from the door. "Do you have a key, buddy?" I asked. He nodded and started fumbling under the doormat. "We can wait inside together for Kermit and Seth," I added.

"Stop." Benjamin's tone was quiet but forceful, and sudden

concern rolled off him in a wave. He stared intently into the dark of the night.

Mikey froze with his hand under the mat, and I looked questioningly at Benjamin as I strained my senses, trying to detect whatever had him worried. Benjamin quickly turned back to us, his eyes wide. "Mikey. Hide, now."

The boy nodded and jumped off the front steps, sliding on his stomach until he was fully concealed under the blue car in the driveway.

"Benjamin, what—" I started, but he held up a hand in a request for silence. Every muscle in his body was tense, like a snake waiting to strike. Then I sensed it, too: another presence in the night.

"Benjamin, is that you?"

The voice didn't sound sinister. On the contrary, she sounded deeply sensual. The woman the voice belonged to also *looked* like a sensual kind of gal. She stepped out from the side of the house and into the moonlit driveway, the pale lighting hugging her curves like the tight black slacks and blouse she wore. *Did she just come from the woods?* She had olive skin, sleek, raven-black hair, and caramel-brown eyes. Her full, blood-red lips smiled when she saw me and Benjamin. That smile didn't reach those brown eyes, though, which was an automatic red flag to me. I let my hand drift down to my side where my gun was holstered. I noticed Benjamin hadn't untensed yet, either.

The woman nodded agreeably. She had one of those ageless faces that made it hard to determine how old she really was, and the moonlight wasn't helping. When she nodded, a lock of shining dark hair fell into her eyes, giving her an even more youthful appearance.

"You two are right to be worried. Foul things are happening." She had a melodious voice, though she whispered that last part, and it came out as a hiss.

Goose bumps prickled down my arms, and my fingers brushed the gun's grip. The woman bent under the caution tape and stopped at the bottom of the steps, looking up at us. She must have registered our twin suspicion because she tilted her long neck back and laughed. She lifted her arms with hands out, palms up. "Relax, I'm probably here for the same reason you are. To investigate the murder that happened last night."

Neither of us moved, and the woman cocked her head to one side. Black hair flowed down her back like a waterfall. "Come on, Benjamin, it's me, Harlow Sinclair."

"Harlow..." Benjamin repeated, recognition dawning in his tone.

"It's been a while. I'm surprised to see you here, I must admit, since this is in violation of our terms with your father."

Beside me I felt Benjamin blush, but Harlow waved a hand as if brushing something away.

"No matter," she said. "I'm glad, because there's something I need to talk to you about." Benjamin nodded but didn't move. Harlow did. She edged closer to us, her melodious voice dropping. "The Council is fractured. There is a faction that has broken off, and they plot to overthrow the current order of things, even as we speak."

A cloud obscured the moon, throwing the woman's face

into shadows as she leaned closer and continued in a whisper. "There are two rogue members, and we tracked them here. To this very spot." Harlow pointed to the bloodstain in the driveway. My goose bumps were back and pricked my arms uncomfortably. *Whose side is she on?*

"Only two?" asked Benjamin. "That doesn't sound like much in the face of the Council."

"These are a special pair." Harlow paused, as if considering something. Her lips curled into a ghost of a smile. "Where are your father and brothers?"

"On their way right now," Benjamin replied.

I noticed that Harlow said "brothers" not *brother*, meaning she must not know that Theo was gone. I also noticed that Benjamin didn't disabuse her of this notion.

"Good, that's good," Harlow said. "They should hear this, too." She glanced behind herself, as if expecting to see the other men there. *Is she acting nervous?* She didn't smell nervous. If anything, the other woman gave off a ripe scent of extreme confidence. *Maybe she really is one of the good guys.*

Harlow turned back to us, looking Benjamin in the eyes. "What do you know about the Serum your brother Theo developed?"

My stomach dropped. *She's not supposed to know about that, unless...* I recalled the note I'd seen in Theo's room and tried to cover my alarm, knowing the Council member would sense it. I chanced a glance at Benjamin. He'd crossed his arms and seemed to be standing somewhat taller and more threateningly.

"What Serum?" Benjamin asked calmly.

"Oh, it's a marvelous and dangerous thing. I'm surprised Theo didn't tell you. Your brother is very talented, you know." Harlow's eyes glittered in the returning moonlight as the cloud passed. "It enhances our powers by incomprehensible amounts—which is why these two rogue members are so troublesome."

She thinks Theo developed it alone.

"You mean Theo made some kind of Serum that boosts... everything?" Benjamin asked with feigned surprise.

"Everything," Harlow said in a deeply sensual tone. "The two rogues I'm tracking took it. They plan to use their new strength to overpower the rest of the Council." She paused, looking Benjamin up and down. I suppressed the urge to growl as she continued. "And to ultimately create a different order in both the Council and the packs."

Benjamin raised an eyebrow appreciatively. "We're at the Council's service, of course."

Harlow gave Benjamin a broad smile. "Of course. The first—"

"Stay away from her."

Kermit's commanding voice cut loudly through the silence of the night. He stepped forward from the side of the house, holding a large compound bow with an arrow nocked and pointed directly at Harlow. The tip of the arrow glistened particularly brightly. *Like silver.* Seth appeared alongside his father. Though he held no weapons, his eyes glinted in the moonlight as if already half Changed.

Harlow turned toward Kermit, and I took the opportunity to retreat to the edge of the porch. I backed up until I felt the metal railing. Benjamin backed away as well, keeping himself between me and the other woman. The latter was still standing at the bottom of the stairs, however, so I busied myself with climbing over the railing. *If I could just get to the other side, I could get a clean shot.*

Harlow smirked, looking unfazed. "Kermit, darling, you know it's against the law to threaten a Council member." She shook her head and tsked disapprovingly. "Where is Theo?"

"He's dead," Kermit spat. "As will you be. You're a traitor to our kind."

Harlow frowned at the news of Theo's death, but then she smiled again, more broadly than before. This time the smile stretched upward, crinkling her eyes with apparent glee.

"Oh, that's where you're wrong, Kermit." Her smile continued stretching unnaturally and horribly, twisting her face like it was made of clay. "You are the traitor, for trying to 'cure' us of our power. And it's not *me* who will be dead tonight." The voice that issued from her twisted face became vicious and raspy, then descended into a low growl. "It's you."

Harlow cackled loudly, revealing sharp, pointed teeth that grew longer as her full lips dissolved and her face stretched into a muzzle. A patchy blanket of coarse fur sprouted in haphazard clumps over her body. She fell to all fours, caught not by her hands but by enormous paws. Those paws pushed into the pavement until I thought it would crack. Her body shuddered as long, disgustingly yellowed claws erupted along what used to be fingers. Each appeared with a sickening *pop*, sprouting like grotesque daisies from a field of flesh.

I was frozen in shock on the porch railing, one leg over the side and one foot still on the porch. Benjamin also stared at the monster before us, and Seth was just as transfixed on the other side of the driveway. Kermit was the only one who remained unfazed, sighting the crossbow and pulling the trigger on the silver-tipped arrow with lightning speed.

He wasn't quick enough.

The moment his finger brushed the trigger, Kermit was knocked down from behind by yet another enormous beast. And by "enormous," I mean really, truly, terrifyingly gargantuan. If I hadn't known it must be a Serum-enhanced werewolf, I would have thought the monster was an honest-to-God Yeti. The beast's shaggy white fur was the longest I'd seen, but it only covered his back, growing in a long stripe from the nape of his neck to his tail, like a mohawk. The rest of the monster's body was mostly hairless. His hide was a deep blue-black in the moonlight, and was covered in the dappled shadows of pockmarks and old scabs. *Gross.*

The impact of the creature made Kermit's shot go wide, skimming past Harlow's wiry fur instead of piercing her in the heart. The arrow landed silently beyond the house in the darkness, and the white beast pushed Kermit to the pavement. A loud thud and the crack of breaking bones resonated through the driveway. The crossbow clattered away from him, and the gargantuan beast snapped its saliva-slicked jaws around it, breaking the bow into pieces.

The snapping sound of the bow (and maybe some of Kermit's bones) plunged through my consciousness like a stone through a winter lake. The shock that had frozen me cracked like a sheet of ice, and my brain jolted into action. Benjamin and Seth must have felt the same, because as I raised my gun, the men flowed into their wolf forms. Benjamin went from man, to wolf, to leaping at Harlow's beastly throat in one fluid motion. I quickly lost track of Kermit, Seth, and the Yeti-beast because I had my own battle to fight. Benjamin and Harlow were grappling directly in front of me, and all I had to do was get an opening for a shot.

Three bullets, two beasts. You can do this, Jericho! I raised my gun, still straddling the porch railing, and fixed my sights on the creature that used to be Harlow. Benjamin's wolf had managed to bite her, latching on with ferocious intent.

I breathed in, looking through the sight to find my target. I absolutely could not afford to miss this shot. The brutal cacophony of the fight rang around me, but I tuned it out. I was in my element. I took a deep breath in.

Benjamin was still blocking Harlow's body, but the monster's head was completely clear. I aimed right between her hateful eyes, knowing this would be a killing shot. I could feel it.

Now!

I exhaled and squeezed the trigger.

Harlow's beast suddenly shook Benjamin off with a guttural roar. She flung Benjamin's body straight into me, just as the silver bullet was exiting the barrel.

My hand jerked upward in surprise, and thank God that it did, because that bullet *barely* missed Benjamin. In fact, he probably sported a bullet-shaped line where it grazed across his fur. *If I hadn't moved...* There was no time to think about it, because a fully grown wolf had just hit me, and together we toppled over the balcony railing and into the grass below.

A cold, wet nose pressed against my face, and Benjamin's chestnut wolf leapt back into the battle as soon as my eyes fluttered open. I was lying on my back in the grass, hidden from the fray by the concrete base of the front porch. The sounds of fighting rang out around me, and it didn't sound good. They needed help; they needed me. I grasped around desperately for my gun. *Two bullets, two beasts.* My fingers met with only grass. Alarmed, I rolled onto my stomach to search.

There! The weak moonlight glinted from something metal in the driveway beside the parked car: my gun. It was probably fifteen feet away. In the middle of the werewolf fight. All I had to do was get it before the monsters got me.

No sweat.

Lots of sweat.

I rose into a crouch and crept to the driveway. I'd reached the edge of the porch. After that I'd be in plain view, so I would have to act quickly. The sounds of bodies crashing and jaws snapping reverberated around the empty yard, and Benjamin's wolf yelped.

One, two, three— I dashed into the driveway, lunging for my gun.

And Harlow lunged toward me.

My movement must have attracted her attention. She whipped her head away from Benjamin as soon as I emerged, kicking the smaller wolf in the face as she leapt. Benjamin's wolf let out a whine and fell to the driveway as Harlow's beastly paws flew over the pavement.

Meanwhile I dove for my gun for all I was worth. I landed hard and empty-handed. My outstretched fingertips were still about a foot away from my weapon. *Damn!* I chanced a look behind me and registered Harlow's monster flying across the driveway, with saucer-size paws and disgusting yellow claws reaching my direction. And a wolf on the ground behind her—Benjamin. He rolled upward, standing shakily on three legs with one front paw lifted and hanging loosely.

I didn't want the last thing I saw to be a monstrous creature's claws and teeth coming to slash me apart. Or a Benjamin so injured he could barely stand. So I turned back to my gun.

Which was now in someone else's hand.

Someone's little hand, belonging to a small but brave boy hiding out under the car while monsters fought on his doorstep.

Mikey flung the gun. It skittered across the pavement toward me, and the hard rubber of the grip smacked into my palm. Time seemed to speed up then, because I rolled onto my back faster than I thought possible and pulled the trigger. The bullet fired up and into Harlow's beastly form as she leapt on me.

I screamed as I shot, and the gun blasted a fist-size hole in the monster at that close range. A spray of blood shot into the night, hanging in a red mist. And so, instead of landing on top of me and ripping off my face, a now-human Harlow tumbled onto my body. I was covered in beast guts—black, sticky, and reeking. And a dead woman. I'd never wanted a shower more in my life. But the fight wasn't over yet.

One more bullet, one more beast.

I heaved Harlow's body off and stood up. I hoped I made for an intimidating sight: my white hair gleaming silver in the moonlight, and my golden eyes burning out of a blood-covered face. I was coming for the final monster.

Though, with the way I felt in that moment, maybe I was the final monster.

I shook out my arms as I stood, flinging werewolf viscera to the ground beside me. I strode purposefully to the savage tumble of teeth and fur that was the men fighting the last Council beast. The wolves were moving with such speed against the Yeti-creature that their coats blended together in a dizzying blur. I raised my gun in two blood-splattered arms, keeping my stance wide and powerful. I was ready.

But I couldn't get a clean shot.

The smaller wolves danced around the beast, as they had with Theo. And as with Theo, this creature only seemed more emboldened each time the other wolves landed a bite or a scratch. It was as if the scent of his own blood running down his blue-black hide was a drug to him, and he was getting *loaded*. To their credit, the guys were all over him. Even Benjamin, teetering on his three legs, leapt back into the fray each time he was knocked down. They were determined. They were tenacious. But I needed them all to step aside.

"*Guys, scatter!*" I yelled. My eye was locked on the target and my finger ready to squeeze the millisecond I got a clear shot.

I couldn't tell if they heard me, but the monster certainly did. He met my eyes with a cold glare and then bit down hard on Seth's wolf neck, viciously flinging the smaller wolf in my direction. *This is my chance!* Seth's body tumbled low so I aimed high, straight for the beast's wickedly glaring eyes.

I shot, and he ducked.

He ducked.

I missed.

The last silver bullet flew harmlessly into the night, and we were now well and truly fucked.

CHAPTER 23

The Yeti-beast reared up on its hind legs, looking all the more Yeti-like as it stood and roared. It was an earsplitting roar—an instant-headache-inducing blast. The Volvo's window nearest the monster burst, raining glass on the blood-soaked driveway. I had the time to register a ringing in my ears, and the time to wonder why nobody else had come out during the fight. I mean, there weren't a lot of other houses across the street, but there were a few. Surely someone had heard *something*.

But then again, would you come out if you saw a monster-battle across the street? I decided it was a good thing no neighbors or police had appeared, because they would have been dead already.

The other wolves, all limping and coated in blood-matted fur, now circled the monster for one last offensive. The roar died away, but the huge beast still had its eyes locked on me. *Whatever, asshole.* I looked back into them, into their black and evil depths, and screamed my loudest. I let out all my frustration, my fears, my dreams, and my desires that now would never be. I put my heart into that scream, and it heartened me in return. I focused my energy into my back leg, ready to spring and run at the creature's face.

If I got lucky, maybe he'd choke on my bones.

A sudden movement to my left made me turn, and pure shock froze me in my place. A tall, dark-skinned man in a business suit was running toward us holding a large, gleaming, metal-handled axe. Have you ever seen something so out of place, your brain simply doesn't compute for a moment? The entire group on the driveway seemed equally stunned, and for one beautiful second, nobody moved. I wanted to yell at the man, to tell him to run the other way and save himself, but my brain wouldn't send the message to my mouth.

Glancing around the driveway as he ran, the man must have assessed the situation and somehow decided it was a good idea to *throw the axe down*. My brain was busily not computing this latest twist in the series of surprising developments when the man leapt. As he did, his suit fell away and he flowed easily into the form of a sleek black wolf.

The scene burst into action once more, like someone pressing PLAY on a movie.

The new black wolf sprang straight for the beast. The monster had turned his head to snap his wicked jaws at the other wolves, leaving his neck open. *Yessss!* The black wolf was about to close on the beast's dark, scabby throat. I could see the monster's veins pulsing and the black wolf's jaws widening to rip them open. Then a large, beastly blue-black arm flew up and connected with the black wolf, snapping the wolf's jaws shut with the crack of broken teeth. The monster spun, and the other wolves fell off him.

They needed help.

My eyes darted around, hoping to find something I could use as a weapon. Anything. A piece of glass from the broken window? A rock? No. There was something even better.

Run, Jericho. I sprinted for the axe, grabbing it in one swift motion as I dashed toward the monster. His back was toward me. He raised an arm to swipe at one of the wolves at his feet.

I didn't let him.

I sprang from the porch steps and landed on the lanky white fur on the beast's back just as I'd done with Theo. He reared up, but I held on. My legs squeezed him for purchase as I hefted the axe above my head. I swung it down, hard.

There was a disgusting squelch as the axe severed bone and sinew, then a loud *thunk* as the monster's head hit the driveway. The beast's body slumped, collapsing onto the pavement beside its head. The hateful eyes were open and glassy, staring sightlessly into the night. The waning moon was reflected perfectly in each of them.

Decapitation.

The bloody axe landed with a metallic clatter as I threw it down. I wiped my bloody hands on my bloody leggings, and *so much more fucking blood than last time*... but somehow none of it belonged to me. I glanced over to the men on the driveway. They were all still in wolf form as they licked wounds and whined at one another. Nobody seemed in danger of dying, and it looked like the wolves were taking care of themselves, so I turned around and crouched down beside the car.

"Mikey?"

He didn't answer. I brushed the broken glass aside and leaned down even further until I was lying belly-down on the driveway. I tilted my head to the side, pressing it against the pavement to see under the Volvo. Mikey was also pressed against the driveway, with his head turned away from me, but he was breathing.

"Mikey, you can come out now," I said gently.

I wasn't going to ask if he was okay, because none of us were. How could we be okay after that? He didn't move or acknowledge that he heard me, though, so I tried again. "The monsters are gone, buddy, come on out."

"I threw up," he said in response. His small voice sounded nasal, as if he'd been crying.

"I did, too, after my first experience with, uh, this stuff," I said. "Don't worry about it. Come on out and we'll take care of it."

"Okay." He shimmied to the side and squirmed from under the car.

When he was fully out, we stood up together. He dusted off his pants as I looked him over. One of the lenses of his glasses was cracked, his elbows were scraped, and the remnants of vomit stained his shirt, but other than that (and whatever mental damage witnessing a mutant werewolf fight causes), he was in one piece.

"Um, you don't look so good," he said, eyeing me. *Pot, meet kettle.*

"We could both use some freshening up," I replied. He nodded and reached out for my hand. I took it, and together we walked across the driveway to the wolves.

Seth was the only one in human form. He must have been the least injured. Benjamin had said that as wolves they had super-healing powers (and I did, too, thanks to the Serum), but I guessed the healing didn't work as well in a werewolf's human shape. Seth sat in the center of the wolves, hugging his knees close to his body, looking for all the world like he and the wolves were communicating silently. They probably were. I cleared my throat as we approached them.

"Hey, guys, I'm going to take Mikey inside to get cleaned up." The wolves stopped licking their cuts, and three sets of wolf eyes fixed me with their stare, along with Seth's human eyes. It was altogether a bit much for me just then.

"So, yeah," I said, turning toward the house.

"Jericho, wait," Seth said, and I paused. "Mr. Night, from the Council, wants to talk to you about something." He nodded toward the black wolf, who briefly wagged his tail in response. I wondered if Night was his real name, but I didn't say anything.

I looked back at Mikey, who still held my hand expectantly. "Go on in. I'll follow in a minute."

He shook his head vehemently. "I don't want to go in alone," he said in a low voice.

I didn't blame him. I supposed I wouldn't, either, not after experiencing a real-life nightmare in my driveway. I felt bad for asking.

Kermit whined in Seth's direction, and Seth nodded. "They need a few more minutes to heal. It's faster as a wolf," he said with a shrug, confirming what I had suspected. "Anyway, my dad will Change in a minute, so I'll go in with Mikey." At this, Seth shifted his gaze to the boy. "That is, if it's okay with you, little dude?"

"He's one of the good guys," I said quietly to Mikey. "And he's Benjamin's brother," I added. *And your uncle...*

Mikey shrugged. "Okay I guess." He dropped my hand as Seth moved to his side, tactfully picking up the shredded remains of someone's shirt to hold over himself as he went.

"So, do you like video games?" asked Seth, as they walked up the steps to the front door.

"Yeah, I do," said Mikey, a little more brightly than before.

"What's your favorite?" Seth's voice faded as they entered the home together.

"Huh," I said, watching a length of ripped caution tape flutter onto the front porch as the door shut. Benjamin's wolf nudged my hand with his nose, and he cocked his head to one side. I looked down at him. "I just had no idea your brother was good with kids."

The chestnut wolf sat back on his haunches and opened his mouth in what looked like a large grin. I looked him over. Any cuts and scrapes he'd gotten were fully healed, leaving behind streaks of bloody fur as the only evidence they'd existed. He was still holding up his front paw, however, and it dangled just as limply as it had before.

I held out a hand to touch his (presumably broken) paw, but he pulled it back with a whine. Before I could admonish him, a deep, rich voice rang out behind me.

"Jericho James."

I turned around and stood face-to-face (well, face-to-midchest-and-bare-pectorals) with the Council member who had brought the axe. He'd managed to find a pair of pants somewhere, which was just as well, because there was a lot of him to cover. He was even taller than I first thought, and had close-cropped jet-black hair. His rich-brown skin took on a bronze glow in the moonlight, and the hard lines of his muscles were clearly defined. Seth had said his name...

"Mr. Night, I presume," I responded, inclining my head slightly in what could have been a polite bow. *How does one greet the Werewolf Council anyway?*

He smiled, his white teeth glinting brightly in the moonlight. "Please, call me Steven." I nodded but didn't speak.

"So," he continued smoothly, "it seems we have you to thank for foiling the plot against the Council?"

"Well, I certainly didn't do it alone," I said.

"No matter," he waved his hand as if waving away a fly. "We don't have too much time before the police of this town show up. They'll have found the wires under their cars chewed through by some kind of animal." He gave me a shrewd smile. *Sneaky, Steven.* "But they'll secure an alternative means of transportation eventually."

I nodded again, and he went on. "These are the facts: You're a human, you're aware that werewolves not only exist but also live among you, and you know we are governed by a Council, of which I am a part." He paused.

"Uh, yes," I said.

"Humans are not allowed to possess *any* of this information. It is the very foundation of our secrecy."

"Er," I, ever the conversationalist, replied.

He continued. "The only way that a *human* with this

particular knowledge can coexist with the Council is as part of a pack." I swallowed hard as muscular Steven Night, tall man and axe-wielder of the Werewolf Council, edged closer to me. He bent to look me in the eye.

"But Kermit assures me that you are indeed part of his pack. And I'm not sure that you're entirely human. Besides, we are in your debt." Steven straightened, still holding my gaze with his. Then he smiled warmly.

I exhaled a breath I'd been holding and tried a tentative smile in return. At least I hoped it was a smile and not a nervous grimace.

"We—the Council—are going to continue funding the Grey pack so they may rebuild the lab and continue their work on the Cure. Not to control the other packs, as the creatures you fought would tell you, but to give our people a *choice*."

"Choice is what matters," Kermit said from behind me. I realized he had managed to find clothes somewhere as well, then spotted an open backpack on the ground beside him. *This clearly wasn't his first post-fight rodeo.*

"As for what else you've been working on," Steven started as he turned to face Kermit, "we'll revisit that later." Steven threw both me and the bodies on the ground a very pointed look before turning back to Kermit. "It seems that you and I have much to discuss."

Kermit nodded solemnly and stood beside me with his hands clasped differentially at his waist. Benjamin's wolf sat to my other side and nudged my hand with his nose. I patted him on the head. He was still favoring his front paw, but it might have looked slightly less limp than before.

Steven stood before us, surveying our battered trio and shaking his head slightly. "Part of the pack, indeed. Jericho James, whatever else you may be, you're a special soul. And no matter what happens, you'll always have a place here."

I wasn't used to being called a "special soul" by anyone, much less an imposing werewolf. I blushed in the moonlight.

Steven's lips tilted up in a slight smile. "You're also in a special position."

I raised an eyebrow at that, because it sounded like a segue into asking for a favor.

He laughed, showing his brilliant white teeth again. "I'd like to make you an offer on behalf of the Council." This struck me as somewhat mafia-like.

I crossed my bloody arms, still dubious. "Is it an offer I can't refuse?" I asked.

Kermit quickly nudged me in the side and hissed my name under his breath while wolf-Benjamin whined.

Steven didn't laugh, but his eyes crinkled in amusement. "You could refuse it, but I'd prefer that you did not." He cocked his head to the side. "And I will offer you a favor in return."

"Okay, what is the request?"

"We—the Council—would like to keep you on retainer as our special investigator," he began.

Wow. I did not see that one coming.

He continued, "I understand that Benjamin here has vouched for your abilities, and you'll be in a fully unique position with one foot in human society, and one foot in ours, so to speak."

I nodded, considering, as he went on. "You'll be able to investigate human activities in ways we cannot, and you can be involved in Council business in ways that we cannot involve the police. We will pay you handsomely for your services."

Kermit nudged my side again and nodded ever so slightly. On my other side, Benjamin's wolf nodded as well and gave me a questioning look, raising his eyebrows. *Did you know real wolves can't raise their eyebrows, but dogs and werewolves can?*

Werewolves. I wasn't sure how closely I wanted to be tied to their Council, considering two of them had just tried to kill me, but on the other hand, I was already involved. *And you just might be one yourself.* So becoming uninvolved didn't seem to be on the table. I thought about Benjamin's lips on mine and decided I wouldn't want to be uninvolved anyway.

I looked back at Steven, standing patiently in the moonlight.

"I accept," I said, "on one condition." I could feel Kermit's and Benjamin's eyes quickly shift their focus to me. I gave them both my best I've-got-this look. Then I turned back to Steven, who had the air of someone who wasn't used to receiving conditions. "I'm going to continue with my regular business, too." Steven looked like he was preparing to object, so I quickly kept going. "I've spent years building up my business. I love what I do, and I'm good at it. I'm not going to lose my connections, and everything I've built, just to sit around and wait for your Council to call me like a—" I was going to say *like a dog* but stopped myself. "Er, I'm not going to sit around doing nothing and wait for your Council to call me."

I registered shock from either side of me—apparently

talking back to the Council was very much frowned upon—but Steven nodded contemplatively.

Finally, he spoke. "Very well. But when the Council does call, you must answer."

"Very well," I responded in kind.

He reached out a large, dark hand, and I shook it. His fingers were long and callused, and his palm warmed mine in the cool night air. "It is done," he said.

"It is done," I agreed, fully aware that I was beginning to sound like Steven's echo. "Oh wait," I said, remembering something. "You mentioned a favor..."

"Ah yes," Steven nodded. "What would you ask of me?"

I shifted my gaze over Steven's shoulder, to something long and metallic and shining in the moonlight on the ground behind him. He turned around but said nothing.

I pointed to it. "I want that axe."

CHAPTER 24

Mr. Night and Kermit agreed that it was time for them to get lost, as it were, so they quickly gathered their belongings. For Kermit, this meant his bag, his broken compound bow, the retrieved silver-tipped arrow, Seth, and Mikey. For Steven, I thought this meant absolutely nothing, since I was the proud new owner of his solid-steel axe, but he announced that he would also remove the bodies.

"Tell the police you slew two infected wolves, and Kermit is burning the bodies to limit disease spread. There will be too many questions otherwise," he intoned in his rich, deep voice.

I didn't argue. I was relieved to not have to deal with human remains when the police showed up. *But...* "Wait, what about the blood?" I asked, gesturing to the dark stains that surrounded us on the driveway.

"It is of no consequence," Steven replied. "They began to bleed in their wolf forms. Should anyone retrieve a sample, the best the analytics will provide is that it's lupine in origin."

I didn't pretend to understand how that worked, but I nodded and watched as Steven placed the decapitated head in a plastic bag and hitched both bodies over his shoulders. Mikey had fallen asleep inside the house, so Kermit was on kid-carrying duty, and Seth wore the backpack.

We exchanged hasty goodbyes (at this point we were all shocked that not a single law enforcement official had appeared), and Steven promised that the Council would help if I encountered any problems with the police. I wasn't entirely sure what form this "help" would take, though, and I didn't want to find out.

When I asked about Mikey, Steven assured me that the foster care paperwork would be taken care of to place him with Kermit. "We have people in the system, you know. Sometimes our kind end up in foster care as pups. We must make sure they go to homes in the pack."

I turned to Kermit, who looked older than before in the moonlight, then shifted my gaze to Mikey, asleep in his arms. "Will you tell him the truth?" I asked.

Kermit tilted his head thoughtfully. "Someday, but not yet. I'll let him get over the shock of what happened here first."

I nodded. "Tell him I said see you later, okay?"

I watched the men fade into the tree line with Benjamin's wolf beside me. The last hint of Seth's backpack disappeared into the darkness, and I sighed. Benjamin's sudden whine brought my attention to him. His ears perked up as he whipped around to face the road. I heard it, too—the sound of breathless panting and squeaking wheels carried up the driveway. I turned to look for its source as a child-size pink bike carrying a rather large policewoman rolled into view.

The woman locked eyes on me with a grimace. The moment the wheels touched the driveway, she dismounted and tried to push the kickstand, still glaring in my direction. The kickstand didn't budge. She growled her displeasure as she flung the bike on the ground behind her. I guessed Steven's wire-works with the police cars had been effective.

"I *cannot even* with this night," she muttered under her breath, though I could hear her clearly. She lightly touched her tidy bun, then marched up the driveway until she was about an arm's length away from me and Benjamin.

"What the *hell* happened to my crime scene?" she asked loudly, placing both hands on her hips. Anger and frustration poured from her, and I steeled myself so as not to be swept up in it. Benjamin leaned against my leg, offering silent support. He was so big that his head rested above my hip. I hoped the officer wouldn't notice that he was bigger than your average canine.

I held up my hands to show her I was unarmed. "Hi, Officer..." I trailed off, glancing at her name tag in the moonlight. "Jackson, ah! I spoke on the phone with you last week, and I met with your father. I mean, the sheriff. I'm Jericho Ja—"

"I know who you are," she interrupted. "That's the only reason I don't have a gun on you right now."

I sighed. This exchange was not starting out how I had hoped, but I supposed I should have expected it, given the circumstances. I hadn't been worried about talking to the police, but now I found myself nervously hoping that Officer Jackson would believe my version of the night's events. I opened my mouth to explain, but she spoke first.

"Tell me exactly what happened here."

I stuck as close to the truth as possible. I started with returning from Kermit's house and finding Mikey in the woods. I admitted that I came back to check for clues, in case the killings of his mother and Katherine were connected.

"I know I should have contacted the police when I got into town, but it was late. I figured it wouldn't hurt if I checked things out on my own," I said apologetically.

"Well, you figured wrong," she retorted.

"Apparently," I muttered, then continued. I explained how we were attacked by diseased-looking wolves (true), and that I shot the first beast (true) and decapitated the second (also true). I pointed out the corresponding bloodstains on the driveway as evidence.

Officer Jackson was equal parts impressed, surprised, and disturbed by the decapitation. She shuddered at the head-size stain on the driveway. "Decapitation. That's a little extreme, don't you think?"

I didn't have an answer for that, so I simply shrugged. "I'm from Florida."

She shot a sideways glance at me. "I see."

I ended with Kermit taking the wolf bodies to burn and returning to his home in the woods with Mikey in tow.

"I ought to charge him with kidnapping," she said, shaking her head. "Did you know we've been looking for Mikey?"

"I didn't think about that. Sorry, we should have told you when we found him in the woods," I replied.

"Damn straight."

"But," I added, "I think that if you check in your system tomorrow, you'll see that the paperwork for Mikey to live with Kermit is all in order." *At least it had better be.*

She raised an eyebrow at that. "Since when?"

"Um, since Kermit got a person who helps with paperwork, I guess?" I shrugged again, doing my best to look entirely innocent.

Officer Jackson peppered me with additional questions—what did the diseased wolves look like? How many people were with you? How did you know this was related to Katherine's death? But she visibly relaxed after each answer. She got as much truth in as much detail as I could give. The only parts I left out were Mr. Steven Night, Seth, and Benjamin. And the monstrous truth, obviously. Eventually she looked mostly satisfied, especially after I promised to come by the station the next day to give a full report. I told her that Kermit and Mikey would stop by as well.

She rubbed her temples and sighed, walking around the driveway. Something small glittered on the ground in the moonlight, and she bent down to retrieve it. She held it up between her thumb and forefinger, squinting. My poor heart jumped—*did we miss something?*

"Did you shoot one with a silver bullet?" She asked.

"Yeah," I said.

"Did you stop by the jewelry store earlier today?"

"Yeah," I repeated, this time hesitantly.

She shook her head. "Aw, hell. Carol will be so sad to hear those bullets weren't destined to become flowers after all."

It was my turn to be surprised. "How did you know that?"

She crossed her arms over her chest. "I'm Officer Jackson. It's my business to know."

She did make a rather imposing figure. Despite the late hour and her unconventional transportation to the scene, her black hair was in a perfect tight bun and her uniform was freshly pressed (aside from bike-related wrinkles). Her brown eyes glittered in the moonlight. I raised my eyebrows, impressed.

"...and my mom is in Carol's knitting group," she added.

I would have laughed if my nerves weren't so strung out after the night's events. I smiled, though, and she returned it with a grin of her own.

Her grin slipped when she noticed Benjamin. "What's that?" She gestured toward the elephant in the room, or in this case, the werewolf in the driveway. He'd been standing beside me the entire time, but I supposed Jackson's mind was on other things.

"Um, my dog?"

"Looks like a wolf. And since when do you have a dog?" She crossed her arms over her chest again.

"I got him from Kermit." *Mostly true.*

She raised an eyebrow. "Uh-huh. What's its name?"

"*His* name is Benny."

"Is he tame? If not, you'll have animal control all over you."

"Sure. Sit, Benny," I said.

Benjamin sat obediently and panted in a gloating sort of way. I scratched him behind his ears, and he leaned his head against my waist.

"My, my. I have never seen a dog look so self-satisfied."

This time I did laugh. *You don't know the half of it.*

She swept her gaze across the driveway again, taking in the gruesome scene. "I still have some questions, and I have the feeling you're not telling me everything here."

I shrugged, looking at the moon. It would be full again in about three weeks. When I turned back, she was looking at me.

"Do I want to know?" she asked.

We locked eyes: Hers were a deep mahogany, a normal human color. I knew mine were glowing golden in the moonlit night, shining brightly from my blood-streaked face. "No," I said. "You don't."

She shivered, looking back to the dark stains on the pavement.

"I'm going to trust you, James. My father does, and Lord knows you come highly recommended." I didn't say anything, and she sighed. "I'll see you tomorrow at the station."

Benjamin and I watched as Officer Jackson walked down the long driveway. She reached the discarded pink bike by the roadside, and we heard her mutter, "Aw, hell." Wolf-Benjamin looked at me, tilting his eyebrows up.

"Want a ride?" I called.

After depositing Jackson and the pink bike at her house, I went back to my hotel with Benjamin. We hesitated at the front. Dogs weren't allowed, but the alternative would raise too many questions. It was a small enough town that there would absolutely be talk if I waltzed in from the crime scene with a strange man. Especially after telling the good officer that it was just me and my "dog."

I needn't have worried, though. The front door swung open easily, and together we stepped into an empty foyer, then up the stairs to my room.

I propped my new axe up on the wall beside the bed. "I'm going to hop in the shower," I told wolf-Benjamin, whose paw was finally looking back to normal. He lay down beside the door in response.

It was the second-best shower of my life. The pressure was good, and the water was hot. I cranked it hotter. I wanted to be positively scalded clean. Steam filled the room as the water pounded out the day's grime and werewolf blood. I stood there until the last vestiges of red circled the drain on the floor.

A clatter of metal-on-metal announced a now-human Benjamin as he drew back the shower curtain and joined me. I'd seen him naked before, but the constant threat of death hadn't allowed me to cherish the moment. Now, though...now I could fully appreciate the man beside me. My eyes immediately caught on the broad pane of his chest. The lines of his muscles were sharp enough to make me forget my own name, though as I followed the groove on the center of his chest downward, I also forgot why we weren't kissing already.

I forced my gaze back to his face. His mane of chestnut hair looked expertly tousled, even after the events of the night. A few stray strands fell forward, but I reached up with my wet hands to push them back. This prompted him to do the same, and his fingers began working their way through my hair, massaging my scalp and drawing me closer.

My fingers left his hair, trailing down the sharp lines of his immaculate cheekbones and pausing on his neck. I was pleased to note the goose bumps that followed, even in the heat of the shower.

He traced my face with his thumb, catching on my lower lip. His thumb followed the seam of my lips until I parted them.

And I licked it.

A deep moan fell from his lips as mine spread in a mischievous grin.

He pulled my body to his without speaking, and I ran my hands back down the hard lines of his muscles. Our bodies could do the talking, and his was beautifully made. I tilted my head up automatically to look into his lake-blue eyes. Our lips met in the steam. He kissed me hungrily, and I met him in kind. My hands ran over his back, slick in the hot shower, as I drank him in. His kisses were deep, passionate, and full of need. One of his hands clutched me to him, and the other hand made its way up my back, his fingers entwining in my hair as he cradled my head in the heat. We kissed in the shower until all that existed in the world was heat and wet and us. He sucked on my lower lip, and I let out a contented sound in response. Then he broke away and trailed kisses down my body as he knelt lower and lower in the shower.

It was the new best shower of my life.

He carried me out of the bathroom afterward, like a groom

carrying a bride across the threshold. We tumbled into bed together, clean and deliciously close under the crisp sheets. He looked into my eyes as he stroked my cheek gently, tucking a silvery strand of hair behind my ear. Something occurred to me, and my smile fell. He dropped his hand to my side.

His eyebrows furrowed. "What's up?"

I pressed myself up on an elbow, peering deep into his lake-blue eyes. I'd thought before that I could drown in them. I still did. But... I swallowed the sudden lump in my throat. "You don't have to do it, you know."

His eyebrows creased. "Do what?"

I gave him a half smile. "Stay with me. With my agency. I know that's what we're going to tell the sheriff if he asks about you." I shrugged as best I could while leaning on an elbow. "But I also know how you feel about your family. Your pack."

He blinked, eyes focusing behind me, which I now knew meant he was deep in thought. "You're my pack, too, you know. I meant what I said back at the house."

"I know. But what's that thing you say? Loyal to the last?"

He nodded once. "To the pack and to the task."

I ran my other hand down his chest, marveling again at the finely knit muscle and the strong and steady heart that beat beneath it. "I was the task... Protect Jericho, keep her away from the Council. But that's done, and your family—your main pack—needs you to replicate the Serum. And help with the Cure."

Still leaning on his elbow, he caught my hand as it roamed his chest. He brought my fingers to his lips, kissing my knuckles gently. It was enough to make me want to take back my words, but I knew in my heart that we had separate paths to follow.

"I told you I would, though. And I'm a man of my word."

I forced a smile. "I know that, too. And I expect nothing less from you, Benjamin Grey. But this is me telling you that you can just be my partner from afar. I'll call you when I need you. And I expect you to do the same for me."

He kissed my hand once more before letting go and breaking eye contact. He lay back on the pillow, his hands behind his head.

"You make a lot of sense, Jericho James. It's a deal—as long as you actually come visit me from time to time. Work aside, I feel like there are some deeper... *investigations* we can do together here."

"I'll do what I can," I said softly.

"And how about this—you stay with me now, just until the next full moon. So if you're going to Change, you won't be doing it alone."

Oh yeah. The tiny issue of me maybe becoming a werewolf. But I wouldn't be doing it alone. My throat was uncomfortably tight, so instead of speaking I simply nodded.

"Thank you for understanding me," he said gently.

"And thank you for the same," I whispered.

He cracked a smile then, a bright white to match the sheets. "Can you say it again?"

I raised an eyebrow. "What? Thank you?"

"No, the part where you said my full name. I like the sound of it on your lips."

His voice was soft and rumbled through me, rekindling

a delicious heat that radiated from my core, unfurling like a fern. I couldn't help but smile back.

"All right, Benjamin Grey."

He grinned against my mouth as we kissed, tumbling together in the sheets.

CHAPTER 25

Going out to the woods alone was a dumb idea, but I'm glad I did it.

The police department and Katherine's parents were ever so grateful that the mystery deaths were solved, and that the creatures responsible for the attacks were eliminated. The mayor personally thanked me, and both Jacksons, sheriff and officer, promised to call me if they had any more trouble.

Steven came through with his paperwork, and Mikey seemed to be getting used to living with Seth and Kermit, the latter of whom renegotiated his deal with the Council to create a more social life for his family. Mikey still didn't know about his heritage, but he was with people who would explain it when the time was right.

Meanwhile I'd acquired a contract with the most powerful werewolf group in North America, superhuman abilities, and a friend. I'd also discovered that the world we know—the world we *think* we know—is so much bigger, darker, and more horrifying, but also more wonderful, than I had ever imagined. The truths we take for granted are just a veneer over a much larger, more beautiful, and more terrifying existence. Like a film of iridescent oil over a deep, dark pool. Who knows what lies at the depths?

But I guess I should start at the beginning. I'm Jericho James, supernatural investigator.

And I'm just getting started.

EPILOGUE

"The first time is easier without clothes on," Benjamin explained. Which is how I found myself naked and shivering in the woods, waiting for the full moon to rise.

We were still in Maine, in a well-forested area for this very occasion. Benjamin wanted us as far away from major populations as possible, "just in case." *Fine by me.* Benjamin also undressed as we waited, so I didn't have to sit naked alone. *Very fine by me.*

We huddled together under a blanket with my skin pressed up against his, which, under normal circumstances, would have been an exciting prospect. As it was, my nerves wouldn't let me concentrate on anything other than trying not to throw up from sheer anxiety. I clutched my knees to my chest and closed my eyes, focusing on Benjamin's warm arm around my waist and the dead-leaf scent that heralded fall's end in the chilly breeze.

Benjamin had told me that older, more experienced werewolves could Change at will. He said, too, that every werewolf felt the call of the full moon, and even the strongest were compelled to Change in her light.

"It's time," he whispered gently in my ear. I nodded and opened my eyes.

He shrugged the blanket off us and laid it on the forest floor. He moved to sit cross-legged atop the thick wool and motioned for me to do the same. The cold night air immediately covered my skin in goose bumps. Cold didn't affect me as much as it once had, but I nevertheless shivered as I sat across from Benjamin.

He took my hands in his. I'd painted my nails the day before, with a color I thought would fit this moment: Once in a Blue Moon. *Hardy-har.* My electric-blue nails weren't visible now, though, with Benjamin's warm palms enveloping mine completely. I barely noticed. My heart hammered in my chest and pounded in my temples, and I continued placing all my concentration on not vomiting. To say I was nervous would be the understatement of the year.

"Jericho, look at me," Benjamin said.

I continued staring at our palms, locked together as humans. *I wouldn't be able to hold his hand as a wolf.* Tears fell, unbidden, from my eyes.

"Look at me," he said again, still gently but with a power behind his words.

I didn't look.

He dropped one of my hands and slid a thumb under my chin, angling my head upward until I was finally facing him. His brilliant-blue eyes shone in the moonlight. *The moonlight!* My eyes widened in panic. The silvery glow edged across the forest floor, creeping toward us as the moon rose higher. I tried to pull away, but Benjamin held my hands tightly, keeping me on the blanket.

"Jericho, no matter what happens, it's going to be okay."

I continued looking into his eyes, but I dropped his hands as the moonlight touched him and he flowed smoothly into his wolf form.

The light glided onward and fell onto my naked skin.

And nothing happened.

I closed my eyes, not daring to move or even breathe, but nothing continued to happen. I cautiously opened my eyes again, wondering if I'd somehow look down at the body of a wolf. But I was still me. I laughed. Relief flowed out of me, like the light pouring from the full moon, and I continued laughing. All cold forgotten, I suddenly felt great. Benjamin's wolf nudged my cheek and licked a remaining tear. I smiled at him.

"Let's run!" I said. I pulled on my tennis shoes and a short white nightgown.

Benjamin barked and broke into a loping run. I picked up speed, easily keeping up with him as we darted through the woods, glittering in the silvery moonlight. I laughed again, joyfully, and together we ran into the night.

The story continues in...

BIGFOOT CONFIDENTIAL

Book 2 of the Jericho James series

ACKNOWLEDGMENTS

There are times when writing a book can be lonely, but there are also so many times when it's not. I started writing this book at the beginning of 2021 when human interactions were still at an all-time low, so thank you to my cats, Candy and Swarley, for always being there. Thank you to my husband for keeping me caffeinated, and to my kids, who have been so excited to tell everyone that "Mommy writes books," even though they're not allowed to read them yet.

Thank you to wonderful authors Kim Tomsic, who pointed me in the right direction when I was getting started, and Breanne Randall, who encouraged me to keep going. Thank you to Adam Wilson for telling me to take the leap. Thank you to my OG beta reader and all-around cheerleader, Deidre Casey. It's so much more fun to write when there is someone actively waiting for the next part of the story, asking for more, and fan-girling over my characters with me. You make writing feel like a party. Thank you to my other beta readers, Megan Khatami and Carol Wicks, for your support and encouragement, and for talking through scenes with me. Jericho James is a stronger character because of all of you. Thank you to everyone who read the opening pages

Acknowledgments

before they were sent off into the world: Brittany Mosby, Chelsea Cupp, Joseph Kline, Jon Carroll, Lorien Gilbert, Camille Check, and Emily Danger. Also thank you, Emily, for teaching me how to properly saber Champagne, and to the rest of my book club for your excitement and support.

Thanks to my mega-smart sister-in-law, Dr. Andrea Jones, for your input on the lycanthropy virus terminology and feasibility, as well as all the other science-related topics.

And to my brother-in-law, Christopher Jones, for giving me lessons on firearm parts and answering my beginner questions, like "Where do bullets go?"

Thank you to the wonderful team at Orbit US, including but not limited to Tim Holman, Bryn A. McDonald, Laura Jorstad, Ritchelle Buensuceso, Erin Cain, Lauren Panepinto, Alexia Mazis, Alex Lencicki, Maggie Curley, Ellen Wright, and Natassja Haught, who are all just as kind as they are awesome. And to Luisa Preissler for the stunning cover art, Six Red Marbles & Jouve India for their fantastic interior design, and Sarah Beth Goer for bringing the audiobook to life.

And to Stephanie Lippitt Clark, my amazing editor, guide through the publishing world, and absolute gem of a human: Thank you. Thank you for finding me, for connecting with Jericho, and for helping her shine. And most of all, for making this dream of mine a reality. Thank you, thank you, thank you. Or as my kids would say, thank you to infinity *plus one*.

But back to writing. Looking back on this list, I realize I

Acknowledgments

was never really alone throughout any part of the process, and I'm so incredibly grateful for all of you.

And last but never, ever least, a massive thank you to *you*, the person reading this right now. It means the world to me. Thank you so much for coming on Jericho's journey.

And she's just getting started.

MEET THE AUTHOR

Lisa Joy Photography

JASMINE KULIASHA was born in Peru and grew up in Guatemala. She spent her childhood traveling, and books were her most constant companions. Today her writing is informed by her adventures abroad and her love of happy endings. She writes from Colorado, where she's living her own Happily Ever After with her children and husband. When she's not writing, she's training for her next marathon or trying to get her personal assistants (two cats) to do anything at all. Follow her attempts at jasminekuliasha.com or on Instagram @kuliashawrites.

Find out more about Jasmine Kuliasha and other Orbit authors by registering for the free monthly newsletter at orbitbooks.net.

www.ingramcontent.com/pod-product-compliance
Lightning Source LLC
LaVergne TN
LVHW032037190725
816567LV00008B/224